# AFTER DARK

## Bette Ford

**Pinnacle Books**
Kensington Publishing Corp.

http://www.pinnaclebooks.com

PINNACLE BOOKS are published by

Kensington Publishing Corp.
850 Third Avenue
New York, NY 10022

First Printing: October, 1997
10 9 8 7 6 5 4 3 2 1

Printed in the United States of America

# One

"Scott Hendricks, have you lost your mind? What are you doing asking me to meet you for lunch in a place like this?" Edmund's Place, where collard greens and macaroni and cheese were served on pristine linen by tuxedo clad waiters, with a grand piano prominently displayed near the lace curtained window. "Who is going to pay for it?"

Taylor Hendricks glanced up at her younger brother as she sank into the soft, cushioned chair he held out for her. Considering their tight budget, they both would be better off at a fast food restaurant.

Scott grinned, wanting to laugh out loud. He could barely contain his excitement. If things worked out the way he dreamed they would, they wouldn't have to worry about money ever again.

"I'm happy to see you, too," he teased. "Close your mouth and take a sip of the wine I ordered for your dining pleasure," he said, determined to hide his own unsettled nerves.

"Okay, where is my brother and what have you done with him?"

At twenty-eight, Taylor was eight years older than Scott. She had not hesitated to take on the added responsibility of taking care of her fifteen-year-old brother when their parents were forced to relocate to a warmer climate, due to their father's poor health. She had put her own career plans on hold in order to provide for them so that he did not have to leave Detroit and transfer to a new high school in St. Petersburg.

He was a great kid. He had worked hard in high school and finished near the top of his class. He had started college on a full basketball scholarship. He was now a sophomore at the University of Detroit. While he credited his sister, she, on the other hand, gave him high marks for staying out of trouble and working hard not to take advantage of the situation.

She had become parent, sister, and friend all rolled into one. Scott wanted her to be happy for him, yet he knew he was facing an uphill battle. How did he tell her his news without upsetting her?

"Why are we here?" she whispered, once the waiter had filled their water glasses and left menus.

Taylor worked at the University and was on her lunch break from her job in the computer lab. She was not due back until two. She enjoyed her work, loved answering student's questions and helping them learn the computer.

As soon as Scott obtained his degree in chemistry and started grad school, she would be able to become a full-time college student and finish not only a Master's in Computer Science but eventually a doctorate. She hoped someday to teach on the college level. Not that she would change their situation. Scott had never given her a bit of trouble. He deserved the helping hand she willingly gave him.

"Okay, what is going on?" she prompted.

"Are you ready to order, sir?"

"A few more minutes, please. The young lady hasn't had a chance to look at her menu," Scott said, winking at Taylor.

"Well?" she insisted, once they were alone.

"I have news . . . good news . . . really good news," Scott said earnestly.

His coffee-tone brown skin shone with good health and youth. At six-eight, he was the prize center on the University of Detroit's basketball team. He was having a phenomenal year. Sports agents and athletic coaches were coming from around the country to see him play, careful not to approach him or jeopardize his amateur status.

He watched his sister wearily, as if he could anticipate her response to his news. She would hate it. The question was: would she grow to accept it, or would she fight him every step of the way?

The importance of education had been drummed into both of their heads by well meaning parents. It was a commonly held belief in the African American community that Taylor whole-heartedly agreed with. Education was the key to eliminating the Black struggle, just as the importance of the Black vote was critical to the race.

"Well, well, well. Detroit isn't as big as I thought," a deep, masculine voice came from over her shoulder.

"Donald, my man," Scott jumped to his feet, his face wreathed in a wide grin. Meeting the Chicago Bulls' superstar had been exciting enough, but having the opportunity to sit down and actually talk to him had been a dream come true.

Taylor turned, getting her first view of the extremely tall man. Her breath caught in her throat at the sight. His height equaled her brother's, something that rarely happened. It was the smoothness of his teakwood brown skin and wide shoulders that almost caused her to gasp at their size. Yet it was the dark beauty of his eyes that caught and held her attention. They were jet black, rich with ebony lights, and they seemed to sparkle with humor. His features were prominent, a throwback to the powerful Africans that ruled ancient Egypt and peopled the most advanced civilization on earth.

"This is a surprise," Donald said, but his dark eyes were glued to the delectable lady who shared Scott's table.

There was only one word to be said about this African queen . . . perfection. She was beautifully curved, her shoulder-length thick black hair curled around her flawless, rich, caramel-colored face. She had small African features, large, deep brown eyes, so dark and rich. His senses went wild as he found himself fantasizing about tracing the generous lines of her lush rose tinted lips, the top lip seductively fuller than the bottom one, giving her a pouty allure.

To his utter disbelief, Donald felt his heart rate quicken and his sex thicken, heavy with longing. What was wrong with him? More important, who was she? Was she tall enough to fill a big man's arms . . . his bed? That question shocked him back to the present.

Hell, he didn't even know her name. Besides, he had enough trouble with women. Every time he turned around there was another one chasing him down. What ever happened to the man doing the hunting? Was a lady a thing of the past?

"Seems like both of us had the same idea . . . soul food," Scott joked, as he gazed with admiration at his hero and new mentor. They had taken an instant liking to each other. Donald did not hesitate to help in whatever way he could.

Taylor looked on, determined to keep her intense reaction to this man from showing. She hid a startling awareness that he was clearly the most attractive man she had ever seen. And she had seen him many times before . . . watched him on television on numerous occasions as he played basketball for the Chicago Bulls. In fact, she remembered he'd been in the news last summer when signing a new multimillion dollar contract to play another two or three years with the Bulls. He was huge, not only bigger than life, but exquisitely male. For such a large man, he moved with incredible grace.

The question uppermost in her mind was: what was Donald Williams doing here in Detroit? And how did her baby brother happen to know him? He was a celebrity.

Donald said, "I try to eat here whenever I'm in the city. I'm meeting my business partners for lunch."

The older home had been cleverly converted into the popular restaurant located close to the theater district and proposed football and baseball stadiums, close to downtown Detroit.

The entire time he was speaking, his attention was on the lovely woman who shared Scott's table. Who did she belong to? A woman like this was never without a man. Surely, she was not Scott's? He was too young for this fine sister.

"Oh!" Scott blushed, recognizing that he'd failed to make introductions. "Donald Williams, my sister Taylor."

"My pleasure," Donald offered a wide smile, hoping she would extend her hand. He couldn't help it. He wanted to touch her, wanted to know if her skin was as soft as it looked, wanted to know if she was attached.

Taylor nodded, her hands were firmly clasped in her lap, but her smile was warm and enchanting. "Mr. Williams. I've admired your prowess on the basketball court."

"Thank you," Donald's naturally deep voice had dropped even lower. He couldn't help himself. His entire body was reacting to her beauty. Hell, he couldn't even see if she wore a ring since her hands were in her damn lap. "Please call me Donald." His eyes lingered on the beauty of her exquisitely shaped mouth. It looked so soft, so tempting.

"Donald, please join us. That is, until your guests arrive," Scott said, eager for more of his company. This man understood the game with an expertise that Scott could only dream about.

"Ms. Hendricks?"

"Yes, please," Taylor managed, in spite of the butterflies in her stomach. Donald Williams! Who would believe?

"Taylor, Donald is an old friend of Coach Gardner's. We met yesterday during practice," Scott gushed.

"More than a friend. Greg was also my coach way back when I attended U. of D." Donald said softly. "I'm from Detroit."

"Oh, really." Taylor nodded, that was apparently the most she could come up with. What was wrong with her? She was acting as if she had never been near a good-looking man. So what if he was gorgeous? He was only human, for heaven's sake.

She didn't need to look around the dining room to know the man was causing a stir. Every female in the vicinity was looking at him. He wore his clothes like a dream. The taupe custom-made Italian suit with the pristine white shirt, teamed with a honey-and-tan striped tie was absolutely gorgeous on him. From the Italian loafers on his feet and the Piaget on his wrist, and the 18k-gold links at his cuffs he looked successful. Yet, none of those things made the man. Donald Williams was no doubt used to feminine attention.

"Do you have family living in Detroit?" If her life depended on it, Taylor could not recall his marital status. He wore no jewelry, just gold cuff links and tie tack. What threw her off balance was why the information mattered. She wasn't interested in a relationship.

"Yes, my sister and her family, as well as our older brother Carl and his wife."

Taylor struggled for a normalcy that she was far from feeling, telling herself that he was no different from any other man in the crowded dining room. Yet, she knew that wasn't true. He was anything but ordinary.

Donald Williams was one of a kind. He was one of the toughest forwards in the NBA. After ten years in the League, he was still at the top of his game. He was also very wealthy. If he was currently without a woman, it was due to choice alone. He didn't have to work to have a woman in his life, nor did he have to put forth any effort to keep one. His looks, his fame, and his income did all that for him. All he need do was enjoy yet another conquest.

"Detroit is home. I grew up on the west side of town. My parents are the only ones not still in the area. They retired to Florida a few years back." He eyed Scott thoughtfully. "You have a very talented brother. He's unbelievably smooth on the court. I saw him play yesterday, and I've heard his name being battered about. It's clear that his future lies with the NBA."

"That's wonderful. Scott's been crazy about the sport since he was little. A few more years and he might be ready to give it his full attention—that is, if he decides against grad school."

Taylor's dark eyes sparkled like precious jewels and her beautiful tinted lips formed a smile that captured his thoughts and seemed to take Donald's breath away. It took him a moment to collect his thoughts.

What was with her? She seemed so warm and lovely, yet her feet were firmly planted on the ground. Although she had smiled at him, she hadn't offered an open invitation to her lush body. And from what he could see of it, it was generously curved. The Lord had blessed her not only with a lovely face but with large, full breasts and a small waist. He was beginning to envy the dark rose-colored wool suit and white blouse that covered her soft skin.

"Sis, you can't imagine how surprised I was to see Donald at practice. Donald, I've admired you for years. The Bulls may have Michael and Rodman, but they also have you." Scott laughed with all the exuberance of youth. "You are what won them the last championship."

"Thanks," Donald laughed. "You're great for my ego. But you, my man, have it going on. I plan to talk to the coach about you. I, for one would be shocked if you don't make it into the draft this year. You are ready!"

Scott looked at him as if he'd been handed a gift-wrapped box on Christmas morning. His eyes danced with excitement. Taylor's eyes also sparked but with indignation.

"This year's draft? What's he talking about, Scott? You're only a sophomore, for heaven's sake! You have another two and half years of schooling ahead of you before you can entertain playing pro ball." Her brother's wide mouth went taut but he did not look past the brim of his beverage glass. "Scott?"

"No, Taylor. You don't understand. This could be my only chance to make the NBA. I'd be crazy not to take the opportunity."

"You'd be a fool to turn your back on a full athletic scholarship!"

"Taylor . . ." Donald said.

"Ms. Hendricks," she corrected tightly. It was to Scott that she addressed her next comment: "The NBA isn't going anywhere." Her agitation was evident in her voice, and both hands were braced on the table.

Donald's eyes flashed in triumph. She was not wearing any rings, engagement or otherwise. He kept his voice even when he said, "Scott's right. If he enters his name into the draft, believe me, I'll do everything I can to ensure he gets a fair deal. I can almost guarantee he'll get a lucrative contract. He's just that good. He might not be from one of the big ten, but he makes up for that with pure talent. He'd be out of his mind to turn a chance like this down."

"This is a family matter, Mr. Williams. That's not open to discussion."

Donald blinked, shocked by her candor. The lady was definitely not interested in impressing him. Nor was she afraid to speak her mind. He could not hold back the grin that spread across his face. She was feisty, yet real. There was nothing pretentious or phony about her. She did not care what he thought of her. A refreshing change for him. In fact, it was like an adrenaline rush going straight to his head.

While Donald was impressed, Scott was horrified. He had never heard his sister offer an unkind word to anyone. The news had evidently really rattled her—not that that was surprising. Her voice had a decided edge to it.

Scott blurted out, "Taylor Hendricks. I don't believe you said that. Donald was only trying to help."

Taylor flushed, embarrassed by her lack of control, but she couldn't help it. It was difficult enough to keep Scott on the right track without interference from the peanut gallery! It was none of Donald Williams's business. This was a family issue.

"I apologize. I didn't mean to be rude. Scott knows how much education means to our family." She frowned. "You have your degree, don't you, Mr. Williams?"

She was not about to step back and let a super-jock like Williams change what they had worked years to accomplish.

"Donald," he said softly, "I admit I finished my undergraduate work before I started pro ball. I went back and got my Masters' in business. The school house is not going to close. He can always go back. I think I know what you're getting at, but things were different when I was coming along. The system is tougher now. The guys start competing earlier. Some of them straight out of high school. Twenty-two can be old for a rookie."

Taylor glared at him, then said through tightly clenched teeth, "Do me a favor? Stay out of this."

They stared at each other. Donald longed to grin his delight. He had waited a lot of years to meet a woman like this. Taylor seemed to possess so many of the qualities he valued. Unfortunately, at the moment he was last on her list. Damn!

Just then he noticed his brother and brother-in-law being seated in the dining room. He waved reluctantly while getting to his feet, he said, "My lunch companions have arrived. Scott, it was good seeing you again. Good luck. You definitely have the talent. Ms. Hendricks, it has been a pleasure. Perhaps we can finish this discussion at another time?" His ebony eyes caressed her small features, lingering for a moment on her beautifully shaped full mouth.

Taylor didn't respond, staring at her plate.

"Thanks," Scott said rising to his feet and offering his hand.

"Any time." His gaze remained on Taylor. Much to his disappointment, she still did not lift her eyes from the meal being placed in front of her. Reaching into his inside pocket, he handed Scott his business card, saying, "Give me a call, anytime. I'll be glad to be whatever help I can."

As Donald walked away, he was thrown off balance by his uncharacteristic reaction to Taylor Hendricks. He had not noticed her when he initially approached the table. The instant his eyes had come into contact with hers, his heart had started to race as if he were in a full-court press during a championship game.

His heart rate had not slowed even now as he joined

his business partners, his older brother, Cart Williams and his brother-in-law, Jess Davis. He couldn't remember being so strongly attracted to anyone after so brief an encounter. What was it about her that instantly garnered his attention? He instinctively knew it was more than her beauty.

Although Carl was speaking to him, Donald's thoughts were on the woman on the other side of the room. His senses sizzled with deliciously sweet anticipation. Hell, he had been mildly aroused the entire time he sat beside Taylor. This was much, much more than sexual attraction. He wanted to know everything there was to know about her. What he wanted, he went after with a vengeance.

He was not concerned that this was the first time his aggressive ambitions had been directed toward a woman. Basketball and then, later, business, had become his passions. He did not understand what was happening to him, but he welcomed the change. His life had become too predictable . . . empty of emotional ties.

Taylor had made herself clear. Not only didn't she like him, she resented his interference in her baby brother's life. Donald did not require a crystal ball to know that getting to know Taylor would be an uphill battle all the way. He was up to the task.

# *Two*

"I don't believe you, Sis. What has gotten into you?"

"You have no cause to lecture me. I did what I had to do. At least one of us has to act like she has good sense," she snapped.

Taylor pushed her plate away. She was too upset to eat. In fact she knew she was close to breaking down. Taylor was so angry she was shaking. She was not going to let that arrogant jerk change the plans they had made for Scott's future. What did Donald Williams know about them anyway? Nothing!

It didn't matter how good looking he was. He had no business meddling in a private family matter. Why couldn't Scott see that? Why was he so upset with her? She'd done what she had always done, looked out for her baby brother.

If Donald Williams had just stayed out of it. They would not be arguing like this. This was all his fault! What she could not get over was the sheer gall of the man to try and influence her brother. It was none of his blasted business!

"Well?"

"Well, what?"

"I don't understand you."

She took a deep, calming breath, forcing herself to ask, "Were you going to quit school without even talking to me about it?"

"No," he quickly denied. "That's why I asked you here to help me celebrate." He searched her face, looking for approval.

Taylor had always been there for him, even before their folks moved down south. They had always been close, even when he was going through manhood and needed more independence. She'd given him space.

No matter what, he knew he could trust her. They had shared first her small apartment and then, later, the small home she had recently purchased. Many times she had been forced to stand in as mother or father, willing to do whatever she deemed necessary to keep him moving forward. Even though the decision as to whether to join the pros or not was his decision alone, he wanted her approval.

He sighed. They'd come a long way as a family. He had earned that basketball scholarship and had completed almost two years of college majoring in chemistry. He was a hard worker and kept his grades high. He'd also worked summers and evenings during the off-season at Randol Pharmaceutical, one of the largest black owned companies in the country. He could almost see his dream of becoming a research chemist blossoming.

Basketball was a bonus. It was the vehicle that would take him where he had always known he wanted to go. He wanted to be a research chemist and he wanted to own his own company. He had been warned against counting on making the pros. They all had. Coach Gardner was a no nonsense kind of guy. Until recently playing pro ball had been nothing more than a pipe dream.

Suddenly, he was not sure what he wanted to do. He faced the opportunity of a lifetime. What if it did not change his life for the better? What if he somehow lost sight of his goals? Should he take the risk? Then there was Taylor. She expected so much from him . . . too much at times. He didn't want to disappoint her. And they were too close for him not to know how she felt. This whole thing was hurting her. Damn! Why couldn't she see he needed her to support him, regardless of his ultimate decision? And then there was Jenna, his lady. He hadn't even told her yet.

"This draft thing came about unexpectedly. The coach has been talking to me about it. He had a few contacts with the NBA. There have been several scouts out watching me play. I've known about it, but I tried to just do my thing and not let it throw my game off.

"I know I keep saying it, but I've never seen anything like it. When Donald walked in, man! He stopped practice just like that," he snapped his fingers for emphasis. "The guys were floored. Man! Donald Williams!" Scott's eyes gleamed with enthusiasm. "He autographed everyone's jerseys. I can't even imagine being able to play with guys like Rodman, Sally, Jordan, and Shaq! Man, oh, man! Williams is all over the floor. He's everywhere and not squeamish about taking a hit, either. Just being able to talk to him about my game was awesome."

"I don't care about Donald Williams! I care about you!"

"How could you treat him so coldly? Man, there is no telling what he thinks of me now after your rudeness! What got into you, girl?"

The last thing she cared about was what a stranger thought of either one of them. Her brother was another matter. Taylor had always tried to set a good example for him. He was right, she had acted out of character. She had no choice but to stand up for what she believed in. Scott's future was worth fighting for. She would go toe to toe with Williams any day of the week if that was what it took to protect her baby brother.

Taylor huffed with indignation, "You could have given me some warning. I really didn't expect to meet a celebrity at lunch. More important, I thought you would have come to me with this, rather than deciding for yourself."

"I had planned to talk to you about it. That was what this lunch meeting was about. I didn't know Donald was going to be here."

Glancing at her watch, she pushed back her chair. "I have to get a move on. Should I expect you and Jenna for dinner?" She threw her napkin down impatiently beside her untouched plate. Scott spent what free time he had with his girlfriend, Jenna Gaines.

"I'll be over after practice. Jenna has a late class tonight."

"Fine. See you later."

Intent on adjusting the heavy black wool ruana over her shoulders as she prepared to leave, Taylor walked right into Donald Williams, who had made use of the washroom off the foyer of the converted house. If he had not caught her, she would have bounced off his broad muscular chest like a quarter on a tautly made bed. His large hands gently cupped her shoulders.

"Excuse me," she stammered, then realizing who was holding her, she quickly stepped out of his reach. Her soft, generously curved mouth was set in a firm line.

"Are you all right?" he asked. His husky voice seemed to come from deep inside his chest, the sound heavy with masculine appeal.

Taylor shivered, in spite of herself. She did not want to notice anything about this man. He represented all that she did not want her brother to become . . . easy wealth, loose women, probably drugs, who knew what other excess. Even though pro ball seemed highly appealing to a young man like Scott, she had no doubt it could also be destructive.

"In a hurry?" he smiled, thoroughly pleased that she was tall, over six feet in heels, and generously curved in all the right places. Oh, yeah, she was all sweetly scented woman. And she wasn't exactly jumping through hoops trying to gain his interest.

Despite her best efforts, her eyes were drawn like a magnet to the firm lines of his strong African featured face. Her gaze lingered too long on his full, well-shaped mouth before she caught herself and looked away.

"Taylor?"

She blinked quickly, disturbed at her keen awareness of this man. It was not welcome. "Excuse me. I have to get back to . . ." she stopped herself, furious that she'd been explaining herself to him, of all people.

What was wrong with her? What difference did it make how utterly masculine he was, how wondrously appealing? She was not stupid! She was not about to fall for a man just because he was good to look at. She would not have her name added to his no doubt long list of conquests.

"I hope I didn't spoil your lunch. I know we had a difference of opinion, but I hope that doesn't mean we can't get to know each other. Perhaps, one evening soon over dinner?" Donald knew he was moving quickly, but he didn't have the advantage of time.

He was taking a late flight tonight back to Chicago. He'd be on the road in a matter of days. He was not prepared to let this lovely woman walk out of his life. He wanted a chance to get to know her, much, much better.

Taylor stared at him, incredulous. No, he didn't! Evidently, he was so used to women falling all over themselves to get next to him that he expected her to do the same. Well, he was in for a disappointment. She could not stand the man! So why in the world was her heart pounding, and why were her senses sharply aware of his male scent?

She was thoroughly infuriated with him and herself.

The highly sensitive tips of her breasts had actually peaked from the brief contact with his deep chest. Her nipples had gone tight and achy as if preparing for his touch . . . his mouth. What was wrong with her? She never responded so quickly to any man. She fought the urge to cover her chest, hide her reaction to his nearness.

With her hands balled at her sides, she said, "I already know more about you, Mr. Williams, than I ever wanted to know. No, thank you. It's enough for me that you're encouraging my brother to give up the one thing he has worked to accomplish all these years—an education." She paused before she went on to say, "You had your degree before you started playing ball, so you had something to fall back on if you were badly injured. What will Scott have? Two years of college. There is not much a black man can do these days to take care of himself and his family without a degree."

Her beautiful eyes flashed with temper as she moistened her lips, unwittingly drawing his interested gaze to the area. "Nowadays, you need a high school diploma just to slap two pieces of bread together in a fast food restaurant. Our family wants better than that for Scott." Taylor knew her voice shook with emotion but she couldn't help it.

"Look, Taylor, if we could just talk calmly about this, I'm sure we could reach an agreement. Scott is a good kid, even I can see that. He's got a hell of a future."

"An agreement between us? Never . . ." she said, turned on her heels and marched away before he could do more than admire the lush curves of her shapely behind and the beauty of her unbelievably long legs.

He might have caught her if he had not been stopped by several female fans who demanded autographs. Damn!

His resolve hardened. He would find a way to get to

know that gutsy lady. Those few minutes of having her in his arms had convinced him that not only could she fit his large frame to perfection with her queen-sized beauty but, more importantly, that she intrigued him mentally. She was not afraid to fight for what she believed in. When she cared, she apparently did so with her entire heart. No half measures for this lady. And she was very much a lady. Imagining that kind of loyalty and devotion directed his way was, frankly, more than he'd hoped to find in any woman. Loyalty, devotion, beauty, brains, and courage . . . what more could any man ask for?

A man would have to be a fool to willingly let a woman like Taylor Hendricks walk out of his life. Donald may be many things, but he was not stupid. He grinned roguishly, realizing that he was actually looking forward to the challenge ahead.

The bumper to bumper traffic on the I-94 freeway had Taylor ready to tear her hair out by the roots by the time she pulled into the driveway of the two bedroom house on the west side of the city.

She looked at the modest home with pride, despite her hovering headache. After collecting the mail, she let herself inside, pausing long enough to wave at her next-door neighbor. The neighborhood Block Club worked hard at keeping their area clean and crime free. No abandoned boarded-up houses or crack houses in their neighborhood.

"Bills, bills . . . more bills," Taylor mumbled, dropping them, along with her keys, on the hall table. She collapsed on the couch, flicking on the television. She didn't expect Scott until after seven. He had basketball practice, as usual. She hoped he stopped for burgers tonight, then thought better of the idea. After springing for lunch at Edmund's Place, he would be broke and looking for a meal.

Lately, she had been lucky if she saw him at all except for Sunday dinner. Between basketball, his studies, and his girlfriend, Jenna, he didn't spend much time with her these days.

Suddenly, her eyes went wide. Fumbling for the remote control, she quickly raised the volume of the set. On Channel 4, the news broadcaster, Carmen Harlan, was interviewing none other than Donald Williams.

When asked if he were involved in the city's empowerment zone project, he said that along with his partners, they had been contracted to build a mini-mall and were working to draw black-owned businesses into the mall. They were willing to offer financial help if necessary.

When asked about his charity work, Donald admitted that he was involved in the development of year round sports camps for inner city kids in both Chicago and New York. In Detroit, he was very much interested in expanding the Malcolm X Community Center, headed by Charles Randol and Dexter Washington, to include the east, north, and south sides of the city. The interview ended with his predictions for the current basketball season.

She sat glaring at the screen, then clicked off the set. He was just as attractive as he had been that afternoon in the restaurant. It had been hours since she had last seen him, but she still hadn't gotten over the sheer arrogance of the man.

How could he think that she would even consider dating him after he had encouraged her brother to quit college and play for the NBA? No way! The trouble with Donald Williams was that he could not believe there was a woman on the planet who could resist his dark masculine looks. Well, he was wrong. She would not waste her time by giving him more than half a second's worth of consideration.

All her energy should be focused on Scott. How close was he to making the type of choice that could alter his entire life? He said he had not decided yet, but he had invited her out to lunch to celebrate. Taylor reached for the telephone, but decided not to call their folks, after all.

Why upset them just because she was worried? No, it was much too soon. What she should be concentrating on was how to convince Scott that he would be making a terrible mistake if he quit now, rather than going ahead and getting his degree. She would support him if he decided to postpone graduate school for a few years to play pro ball.

Scott called while she was changing into an old tee-shirt and sweat pants, to tell her not to bother with cooking, since he was bringing Chinese carry-out. She was absently thumbing through the latest issue of *Essence* magazine when he arrived.

"Hey, Sis. Hope you're hungry," Scott said, placing a large bag on the coffee table with a forced grin. His dark gaze was troubled.

"I'll get the plates and silverware," she volunteered, hurrying into the kitchen. She was annoyed with herself when she acknowledged that she had not expected Scott to be alone. For an instant, her heart had accelerated at the thought of Donald accompanying him. Thank heaven, she'd been wrong. One encounter with that smooth womanizer should have been enough to last a lifetime. He probably had women crawling out of the woodwork just to be near him. Well, he need not lose sleep at night worrying about *her* chasing him down.

"I brought two quarts of pepper steak, almond chicken, shrimp fried rice and mixed Chinese vegetables."

Taylor nodded, handing him his utensils.

"You should be starving. You didn't eat any lunch."

She shrugged, trying not to start another argument. What was the point? It would just get his back up before she could make her point. They had to talk about this calmly without emotions getting into it. The trouble was she was his big sister and she knew she was right about this. She just had to make him understand.

"What is this, Sis? You not talking to me?" He knew he was on edge, but he expected his sister to give as good as she got. She was a fighter.

Taylor looked up from filling her dinner plate. "Sorry. I just have a lot on my mind." Studying her brother, she asked, "Why didn't you tell me?"

At his puzzled look, she clarified, "About the scouts coming to see you play?"

"There haven't been any offers. I didn't take it seriously. Coach has been talking about it for some time, but I thought it was his way of keeping me on my toes, keep me working hard."

"Are scouts supposed to talk to you, try to recruit you? Doesn't that jeopardize your current status?"

"Yeah, but they have been cool. No one has approached me. I've just been told when they're in the gym. A lot of the guys were under scrutiny, not just me. With March Madness coming up, it is going to get crazy."

"So no one has propositioned you?"

"No. Everything is cool."

Taylor had her doubts but she didn't voice them. At this point they did not need an overeager agent or scout causing him to lose his athletic scholarship. It was too scary to even think about. Thank goodness the collegiate finals were fast approaching. The basketball season would be over soon. He would have all summer to decide, wouldn't he?

"I had no idea you were even considering playing pro-ball. This has come out of the blue, a complete surprise." More like a slap in the face, Taylor decided but, wisely did not voice.

"Yeah!" Scott broke into a peal of laughter.

"There is always time for the pros, after college. Why does it have to be now or never?"

"Don't go ballistic on me. I haven't made a decision, Sis."

"You may love the game, but your education will determine your future, good or bad. I thought you admired Charles Randol, wanted to own your own pharmaceutical company some day?"

"I do. I also admire Donald Williams. We have a lot in common. He's from Detroit. He played for U. of D. before he was drafted by New York. He's good people." He sighed heavily before he went on to say, "Let's look at this objectively. I'll be twenty next month. I'm in top shape. I'm strong and I'm healthy. College ball is no picnic. We play to win. We're having a great season and we're going to win the championship."

"But Scott . . ."

"No, let me finish." His eyes pleaded with her to understand. "I know I could be hurt at any time. If that happened, then you tell me what kind of chance I'll have to enter the pros after college? Very little. I'm not stupid. I can't just turn my back on a chance like this."

"Easy money! We're talking about dollars and cents. You always told me that you wanted a career in chemistry. Have you changed your mind about that also?"

"No!"

"That means a degree and then graduate school."

"I know that. Do you have any idea what I could make playing pro ball? I'm talking about millions. You would have the money to go back to school full time without having to work. Money that Mama and Daddy could use to build that dream house they've always wanted. We could see them more often."

"If you do this you are doing it for yourself not us . . . certainly not me."

He chose to ignore the last and went on as if she hadn't interrupted. "The money will take a worry off the folks' shoulders. Dad can have whatever treatment he needs, no matter how expensive. Do you have any idea how proud this will make me? To be able to help my family? Jenna and I wouldn't have to wait to marry."

"Marry?"

"We've been talking about it after college. This way we wouldn't have to wait. We're together as much as we can manage it now. I want to be able to pay for her schooling so she won't have to worry about it. I love her, Sis." He said, closely watching her reaction.

Taylor was somewhat traditional in her views. She knew he spent more time with Jenna than he did at home. Taylor didn't like it that they were practically living together, but there was nothing she could do to stop it. She had purposefully not mentioned it to their parents, not wanting to upset them. He knew that Taylor felt he was rushing things and he was too young to be so serious about any one girl.

Yet, she also loved Jenna. She was a wonderful girl and she had been so good for Scott. But marriage? Now was not the time to further complicate an already complicated situation.

"This decision should be about you, Scott . . . only you. What does Coach Gardner say about it?"

"Are you kidding? He was all for it."

"That doesn't make sense! He should be encouraging all of you to finish college. Good grief! The man is an educator, for heaven's sake!"

"Come on, Sis. He'll look damn good if I'm picked up early in the draft. It also draws attention to U. of D.'s athletic department. It's a win, win situation for the college. Just look what Donald Williams's success has done for the college's reputation."

Taylor tried to concentrate on her dinner, even though she had lost interest in food. She nearly choked when Scott asked, "What do you think of Donald? I saw you talking to him in the foyer."

Taylor did not welcome the question. And worse, she didn't have an answer. She had been unable to think of little else besides Donald Williams.

It had been years since she had been so taken with a man, not since she had been used by someone she cared about. She had made it her business to stay away from men, especially the good-looking, womanizing variety. When she dated now it was no different than when she went out with a girlfriend, nothing more than casual friendships.

"Sis?"

"What?"

"I said . . ."

"I heard you. Shall we change the subject?" Taylor was on her feet, having discarded her plate. She paced the brightly furnished living room done in shades of rose, from the deepest burgundy to the palest blush.

"That's too bad, because he asked about you."

"What? Scott, I don't want to talk about him. He's your hero, not mine. I would have been perfectly happy not to have met him at all."

"Well, he is interested in you. He wanted your phone number."

"Maybe he was trying to reach you?"

"He wanted to know about you, not me," Scott was trying not to grin. He found the whole thing amusing.

"He questioned you about my personal life?"

"Yeah!"

"What did he want to know?" She could not stop her-self from asking.

"The usual. If you're single, involved, or dating that kind of stuff."

"And you told him?" Her voice was filled with accu-sations.

"Why not? You're not serious about anyone and haven't been for a long time. The guys you go out with are friends, nothing more."

"You should know when to keep your big mouth shut!" Scott roared with laughter. "Why?"

"It's none of his business, that's why!" Taylor snapped. Scott chuckled. "Liked him, did ya?"

"No!"

"Yeah, sure. What else is new? The sky falling?"

"I said . . ."

"I don't care what you said. I saw the way you were looking at the guy. You should be pleased that he's in-terested. He's a great guy."

"Scott! The man has women falling all over his feet everywhere he goes. I'm not joining that crowd."

"I don't think there's a problem. Just because he's in the NBA does not mean he is a player."

"Sure."

"Taylor . . ."

"Not interested."

"And if he calls?"

"It's not likely. My guess is you will talk to him before I do."

"I have his number if you're interested."

"Bury it!"

Scott almost fell on the floor laughing.

"Forget Donald Williams. We are discussing your fu-ture." She hesitated, her worried gaze directed at her baby brother. "Do me a favor, kid?"

"What?"

"Don't rush this decision. Talk to the folks. Talk to Jenna. Maybe she might not want to be married to a college drop-out? We haven't even talked about you getting seriously hurt. One serious injury and your career goes down the drain. That has to be considered. This would change your whole life. Maybe not for the better? Think about it."

"Okay," he said, collecting the plates and the uneaten food. He started carrying everything into the small kitchen in the rear of the house.

Taylor was right behind him when she said, "Okay? That's it?"

"I agree with you," he said, placing dirty dishes in the sink, then turned to face her. "I'll take my time deciding." He leaned over and kissed her cheek. "I have to get going. I want to meet Jenna after her night class. I don't want her walking home."

Taylor followed him to the front door. "Be careful."

"I will. But you have some thinking to do also."

"Me?"

"Why are you so reluctant to give Donald a chance?"

"I just met the man."

"This has everything to do with Alex."

"No way!"

"Then why don't we ever talk about what happened between the two of you?"

"It's ancient history," Taylor explained quickly. "There is nothing to discuss."

"If he's history then you should be over the man by now. Sis, you've been using him as a shield to protect yourself from other men. It's time to stop. I love you and I want you happy. You're twenty-eight, not a hundred and twenty-eight."

"Get going! Isn't Jenna waiting for you?"

Taylor finished in the kitchen before she prepared

for bed. It was still early, but she was exhausted. It had been a long, emotionally draining day.

As she slowly sank into a sudsy, hot bath, she vowed to pretend that she had never even met Donald Williams. He was not for her. The man of her dreams was strong, sincere, capable of loving one woman and devoting himself to her alone.

She had waited years to find such a man. In fact, she had given up hope of ever finding him. Nowadays, she concentrated on her personal goals. She read and studied, worked hard in her classes as she prepared for an eventual teaching career in computer science. It would take years, even if she could afford to take classes full-time. Unfortunately, her days of being a full-time student were behind her. She had to keep her job at least until Scott graduated. Only then could she afford to work flat-out to complete her master's degree and eventually, a doctorate degree.

She had never considered the sacrifices she had made to help Scott as a hardship. They were family and family meant everything. She wanted Scott to have all the advantages available to him. She didn't consider having a career in the NBA to be living up to his full potential. His dreams were much higher than shooting hoops for a price. Now, if Donald Williams stayed out of both their lives they would not have a problem.

# Three

Donald had very little free time these days. His schedule had little room for extravagance. Although he owned Williams Enterprises, with his basketball schedule, he really didn't have as much time as he needed to devote to the rapidly growing business. He relied on Carl and Jess to handle the day-to-day operations.

The three partners had a variety of business interests, including real estate development, and new housing starts, as well as giving minority businesses support in getting started. Currently, they were working with the mayor's task force, recruiting Black-owned businesses for Detroit's empowerment zone.

Charles Randol had contacted Donald in hopes of getting him involved in the expansion of the Malcolm X Community Center throughout the city. Charles had met Donald in Washington while taking part in the Million Man March and he had learned about Donald's work with teens in Chicago and New York. The two had become friends, realizing they had more than business interests in common but also similar views on the black man's role in insuring black boys' survival.

Donald had spent most of the day in meetings, the high point had been meeting Taylor Hendricks. She hadn't been far from his thoughts, even when he arrived at the Randol home exactly at seven for his scheduled business dinner.

"Welcome," Charles Randol said at the d█ smile, offering his hand. The African-America█ tycoon wasn't a small man, but he didn't quite equal Donald in height—but then few men did.

"You're sure I'm not imposing?" Donald asked as he stepped into the foyer.

"No problem. My wife enjoys entertaining. She's a jewel." Charles smiled easily.

"Sounds like you are a lucky man."

Charles nodded. "I have no complaints. This is Dexter Washington. Dex runs the center."

Donald accepted the other man's outstretched hand. "Great to meet you. Charles speaks highly of you."

"It's good of you to take time to meet with us," Dexter said quietly.

"No problem," Donald assured them. "Sorry it had to be so late in the day."

"Come on in. I bet you could use a drink." Charles led the way into the elegantly furnished living room.

"Sounds great." One thing Donald liked about Charles was that he was not star-struck, there was no hero worship, no cheesing.

Charles's dark eyes sparkled. His gaze lingered on his lovely wife who was seated on the sofa. Her eyes danced with pleasure as they locked with her husband's.

"Look who's here," he announced, then dropped his gaze to the pretty little girl on his wife's lap. Madelyn, fourteen months old, giggled, "Da-Da," holding up her chubby little arms. She was a tiny replica of her very beautiful mother, from her toffee-tone skin to her large dark eyes and thick black curls.

Charles laughed, kissing her plump cheeks and tossing her up into his arms. The baby giggled with delight.

Donald watched the intimate family scene. The deep love that the couple shared was easy to discern. Yes, Charles was a damn lucky man. He had what Donald felt was missing from his own life, a loving woman to fill his arms and soothe his lonely heart.

Realizing his oversight, Charles hastily said, "Oh, sorry. Donald Williams my wife, Diane Rivers-Randol and our daughter, Madelynn."

"How do you do, Mr. Williams. Please, have a seat."

Donald smiled, comfortable with her warm easy manner. "Please, call me Donald. You have a lovely home."

"Oh, thank you. We're constantly finding things to work on."

"What ya drinkin'?" Charles asked.

Donald noted the beer Dexter was holding, then said, "Water. Season's on," he explained.

Once they were all comfortably seated, Charles and Diane side by side on one sofa, the baby in her father's lap, Diane said, "I'm sorry I'm not much of a sports fan, but we're honored to have you in our home. Chucky has told me what a busy man you are and I would like to thank you for finding the time to work on this project with him. It means a lot to us."

Donald smiled. "Unfortunately, it is necessary work. I apologize that I have to intrude on your family time in order to meet with Charles."

"I assure you, it is not a problem."

Donald was conscious of the tenderness and genuine love and warmth these two shared and probably took for granted, just as he was when he was around his sister and her husband or his brother and his wife.

It built in him a longing that was always there, no matter how full his own life seemed. The problem was, he didn't have a special lady in his life and in his heart. Because of it, the road ahead seemed longer and lonelier with each new day.

The evening proved to be pleasant and Donald found he was able to relax as they discussed the year-round sport camps that he had developed and that were working so well in Chicago and New York, as well as the community center here in the Detroit area.

It was while he was on his way to the airport that he realized his thoughts had never strayed far from Taylor Hendricks. She had captured his attention in a big way without any effort on her part. She clearly had no idea what she had done to his equilibrium . . . shot it to hell. He had been completely thrown off balance when she flounced out of the restaurant, refusing even to listen to him. He had no choice but to seek out her brother.

He noticed everything about her, from the way she dressed—fashionably chic—to her thick black curls. There are some things a woman can't hide. Taylor's figure was lush and provocative, while her features were downright alluring. The woman's pouty sweet mouth looked as if she were begging for a man's tongue. What was that old saying? Something about sopping up like a biscuit? Oh, yeah, he grinned roguishly. It fit. He felt as if he could swallow her whole.

What was it about that woman that he found so incredibly appealing? It was more than her looks. Her smile had caused his breath to quicken and his heart to race. She was so feminine, from the way she smelled, to the way she moved her head, down to the sound of her voice. He found the entire package fascinating.

Curiously, her resentment toward him was not a turnoff. In fact, it was a clear challenge. She had formed that opinion based on a single brief meeting. How difficult would it be to get her to change her mind? He was almost certain that she had been as aware of him as he had been of her. He would be stupid not to try to capitalize on that awareness. He wasn't prepared to walk away. His instincts told him Taylor's warmth and sweetness were worth any sacrifice.

He didn't often meet opposition from women. In fact, he couldn't honestly remember the last time his advances had been rebuffed. Donald almost laughed aloud. His cockiness was showing. He considered pride as part of manhood. If he didn't believe in himself, who would believe in him? No one.

The absolutely crazy part of it was that he had wanted Taylor to notice him, to like him, had wanted her to give him a chance.

For the first time in memory, his professional basketball status hadn't helped, instead, it had hurt his cause. Taylor hadn't fawned over him when they had been introduced. Her smile had held a natural curiosity, nothing more—until she realized he had encouraged her brother to quit college in favor of pro ball. After that, it was downhill all the way.

Donald jogged to the hangar where his private plane was waiting for him. He would be the first to admit that he was somewhat set in his ways. He preferred a late night flight rather than staying over. He spent his nights, whenever possible, in his own specially designed bed, made to accommodate his super-sized frame. Lately, he found the traveling tiresome; waking in a different city, surrounded by unfamiliar furnishings, had lost all its appeal.

As the plane started to climb, he stared absently out the window. His laptop was beside his oversized leather armchair, his briefcase was open on the seat of the matching leather chair next to him. As he looked down on the twinkling lights of the city far below, he realized that leaving Detroit meant leaving Taylor. He didn't have to close his eyes to recall her scent . . . it was a light, airy scent, almost like jasmine. He remembered leaning toward her in hopes of drowning his senses. Damn! He shifted uncomfortably in his seat. He'd been semi-aroused since meeting her earlier that day.

It had been quite a while since a new woman had captured his interest. He'd been turned off women, turned off by the greed he saw in their eyes once they recognized him. They saw dollar signs, not the man. As with most pro-ballplayers, women were constantly making themselves readily available to him. After ten years on the basketball court, it was, frankly, a bore.

Hell, he'd given up on meeting a normal, down to earth woman who would not fall instantly in love with his bank balance . . . that was, until today. Taylor's heated reaction to him had given him something that he'd thought he'd lost . . . hope. He was hopeful that she might eventually be interested in him as simply a man . . . no different than any other. He grinned. He could not help but respect her views and applaud her courage in standing up for them. A woman of conviction.

Carl would have a good laugh at his expense, that was, if he were dumb enough to tell his brother about the situation he had gotten himself into. Imagine, Donald shook his head in dismay, he was wildly attracted to the one woman in America who could not stand the sight of him.

It had been going on for years, yet he still was amazed at the things women had done to obtain his interest. More often than not, it was downright disgusting. There were no limits. He'd been stalked, he'd been propositioned. A few women had tried to trap him in false paternity suits. Simple blood tests had cleared his name every single time, but the publicity had been nasty.

Thank the Lord, he had the good sense to listen to his father and his older brother. Without fail, he had used a condom, even before the advent of AIDS. It had saved his neck on more than one occasion. Eventually, he had gotten so fed up with casual relationships that never touched his emotions, or spirit, that he'd finally opted for celibacy. It was a fact he shared with no one, not even Carl. And the two them, along with his brother-in-law had few secrets. Yet, this was too private to share with anyone.

In spite of all the craziness, he knew he had been truly blessed. He had been born with a talent and an intellect that many envied. He had been able to make his own dreams come true and he had been able to help his family. Now he wanted to concentrate on giving a helping hand to his people.

Sighing as he massaged the tight muscles in his neck, he covered a yawn. He had asked his secretary to fax a report on the progress of the mall the company was involved in in Denver. He'd read the same page three times and still had no idea what it said.

He was dog tired. He felt as if he'd just come off a long road trip, thoroughly beat. Yet, as tired as he was, his mind returned time and time again to the caramel-toned beauty who had him so damn hard he hurt, all without even trying. Taylor was downright dangerous to his well-being.

Did she have any idea how lovely she was? There was not a single doubt in his mind that she had men falling all over themselves trying to get close to her. She could send a man's blood pressure soaring with a seductive blink of her long ebony lashes. And brother, could she fill a bra. That last thought caused his entire body to pulse.

Taylor had done nothing more than look at him with those dark brown eyes and those luscious rose-tinted lips and he was a goner. Had he ever responded so quickly to any woman, no matter how good she looked? He spent the entire time they were together aching to make love to her.

Hell! Donald was not eighteen any more. He knew what he wanted from life. He knew the type of woman he wanted to share that life with. The difficulty had always been in finding that special lady. Now, suddenly, he found himself wondering if Taylor Hendricks was that woman.

Would she even let him come close enough to find out? It was as if she had built a brick wall around herself. Why? Had she been hurt by a man? Someone had caused her to put her defenses firmly in place.

Just thinking about the enticing softness of her mouth, the top lip fuller, almost pouty, made him hungry. He had no trouble visualizing her in his arms. He had no doubt she would fit him to perfection, all those lush curves and long beautiful legs. He had never been aware of an attraction to full-figured women before, but suddenly he was a number one fan. Taylor was enough woman to hold on to, woman enough to satisfy this big man's potent needs.

As the plane began its descent, he realized he had a problem. He was in no condition to be strolling through the airport. What he needed was a cold shower. Damn! Maybe he was just plain horny? It had been a very long time since he had enjoyed a woman's soft body.

He wanted more for himself than the jock queens who trailed the team and frequented the night spots the fellows preferred. He deserved better.

He deserved a woman like Taylor. A woman whose life revolved around her family, her friends, and her career. A woman with enough love to share her sweetness with only one man . . . her special man. He wanted to be that man. He longed to be the center of her heart. Now all he had to figure out was, how?

The team left for L.A. tomorrow afternoon, the game was on Sunday. He would not be back in Chicago for a couple of weeks, then it would be another week or more before they would head out to play Detroit. He had less than a month to weaken her resolve. How could he use the time to his advantage and lure her his way? By the time he returned to the big D, he wanted her at least willing to see him.

Tickets for the game with the Pistons was too obvious. They may have impressed Scott, but they probably wouldn't faze Taylor. What would it take? What would cause the stubborn African beauty to turn her sweet smile loose on him?

He couldn't remember wanting anything more than he wanted her. He longed to have those large dark eyes gazing at him with warmth and interest. Three weeks. . . .

Taylor had worked late the following day. She was especially tired when she climbed her front steps. She was collecting the mail when she heard her next-door neighbor calling her name.

"Hi, Mrs. Burns. How's the shoulder?"

"Don't need no weatherman to tell me it's going to rain tonight. My shoulder does the tellin'. How you, baby? Keep yourself so busy you don't have no time for a cup of coffee these days. Made some apple cobbler," the elderly woman offered.

Taylor flushed, realizing she hadn't been over to visit with the older woman in some time. "We'll have to fix that soon. How's your grandson?" she asked, pulling her trench coat tight around her in an effort to ignore the damp air and her tired feet.

"I suppose he's well. Ain't heard from him in nearly a month. You know how some folks can get uppity once they get them high-payin' jobs. Working on the city council has sure gone to his big head." She shook her head. Her snow white hair was bound in a tight bun at her nape, and her brown face was lined over the years. "Delivery man left something for you. Told him you don't come home until after six most days. Said he'd remember. I'll get the box."

Taylor crossed over to the other yard to climb the steps to her elderly neighbor's porch so she wouldn't have to come out in the cold air.

Although spring was technically almost a month away, it wasn't apparent in the crisp Michigan evening. Snow banks still littered the ground in spots, while the majestic trees were still bare of any hint of spring leaves.

Taylor was shocked when she was handed a florist's box trimmed with a huge pink and yellow bow with trailing ribbons.

"New young man?" Mrs. Burns beamed approvingly.

"No! There must be some mistake," Taylor insisted.

"Your name and address are printed on the order form, plain as day. See."

Taylor was forced to agree. It was for her. But who?

Mrs. Burns's eyes gleamed with maternal interest. "A pretty girl like you should be married with a family of her own."

Taylor's heart ached, but she hid it behind a smile and leaned over to give the petite lady a kiss on the cheek. "I have kept you out in the cold long enough. You go on inside. May I come by Saturday morning for a chat?"

"Of course, darlin'. I'll make some of my walnut coffee cake to snack on. You like that, don't you?"

"Too much!" Shaking her finger at Mrs. Burns, she insisted. "Don't you dare do that. That's all I need is another five pounds on this body. No, thanks. I'm determined to start that new diet everyone is talking about."

"Girl, you don't need a diet. What you need is a good man to appreciate you just the way you are."

Taylor laughed. "Love you. See you on Saturday." She waved before heading toward home.

Taylor remembered when all she wanted in the world was to fall in love with a wonderful man and have a family of her own. She wanted what her own mother had, a loving relationship that could withstand the test of time. She had come to accept that, in her case, it was nothing more than wishful thinking.

It had been her experience that many black men preferred cute and petite women with figures to match. Or at least the brothers she had contact with had a problem with a tall, full-figured sister.

Taylor's hands were shaking as she let herself inside while balancing her briefcase, the mail, and the florist's box. Who in the world could have sent it?

She had only been serious about a man once in her life. It had proved to be a huge mistake. A mistake that had broken her heart and caused her to distrust men, especially the tall, dark and handsome variety. She had once been attracted to the type of man who could have any woman he wanted. One woman had not been enough to keep him satisfied. From him she had learned a very valuable lesson: how to keep men at arm's length. What woman in her right mind wanted that kind of heartache?

No, she was better served by concentrating on her career. In order to excel at the university, all she needed was to keep herself firmly focused on her academic goals, in addition to helping her brother finish college. Later, after she had completed her master's she would be able to apply for a position as a full fledged professor. Perhaps that future would also include spending the summers in Africa, seeing the motherland?

Donald Williams's strong African face flickered through her mind as she stared at the unopened box. It simply could not be from him. He had to have women practically flinging themselves at him on a daily basis. Why would he send *her* flowers, of all people? He could have any woman he wanted by crooking his little finger. He had his pick of some of the most beautiful women in the world . . . fashion models and movie stars were not beyond his reach.

How could she wonder, even for a moment, if he had sent her flowers? It was ridiculous. Scott was wrong. Donald might be looking for sex, but he was not looking for love.

She stubbornly refused to peek at the card or open the box. She forced herself to focus on mundane chores such as putting away her briefcase, and putting her coat away in the hall closet. She carried the box into her bedroom, and hung her suit in her bedroom closet before she allowed her gaze to return to the unopened box. She told herself it didn't matter who had sent them, as she changed into white leggings and one of her brother's oversized T-shirts.

Hadn't she stalled long enough? She didn't want to admit she was afraid to open the box, afraid of what she would discover.

Slowly, she slid the ribbons from the long white lacquered box. "Oh!" she gasped. Inside the tissue were a dozen pink and yellow roses, surrounded by fluffy white baby's breath. They were so lovely, absolutely beautiful. She dropped the card three times before her hands were steady enough for her to break the seal. "It was my pleasure meeting you. Donald."

Taylor covered her mouth to hold back the sound. Donald Williams! Had they exchanged one kind word? Hardly. She had made herself perfectly clear—she was not interested in dating him. She wasn't interested in knowing him. She couldn't stand him. How could he possibly forget that single glaring detail? And why did he have to be so darn gorgeous? His big muscular frame could make any woman weak in the knees.

How could he have done such a thing? She was not

even his type. She was five-ten in her stocking feet. Her hips and breasts could only be described as ample, and her thighs . . . goodness, she didn't even want to think about them. She could exercise herself silly and her body stayed the same. Losing weight only made her small waist even smaller and her midriff leaner . . . the hated hips and full breasts even more pronounced. Of course, that did not stop her from trying.

Donald! He had no right to try and influence her brother. Didn't he understand how much Scott admired him? He had the power to change the course of Scott's life. Whether he liked it or not, impressionable young men held him in high esteem. Men like Michael Jordan and Grant Hill did not overshadow Donald. He was an icon, for goodness' sakes.

Taylor decided it did not matter if she had piqued his interest for about a half a minute. He was not for her. His money would be better spent romancing a woman whose hardest decision for the day was which shoe to wear with which outfit. She had more important matters to concern herself with.

She had to find a way to disarm Donald's impact on her Scott. She must help him see that he was not using his head to decide, but letting a fantasy of wealth and fame overwhelm him. He longed for the glamour of pro ball, not the harsh reality. Yes, the NBA did give away million-dollar contracts, but that money had to be earned. Not every player was star material. Everyone didn't make top dollar . . . only a select few. A wrong decision now would impact on the rest of his life.

She had reached for the telephone time and time again to call their folks, but had stopped herself each and every time. This had to be Scott's choice. It was difficult to keep quiet, but upsetting their folks or harping on it would only raise his defenses and thus weaken her cause.

How could he possibly overlook the fact that they had been raised to appreciate the value of a good education? Their parents had struggled to give them the best start in life. Didn't he see that by quitting he would be turning his back on their family, on their values?

They were both so lucky to have been blessed with such caring, loving parents, who hadn't thought twice about the sacrifices they had made to prepare Taylor and Scott for a solid future.

How could Scott have changed so much in such a short time? Their ancestors had given their lives for the freedom to be educated. How could Scott have forgotten their history?

No, it was not all Scott's doing, she decided through gritted teeth. Donald Williams's shoulders were wide enough to carry a large portion of the blame. She was not about to forget that important fact. She had more sense than to let a few flowers, a handsome face and a long muscular body go to her head.

# Four

"What's wrong, Taylor?" Jenna Gaines had called her name three times without getting a response. "Hey, girl. Scott just made another basket!"

Taylor blinked. She had been a million miles away from the stadium and the college basketball game.

She and Jenna had gotten to know each other well in the year and a half the girl had been dating Scott. In fact, they had become friends, despite the difference in their ages.

"I'm sorry. I can't keep my mind on anything more than half a second." She sighed, then said, "I know Scott told you about meeting Donald Williams. Jenna, he's really thinking about quitting college." She blinked back tears. "Although I told him how strongly I object to it, I'm really trying not to pressure him. Oh, Jenna, I'm so worried."

"So am I. We've talked of little else lately," Jenna said softly. For the past six months the two of them had shared a small apartment near campus.

"What do you think?" Taylor had avoided asking her opinion, afraid Jenna would agree with Scott.

"I don't know what to think. He's so excited, so happy about the prospect of being in the NBA."

"I know." Her gaze followed her brother on the basketball court. He played well, perfectly at ease on the court. "His education had been so important. Even if he enters the draft and he makes one of the teams, that is not the end of it. What if he gets hurt? How will he be able to take care of himself without a satisfactory education? He won't even know how to keep the money he makes. There are so many people looking to part a fool from his money. How will he know who he can trust?"

"Ain't that the truth!" Jenna said, with a frown. "I know you haven't asked, but I agree with you. Until recently, he's been so motivated to finish and go on to grad school. As long as we've been dating, he's had dreams to become a great chemist . . . own his own company some day. He loves chemistry so much and he is so good at it. He has been looking forward to working part time in the lab at Randol Pharmaceutical once the season ends." She sighed heavily. "Since talking with Donald Williams he's had nothing on his mind but NBA."

Jenna knew Scott was totally absorbed in this decision. She tried not to mind that he had purposefully not asked for her opinion. He knew how she felt.

Taylor grimaced. The last didn't surprise her in the least. Donald Williams was Scott's hero. Having his support seemed to mean the world to her brother.

"I'm trying not to influence him. He's not going to blame me for making a mistake that may cost him his future. Somehow the word has leaked out. The girls have been following him around campus like white on rice. It's sickening!"

Taylor shook her head. It was hard enough for a young man to make a decision that would affect his whole life. Female adoration could really turn a young man in the wrong direction for all the wrong reasons.

The sheer number of women who chased after college players was ridiculous. Taylor imagined the NBA players really got the feminine rush. They quite literally could have any female they wanted, and then some.

A handsome, highly successful player like Donald probably had more women after him than he could count. Not only did he have the education and the income, but he was too darn good looking for his own good. So why was he wasting his time with her? Why was he sending her flowers? Every evening she received one perfect pink rose and one equally perfect yellow rose.

"I love him, Taylor. I don't want to lose him," Jenna confessed softly.

Taylor squeezed her hand reassuringly. "You two haven't quarreled, have you?"

"No, not really. But it really gets on my nerves. All those heartless females chasing him. If he enters his name in the draft it is only going to get worse. I don't know what is going to happen. I don't know how it will affect our relationship. That really scares me."

"Jenna, Scott cares deeply for you."

Jenna nodded. "I know. I love him, but I won't share him."

"I don't blame you."

Taylor suspected that if Donald was her man, she wouldn't be so easy going about other women, either. She almost laughed out loud. The woman who purposefully got involved with him and gave him her love would have to be out of her mind. Talk about asking for trouble.

"I'm doing everything I can to keep his feet solidly planted on the ground. His education will take him a lot farther in this world than a contract with the NBA," Jenna said.

"It all came out of the blue. I know he'd hoped the team would make it into the finals. Why in the world do they call college playoffs 'March Madness'?"

"Your guess is as good as mine," Jenna giggled. "So tell me, what do you think of Donald Williams?"

Taylor jumped as if she had been stuck with a pin. Striving to sound uninterested, she shrugged. "What's to think?"

"The brother is gorgeous. Scott seems to think he's interested in you." Jenna studied her closely.

Taylor tried to keep her face placid, yet her heart picked up a beat at the mention of his name. "That's ridiculous. I only met the man one time. And wouldn't have met him at all if we hadn't run into him at Edmund's Place."

She couldn't get over the fact that he was interested in her. He was too good looking for her peace of mind. She didn't want to remember him. Yet, she couldn't forget him nor could she get him out of her mind.

"That's not the point, and you know it. What do you think of him?" Jenna did not wait for an answer—instead, rushed on to say, "The man is so sexy."

"I imagine half of the women in America agree with you."

"Which half are you in, Taylor Hendricks?"

"The stupid half," Taylor almost said aloud. Instead she reluctantly admitted, "He's attractive, but so is Denzel Washington. I'm not dating him, either." Yet, it was not the popular film star who had been sending her flowers on a daily basis for a solid week.

Jenna laughed. "All my girlfriends will give you a run for that prize."

"Huh, Donald is no prize. He's a very attractive man who is, as far as I'm concerned, completely out of touch with black folks' reality. Not only is he a multimillionaire but, according to Scott he heads a very profitable business."

"What does that have to do with the price of bread?

He's one fine, tall drink of water. And he is interested in you according to your brother."

"My brother is an okay guy, but he has a big mouth. Remind me to smack him, will you?"

Jenna giggled. "Taylor, will you be serious for a second?"

Taylor looked away, feeling as if her heart had lodged in her throat. There was no doubt about that. The brother was good to look at. She would be lying to herself if she didn't admit the truth. Yes, as much as she hated it, she was dangerously attracted to the man.

"Are you going to answer?"

"I forgot the question."

Jenna shook her finger at her. "Donald Williams."

"Thanks, but no. I have enough problems. I don't want a man if I have to spend half my time wondering what woman is after him now and will she catch his roving eye?"

"You don't think he's capable of a committed relationship?"

"Get real, girl. Of course not!"

"But he is interested in you, girlfriend."

"We don't know that for sure."

Taylor was not certain why she hadn't told anyone about the flowers, but it was something she preferred to keep to herself for now. As much as she trusted and loved Jenna, she was not ready to share this. Perhaps because her awareness of the man frightened her? She didn't want to have tender feelings for him. He was the enemy, for heaven's sake.

Jenna clearly could not believe her own ears. "Well, you better start paying attention. He asked for your phone number. He just might call you, girl."

"Will you stop? I'm nothing like the glamorous, sophisticated women he normally dates. I am a normal woman who works for a living. I have both feet firmly planted on mother earth. Jenna, I am no beauty queen. These hips and thighs remind me of that every time I look in the mirror." There was no way she would even try to compete with the tall, slim beauties who were trying to get into his heart.

He was a pro athlete at the top of his game. What could they possibly have in common other than the fact that their ancestry came from the Motherland? Nothing! He probably never considered not starting his day with a strenuous working out. Taylor's brand of working out was peddling for fifteen minutes on her stationary bike while watching morning television.

"You joke, but Scott seemed to be serious when he said Donald was very interested in you."

"Jenna, you're beginning to sound like a broken record, girl. Besides, Scott's my brother. He's supposed to think I'm special."

Suddenly the crowed surged to their feet, shouting and cheering. Jenna and Taylor exchanged a guilty look. Neither one of them were the least bit aware of what had been going on. They both sighed with relief. U. of D. was ahead by ten points and Scott had not been the one to score. Sooner or later, Scott was going to ask what they thought about the game, in detail.

"You know he's going to ask," Jenna said, then broke out into a peal of laughter.

Taylor joined in. It was good to see her happy. Jenna was twenty-one, a year older than Scott, but she was on her own. She had no family to speak of. She had been in the foster-care system for sixteen of her twenty-one years. She was on a scholarship and working her way through college. She was one of three children that had been separated in the foster-care system. Her older brother had been adopted and moved out of state, while her twin sister was rumored still to be in the area, but Jenna had no knowledge of her . . . no way to locate her.

Taylor was proud of Scott for picking a girl who was so down to earth, and also, kind and intelligent. In fact, Taylor found herself rooting for them while at the same time concerned that they were too young to be getting so serious about each other. Jenna was also majoring in computer science and making the Dean's list every term.

The final score was ninety-eight to eighty-nine. Scott's team won. One more win and they would be coming into the finals in March.

"Are you going to wait for him?" Taylor asked, collecting her things. They had driven to the stadium together.

"No. It may be hours before he comes down enough to remember my name," Jenna teased. "You don't mind dropping me off?"

"Of course not, silly."

The two chatted about the changes going on at the University. Jenna was determined to catch up to the junior class. She was a hard worker. She had started later than her classmates due to financial difficulties.

Taylor had known Jenna longer than Scott. The two had met in the computer lab where Taylor worked as a technician. Scott had stopped in to chat with Taylor and completely forgot his sister after one look at the striking Jenna. She was tall, with creamy brown skin and curly brown hair.

Taylor couldn't help but admire Jenna's determination to succeed. She was still so young and a good influence on Scott. Taylor had found herself defending Jenna to their parents when they worried that Scott was too involved with the girl. It wasn't that Taylor was a prude, but Scott had been her responsibility for so long that she found it hard to let go. Yet, she also knew Scott was in love. She felt as if she were balancing on a tight-rope trying to stay out of their relationship but worrying that they both were moving too fast. Mostly, she found herself praying that their relationship would mature and grown naturally, telling herself to relax and let time solve this puzzle. But she didn't want to see either of them hurt. Her own experience in love had proven how painful failed love can be.

The parking lot, like the gymnasium, was crowded and Taylor had to concentrate to get them safely on the road. It wasn't until she pulled in front of the modest two-family home where they shared the upper flat that Jenna touched her arm, saying, "Think about what I said, Taylor." At her raised brow, she went on to say. "Donald may be serious about getting to know you. Are you going to let your feelings about Scott get in the way? He might be a really nice guy." Jenna paused before saying, "What are you going to do when he calls?"

"Call you!" Taylor laughed.

Jenna sighed, realizing Taylor refused to even consider the possibility. She shook her head. "Night," she called.

Waving before she pulled back out into traffic, Taylor knew she didn't even want to seriously think about the possibility. She told herself over and over again that that man was not really interested in dating her. What he was really interested in was Scott playing for the NBA, not her. She was nothing more to him than a means to an end. Just as long as she remembered that very important detail she had nothing to worry about from Mr. Williams. All she had to remember was how to say N-O to whatever he was offering . . . the good-looking womanizer.

\* \* \*

Taylor opened one eye to glance yet again at the bed-side alarm clock/radio: three-fifteen. Doggone it! She flipped over, punching her pillow impatiently. Tomorrow was a workday and she could not get back to sleep. She wasn't sure what had awakened her in the first place, but every time she closed her eyes she would see Donald's dark, handsome face. Goodness, she needed her rest. She did not have the luxury of sleeping late in the morning. Her boss, Dr. Richard Hawkins, would be in before eight. He was like a robot, always on time. He was a hard taskmaster and expected no less from others than he did from himself.

Richard was good people; he was highly respected in both the academic and black communities. And he was single. Taylor smiled thoughtfully. Most of the single women over the age of twenty on campus were after him, while he was so lost in his computer world that, unless she was a new program or application he would not even notice her. Thank goodness, he was not the least bit attracted to Taylor, nor was she attracted to him. They were such good friends that he often used her, with her permission, as a buffer. When he had to have a date, he called Taylor. She was safe with Richard and vice versa.

Donald, on the other hand, was a long muscular length of raw male power. He had the physique to make even a tall woman feel small and feminine. Even in three-inch heels she had to look up to him . . . something that rarely happened to her. The top of her head barely reached his shoulder. She would not be able to reach his wide, sexy mouth unless he permitted the caress. Heavens! What was she thinking? What difference did it make that his chest was deep and his shoulders were so wonderfully wide?

Unfortunately, there were other things she had no business noticing about him, such as the way his muscular thighs moved beneath his trousers. So many details she had not even been conscious of recording in her mind. She found herself imaging him filling a pair of tight jeans, the soft fabric molding his firm well-shaped butt, cupping his sex like a second . . . No! She moaned aloud, turning onto her side. That was none of her business! He obviously knew what he was doing and could keep the women coming back for more, judging by the ladies that mobbed him in the restaurant.

Was he a good lover? What difference did it make? It did her no good at all to waste her time wondering if he took his time, putting his lady's needs before his own. Taylor suddenly realized that that was exactly what she had done, imagined herself in his arms. She blushed, pressing her hands to her hot cheeks. The next thing she knew she would be going buck-wild over a man who would wind up hurting her.

The smell of more than a dozen long-stemmed pink and yellow roses in the crystal vase on the nightstand did not help to curb her thoughts of him. He had not called as of yet, but the flowers kept coming.

She was still waiting for the other shoe to drop, so to speak. She was waiting for him to make his next move. For almost two weeks the florists had stopped at her door every blasted day. No message on the card—only his first name.

What kind of game was he playing? If he was trying to obtain her attention, he'd been wildly successful. But he was wasting his time and his money. She certainly was not likely to forget him after the way they had met. Oh, he had made a lasting impression on her, all right. She could not stand the man.

Even if she had not been trying to forget him, she was doomed to failure. It seemed to Taylor that Donald was all her younger brother ever talked about these days. He had admired Donald's athletic talent on the basketball court for years. Since the two had met and he had found Donald so approachable and knowledgeable, Scott had developed a deep respect for the man. Scott now followed his games, knew where he was playing and when. Donald's name came so easily to mind that Taylor was close to losing patience with her beloved sibling. So instead of snapping at him to shut up, she bit her lip and ground her teeth together.

Although she'd really rather not know, nevertheless, thanks to her brother she now knew the exact date when the Pistons would be playing the Bulls in the big "D."

Why? Why hadn't he given up? Why didn't he leave her alone? What did he want from her? She almost snorted as that crazy question popped into her head. He wanted what all men wanted from any willing woman: sex. But why her of all people? He had his choice of females. She was not his type. Why couldn't he see that?

Hadn't her ex-lover taught her a painful lesson about men? Alex Adams had made sure Taylor learned the hard way that good-looking men were not to be trusted, unless you were after a broken heart. She had learned to protect herself from men like Donald and him. She never would make that same mistake again.

If only Donald would leave her alone. She had done everything she could to stop the flowers. She had gone so far as to call the florist and demand the order be canceled immediately, but they refused, saying that the client had a standing order and only he could cancel it.


Donald tossed and turned, unable to find a comfortable position in the hotel bed. One more night and he'd be back home in his own custom made bed, especially designed for his long frame. He found that he was getting set in his ways.

He grunted, knowing perfectly well it was not the bed that kept him awake, but empty arms and an aching groin he could not do a thing about. Thoughts of Taylor's beauty with her long, shapely legs and the graceful sway of her lush hips, was his problem. He could not get her out of his head. She had thrown him for such a loop after an all-too-brief meeting and would not seem to let go.

He wanted to see her again, spend time with her, get to know her. They weren't playing in Detroit until week after next, but luck would have it that he had been scheduled for a speaking engagement in her city on Sunday. Not soon enough, he grumbled. Yet, he had vowed not to see her or call her. She needed time to get over her snit with him.

"Detroit . . . home," he mumbled, getting up, having given up all pretense of sleeping. He had been tempted to pick up the telephone so many times. He wondered if the flowers were doing the job, softening her attitude. That beautiful lady had a thick protective shield around her. He would have given anything to know why.

What made her so uptight, so distant with men? Had she been hurt in the past? Or was it only him she disliked so thoroughly? There had to be more behind her hostility than his support of her brother. Her anger had been too volatile, too fiery. Or maybe it was just her way? Maybe she was a fighter? Was she a hot-blooded female who burned with an inner fire that would keep a man coming back again and again?

Donald moaned huskily as he realized just where his thoughts were taking him. The last thing he needed was to add fuel to the fire burning inside of him for Taylor. She made him hot enough as it was. The woman kindled a spark . . . a spark that was raw and blatantly sexual. He could not explain it, did not truly understand it himself.

As he stood staring down at the late night Los Angeles traffic, he didn't bother to analyze his keen interest in her. This need was out of character for him. It was something he did not recognize within himself and it had thrown him off balance. He did not know how to control his emotions, did not know how to make it go away. He certainly was not a man who flew by the seat of his pants. He'd always known his motivation, known his own mind. Suddenly, all that had changed.

Now all he could be certain of was that it was critical to his well being that he change her mind about him. His interest in Taylor was as sharp and as ripe as anything he had ever gone after in his life.

"A little taste of her sweetness is all I need," he whispered aloud. The thought soothed him, eased his restlessness. A few hot, wet kisses should do the trick. Donald found himself laughing. Who was he trying to kid? He'd never been appeased with a little of anything. He was a big man with a tremendous appetite for life. He adored sex, a lot of it. Nothing else took the rough edges away, nothing else eliminated the deep hunger inside of him. Yet, he had been so turned off by the games women played to separate him from his wallet or to gain his name that he had been forced to deny his own sexual needs. He had been celibate too damn long.

The trouble with his fascination with Taylor was that his sexual desires could no longer be ignored, nor could they remain buried beneath the demands of his career.

That was it, he assured himself. It was a sexual thing. Nothing more, nothing less. Sex, he could handle. Love was out of the question. He did not plan on making himself that vulnerable to any female. No woman was ever going to control him. Over the years he had seen the devastation love had done to some of his teammates when it didn't work.

He had to be careful. He didn't want Taylor or himself

to hurt. She was a lovely woman and she deserved only the best. He planned to give it to her while they thoroughly enjoyed each other.

# Five

As Taylor dressed for an evening out, her eyes strayed time and time again to the huge bouquet of roses on her nightstand. It seemed strange to be going out with one man while she continued to speculate about another.

She was confused by her reluctance to spend the evening with friends and co-workers, but she answered the door. She usually enjoyed these things. It gave her a chance to chat with old friends.

"Ready?" Richard Hawkins asked with a smile, not bothering to come inside the foyer.

While women found his deep bronze face pleasing to look at and his tall, lean body attractive, he generally was oblivious to their interest. He lived and breathed computers. Most women made him decidedly uncomfortable, even though he had a healthy male appetite which he tended to ignore. Taylor was the exception; with her he could relax and be himself.

"Yes," she said, buttoning her black velvet coat and closing the door behind her.

The freeway to Cobo Conference and Exhibition Center in downtown Detroit was crowded. Traffic was backed up due to construction. The ballroom that had been cleverly partitioned off—one side for dining, the other for dancing—overlooked the Detroit River and the Canadian river-front beyond.

Several members of the University and the computer department were active in the NAACP's community-based organization and shared a large table. Taylor and Richard were welcomed heartily. The room was already bustling with activity.

As Taylor slid into the chair Richard held out for her, she glanced around her with interest. It was like an informal fashion show. Taylor did not feel as if she were in competition with anyone. She wore the same black, silk, figure-flattering sheath dress with black sequins on the straps that crisscrossed low in the back, that she'd worn last year. She also wore black satin covered, three-inch heels, overlooking the fact that even though she and Richard were nearly the same height, in heels she towered over him.

Not that they would be dancing later, since Richard hated dancing. In spite of her height, Taylor loved high heels. Diamond and pearl earrings adorned her ears and tiny, heart-shaped gold charms wreathed her ankle.

With Donald she hadn't even considered her height. She'd been too busy arguing with him. He'd towered over her with his broad shoulders and deep chest so that she had actually felt small. Stop this! He was the last person she wanted to think about. She refused to let thoughts of him spoil her evening.

"You okay?" Richard asked.

"Yes," she smiled. "Why do you ask?"

"You were scowling."

"Sorry." Taylor made a point of putting a generous smile on her lips.

"It looks like we're going to have a big crowd," Richard said, studying his program.

Taylor nodded. Her eyes were on the head table on the raised dais facing the diners. More than a dozen chairs. She hid a frown at the prospect of long lengthy speeches. Thank heaven, dinner would be served first, then the speeches and then awards would be given out, followed by music provided by the live jazz band.

All the tables were draped in pristine white tablecloths and were topped with fresh flowers. Uniformed waiters were bustling about, preparing for their meal.

"Did you see that dress?" Gloria Bishop, who worked with Taylor in the lab, asked in a whisper. "That is Heather Montgomery, the criminal attorney's wife. She and Diane Randol have on the same dress, although hers is in white and Diane's is red. Talk about classy. I heard they were good friends." The two were escorted by their husbands.

"Lovely." Taylor had no trouble recognizing the two prominent couples being seated at one of the VIP tables in front. Taylor could tell by looking that each couple was very much in love. The Montgomerys were openly holding hands, while Charles Randol was whispering in his wife's ear, his hand caressing her nape.

Taylor dropped her eyes, studying her hands as she wondered what it felt like to know you were adored and treasured by one special man. She had never been on the receiving end of such warmth and male attention. Once, long ago, she had imagined herself in just such a relationship—that was, until Alex had opened her eyes to the real world. She no longer yearned for love or fidelity. Both seemed to be in short supply in this day and age.

Alex Adams had taught her many things, including that handsome men are good to look at but are not to be trusted. Temptation from readily available females who don't believe in limits when it comes to what they wanted proved to be their major downfall. Taylor was fresh out of fantasies about happy ever after. Her time was better served focusing on her career goals and helping her brother.

"Looks like there is going be a nice program. They

are honoring . . ." Richard began listing the names of those scheduled to receive an award. When he said Donald Williams's name Taylor's stomach did an immediate flip-flop.

Donald? Here in Detroit? She clenched her hands in her lap, taking deep calming breaths as she tried to prepare herself. Why was he here, of all places?

The president of the local chapter greeted everyone and asked the audience to stand as the twelve honorees and guests filed in to take their places on the dais.

Taylor had eyes for only one man. He was every bit as well-built and easy on the eyes as she remembered. He was dressed, as all the men were, in a black tuxedo and stood head and shoulder above the other men. He took his place, seemingly perfectly at ease. It was his warm smile that caught and held her attention. Goodness! There ought to be a law against any man being so good to look at. No wonder he attracted women like bees to a honeycomb. Why hadn't he stayed in Chicago where he belonged?

When Richard said her name, Taylor nearly jumped out of her seat. She realized they were starting to serve their meal. As hard as she tried, she could not seem to follow the conversation going on around her.

Yet, she knew the instant Donald spotted her. Her dark lashes lifted and she found herself looking directly into the ebony depths of his eyes. She managed to smile in response to the smile and nod of hello he gave her. Was his smile meant for her alone? Stop it! She scolded herself. Just stop it this instant! It did not matter who that teakwood giant was smiling at. It was no concern of hers.

If asked, Taylor would not have been able to tell anyone what she had eaten. It didn't seem to matter. Her eyes returned time and time again to the head table on the dais. Each time her eyes seemed to collide with his, she blushed, realizing he was watching her watching him.

She would instantly drop her gaze, forcing herself to respond to Richard's conversation. For the life of her, she could not follow his dialogue but she felt compelled to try, nonetheless. She missed the dark brooding gaze Donald continued to direct her way.

Once the awards ceremony started, she finally had a legitimate excuse to stare at the head table. Taylor had no idea why she anxiously waited for Donald's turn. He was being recognized for his work with helping minority businesses get started in not only the Detroit and Chicago area but all over the country. Finally, he stood at the podium a wide smile gracing his dark handsome face. As he spoke, Taylor acknowledged that he was much more than a pretty face.

Donald's acceptance speech focused on his pet project. "It's time that we black men stop looking to the Michael Jordans and the Donald Williams of the world to be role models for our young black men. Fathers, brothers and uncles are the real role models. Every black man should take a keen interest in some youngster's life. We must take on that responsibility before it is too late. Too many of our boys are being lost to the streets. We can't look to Washington to do this for us. This is something we must do for ourselves. Get involved. Let's not leave it to the sisters alone to raise our boys. Only a strong man can teach a boy to be a strong man, not only intellectually but emotionally as well. It's our job as black men . . . no one else's."

The applause was thunderous. Taylor was on her feet, like everyone else, thoroughly impressed by Donald's sincerity. Admiration was the last thing she expected to feel for him. He had it all, multi-million-dollar contract with the number one basketball team in the country, prosperous business and tremendous appeal to the opposite sex. So why was he so determined to influence her brother's life? Didn't he have enough to keep him busy?

It appeared as if he had a gilt tongue. Any woman would consider him a dream come true. Taylor blinked in dismay. Surely, she wasn't that vulnerable, that much in need of a man? But it was not just any man. It was Donald Williams who constantly filled her thoughts. At the moment, his charm was harnessed. She prayed he wouldn't release it in her direction. At the moment, she wasn't positive she could resist.

"What do you think?"

Taylor blinked at her escort, trying to figure out what he was talking about.

With the awards ceremony and keynote speech complete, the dignitaries joined their families and friends in the audience. As Donald threaded his way through the crowd, he was stopped time and again and congratulated. He paused to shake hands with Charles Randol and his wife, and paused to meet Quinn and Heather Montgomery. He shook hands with Mayor Archer and met his wife and family before he moved on to join his own family at their table.

"Congratulations, son." Greg Williams stood and hugged his son. He was every bit as broad shouldered and shared the same teakwood coloring and strong African features with his sons. Although over six three, he did not quite equal his famous and youngest son in height.

Donald found himself getting emotional as he grinned at the man he most admired. His father was a devoted family man who had worked hard over the years to build his hardware business and provide for their family. More important, he had always been there for him.

"Thanks, Daddy," he said before he leaned down to embrace his mother. "Give me some sugar," he teased.

Ellen Williams laughed through her tears, kissing his cheek. Her dark eyes filled with love. "I'm proud of you, son." Her soft brown face was as smooth and unlined as her daughter's.

"Thanks. I'm glad you and Dad made it." His parents had flown in from Orlando, Florida, for the dinner. Donald accepted a kiss from his sister, Megan Williams-Davis. She shared their father's coloring but was petite like their mother. He shook hands with his sister's husband, Jess.

Donald received a hearty slap on the back from Carl. The two had always been close and when Donald needed someone he could trust at his back the first person he thought of was his brother. His sister-in-law, Margie, was not about to be left out and gave him a hug and kiss of congratulations.

Donald was glad to sit down. And didn't think twice about taking a swallow of his brother's drink. "I'm glad that's over. Next time someone asks me to speak, remind me to say no."

Although pleased by his family's support, his eyes strayed time and time again to where Taylor was seated across the room. It was true he hadn't expected to see her tonight. Yet, he certainly hadn't been prepared to see her with another man. He was amazed at how much he resented it. Everytime he saw her speaking to her date his entire body tightened with anger. Dislike was too mild a word; he hated the situation he found himself in. She should have been his date for the evening.

"Now, if people would take the next step beyond the Million Man March, then we would have no need for reminders like this." Greg said thoughtfully.

"It's a matter of black male involvement. Well done, kid," Carl grinned.

"The test will come when we leave here. How many men will take the message away and use it in their everyday lives," Donald said, broodingly. His eyes were once again on Taylor.

"Why no date?" Megan asked, curiosity getting the best of her. She ignored the censuring look her husband sent her way. Something was not quite right with her brother and she wanted to know what was wrong.

He could have said that his lady was a few tables away with another man but thought better of it. "Decided to go stag," he grumbled, his voice tinged with bitterness. He was unaware of the way his family looked at him and then each other in surprise.

"You feeling all right, honey?" his mother asked with concern.

Donald had been so absorbed in Taylor that he didn't realize how oddly he was behaving. He flashed a quick smile, hoping to sidetrack his family's curiosity which could swiftly move to pointed questions that he wasn't ready to answer.

"Couldn't be better. You are looking awfully cute in that blue dress, Mama. You better keep your eye on her tonight, Daddy," he teased.

His mother giggled and his father roared with laughter, but his siblings exchanged a knowing look. He might fool their parents but something was obviously going on with him. He just was not talking.

"The music is starting," Margie said, looking pointedly at her husband. Everyone laughed. She was a great dancer and loved to be on the dance floor.

Carl grinned. "I can take a hint," he said, his voice throaty. He was looking forward to having her in his arms as much as she wanted to be there. He rose to his feet. "Excuse us," he said as he led her away.

Donald ordered a scotch neat, causing Megan and Jess to exchange a surprised look. He rarely drank hard liquor, particularly during basketball season.

"What the matter, son?" his father asked.

"Nothing. Excuse me," he said, unable to sit longer and passively watch another man make a move on his woman.

Although his head told him that was not exactly true, his heart told him it was close enough. What if Scott had been wrong? What if she were seriously dating the man beside her? A muscle jumped in his jaw at the hated thought. It didn't slow his steps, as he realized it would not stop him. If that was the case then she could very well tell him to his face. She was the only one who could stop his pursuit.

As he weaved his way across the room he was intercepted time and time again by well wishers. He was forced to curb his impatience. He gave a sigh of relief as he finally neared her table, while his heart thundered with excitement at being close to her again. He did not give himself time to worry about her level of resentment toward him. He was counting on the fact that she would not embarrass them both in front of others by refusing to dance with him.

She was engrossed in conversation with her boss, and she looked up in shocked dismay when a deep male voice said, "Good evening, Taylor. How have you been?"

Donald's presence was so profound that it brought complete silence to the entire table. "Good evening," Taylor said, forcing a calm she was far from feeling. She was well aware of the fact that her co-workers had no idea she even knew the man.

Richard was on his feet, smiling warmly, eager for an introduction. Donald Williams was a popular figure and clearly the man of the hour. Taylor had no choice but to make introductions all around. Everyone seemed eager to meet the man and tell him what they thought of his speech, his team and whatever else they could think up. Taylor was annoyed at how casual and natural he was, not the least disturbed by the attention he garnered. Donald was invited to join them.

His smile was warm and charming when he said smoothly to her date who had made the offer. "Thank you. But I was hoping Taylor would join me on the dance floor. Taylor?"

Although he spoke to her, his gaze was on Richard. He watched the other man closely. When Richard quickly nodded, as if the decision was his, Donald was thrown off balance. What was with this guy? He was with the most beautiful woman in the room and not showing any sign of possessiveness. If the situation were reversed, Donald knew he would not be quick to hand her over to another man.

Aware of practically every curious eye at the table on her, Taylor knew she had no choice but to accept unless she was prepared to make a scene. Donald's keen gaze locked with hers, a hint of amusement twinkled there as he awaited her response.

She was even more lovely than he remembered, he decided thoughtfully. How had he managed to wait so long before seeing her again? He was so hungry for her that he could hardly wait to have her in his arms, pressed close to his frame. Her response was so long in coming that he steeled himself, preparing for her refusal.

Taylor slowly rose to her feet, acutely aware of his dark scrutiny. She managed to smile, but it was for the benefit of the others at the table, not Donald. Her back was ramrod straight as she made her way between the tables, aware of his hand on the small of her back just above the flare of her hips.

Was he looking at her body? Was he aware of the way the fabric clung a little too closely to her hips for her peace of mind? She shouldn't have worn the dress. She should have worn her velour bathrobe . . . at least it covered from shoulder to toe.

Donald was watching, alright, and loving each sweet movement of her sexy behind. He didn't see anything that he didn't like. In fact, he could not possibly see too much of this delectable beauty. Donald slowed, reluctantly, on occasion to nod to or greet someone in the crowd, but he kept his hand firmly on her small waist. He was not about to let her get away. He had waited weeks for just such a moment as this. Just think: he had not intended to call her while he was in the city. He had thought it was best to give her more time to get used to the idea that he was interested in her. He must have been out of his ever loving mind.

His heart was racing from the sweetness of anticipation when he finally took her into his arms. He took care not to crush her lush breasts into his chest as he longed to do. Nor did he thrust a muscular thigh boldly between her soft ones as he hungered to do in his need to get as close to her as humanly possible.

Taylor was a lady and deserved to be treated well. Of course that knowledge did nothing to soothe his masculine hunger. He lowered his eyes, drowning his senses in her essence. He breathed deeply drawing in her feminine scent.

She was so incredibly soft. Everything about her brought forth all that was uniquely male within him. His senses seem to soar. No matter how he fought his own body for dominance, he could not control his male response to Taylor. She turned him on big time, without even trying.

Unnerved by his continued silence, Taylor felt obligated to say, "Thank you for the roses. They're beautiful." She had no idea how he knew that she adored roses. Having fresh flowers in her home daily was a wild extravagance. She had no doubt that he was ruthless in his pursuit of what he wanted. She had piqued his interest. The question was for how long?

She could not stop herself from asking, "Why? Why did you send them?" On their last meeting she had made it perfectly clear to him how thoroughly she resented him and his interference in her younger brother's life. She had come right out and told him that she didn't want anything to do with him . . . ever!

Donald chose not to answer. For now his motivation was his alone. Instead he said, "I'm glad you like them. I thought you might like the soft colors, considering how pretty you looked in that deep rose suit the day we met. Perhaps I was wrong? Black does wonderful things for you. You look beautiful tonight."

Taylor trembled, feeling the warm caress of his deep throaty voice. She imagined the sound of his voice in the dark, surrounded by his masculine strength. He was so wonderfully large, making her feel so feminine. Goodness! He practically oozed male charm, she noted, hating the way her breath caught in her throat in spite of her best effort to distance herself from him. He was dangerous to her peace of mind. He could so easily slip beneath a woman's skin and into her heart. Taylor was determined not to let that happen to her.

"What's your game?" she said in self-defense. "Looking for an easy conquest?"

Donald chuckled, thoroughly intrigued by the lady. "Aw, a woman who shoots straight from the hip. No playing around." He could think of nothing he wanted more than to play with her. He was up to the challenge of making her want him as badly as he wanted her.

"Why me? We aren't exactly contemporaries."

"We're not enemies either, are we?"

"We are nothing what-so-ever, Mr. Williams," she insisted, determined to ignore how wonderful it felt to be in his arms. Their bodies fit together like a hand and glove . . . perfection.

He was all man. His chest was wide and deep, his

shoulders unbelievably broad, his thighs were as muscular as his arms. She had to look up to meet his unrelenting gaze. That didn't happen often, considering her height. Three-inch heels didn't do much to eliminate the difference in their height. She couldn't reach his chin. His mouth was inches from hers.

Goodness! What was she thinking? She didn't want this man! All she wanted was for him to leave her and her brother alone.

His lips parted as he moved the tip of his tongue over the firm surface of his bottom lip, unaware of her interest. Taylor trembled, unable to look away.

"That can easily be changed. And you know my name is Donald. Use it."

"No!"

"Go out with me, Taylor. I'd like to get to know you. We . . ."

Taylor shook her head even before he finished speaking. "I don't think that's a good idea."

"I disagree. I can't think of a better arrangement. You're a lady. I'm a man. That's all I believe is necessary." His brow lifted pointedly.

# Six

Taylor glared at him. Her lovely mouth held tight, drawing his dark eyes to its sweet bounty. "It's going to take more than roses to change my opinion of you, Mr. Williams."

"Donald," he grated, with impatience. He was certain it was her purpose to antagonize him. "I wouldn't think you know me well enough to form any kind of honest opinion."

"I read the papers, Mr. Williams."

"Donald . . ."

She sighed, giving in. "Donald. I'm not interested in dating you."

"How do you know? If your information about me comes from the news media, then you don't know the first things about me. Get to know me, find out the truth," he invited, his smile as deeply seductive as his ebony eyes.

Taylor shook her head. "I already know enough. The way you've influenced Scott. Isn't that illegal? Can't he lose his scholarship if it becomes public that he's friendly with you?"

"Is that what you think I'm doing? Trying to recruit your brother for my team?"

"Exactly."

Donald was scowling. "When is the last time you looked in the mirror, Taylor? If your date does not have sense enough to tell you, then I'll be happy to correct the error. You are one fine, good-looking sister. I like a woman with some meat on her bones. A woman I can hold on to.''

Taylor knew that her mouth was hanging open, but she couldn't help it. She could not believe her ears.

She trembled in reaction to him, unable to collect her thoughts.

''I'm interested in you, sugar, not your brother. Now that that's settled, tell me about your date for the evening. Is he your lover?''

''What!'' Taylor nearly yelled at him. She would have walked off the dance floor if he had not been holding on to her. The music had stopped but he still did not let her go.

''Is he?'' he persisted, grateful when the band played another slow tune thus giving him a reason to hold her.

''Not that it's any of your business, but Richard is my boss and friend. Now about my brother . . .''

Donald hid the relief he felt. ''No. This isn't about Richard or Scott. This is about the two of us.''

''How many times do I have to tell you no? Or hasn't a woman ever said no to you before?'' Taylor was trembling with rage. Having given up all pretense of dancing, she dropped her arms to her sides then hissed, ''Let me go.''

A muscle jumped in Donald's cheek as if he were clenching his teeth, but he did as she asked. He let her go. Taylor turned on her heels. Too shaken to return to the table, she rushed out into the hallway, intent on reaching the ladies room, desperate to control her pounding heart.

''You're frightened. Why?'' Donald was beside her, his long legs making a mockery out of her shorter steps.

''What is this? Why are you following me?'' she snapped. ''I made myself clear.'' She wanted to scream at him but she worked to keep her voice low in a effort not to be overheard.

The hallway was crowded. He was easily recognized. The last thing she needed was to end up on the pages of the society column or one of the tabloids.

Donald was not bothered. He had waited too long for an opportunity to be with her. He was not about to let her walk away from him.

"You're afraid of me, afraid of getting involved. Why, Taylor? I won't hurt you," he whispered close to her ear. They had stopped on one side of the crowded corridor. Aware of her discomfort, he caressed her soft cheek with a fingertip, his eyes never leaving hers. Donald had no idea why her answer was so important to him, but it was. He wanted to date her. He would be lying to himself if he didn't admit that he wanted much, much more than that. He was willing to do whatever it took to have her.

"I'm not afraid of you." He wasn't a threat to her. He had too much influence over her brother. That bothered her. If only he could be persuaded to see that it was not in Scott's best interest to quit school. But how?

"Then you'd be willing to go out with me?"

"I . . ." she hesitated. Could she convince him to help her cause? Did she dare try? She had no choice but to try.

"Yes? I'll be back in town in two weeks. What about Friday after next?" He was clearly issuing a challenge.

He was right. She was afraid of getting involved with him. Yet, it was a risk she must take for Scott's sake. "One date," she reluctantly agreed, while silently praying she was doing the right thing. If they could sit down and talk, then perhaps she could calmly and unemotionally explain her side of this issue. He was a rational man. Surely, she could convince him to agree with her and help her cause.

Donald didn't question her reversal. There would be

time for that later once they were alone. He simply said, "Thank you." His voice was deep, husky when he went on to say, "I'd like you to meet my family before I take you back to your table."

"I don't think that's a great idea," was on the tip of her tongue, but Taylor decided it was too petty to voice. What would it hurt? She had already agreed to spend an evening with him. A few minutes with his family should not matter. She knew that she would never let herself care about him. She had no intentions of getting romantically involved with him. This so called date was for Scott's benefit, nothing more.

Donald was the one surprised when she merely nodded her agreement. He didn't question why. Her agreement was too important to him. He would like her to know the real man, not the one that was displayed in the media. As far as he was concerned, meeting his family was a sure-fire way of getting to the heart of the matter—or rather her getting to know the real man.

Although there were many curious eyes following their progress as they reentered the ballroom and threaded their way through the tables, Taylor kept her eyes straight ahead. Even though Donald made no move to touch her, she could feel his long powerful length close beside her. She had never been so aware of a man in her life. There was something about him that made her cognizant of her own femininity.

All three men came to their feet at their approach. Donald easily made the introductions. Taylor couldn't help noticing the strong family resemblances that both Donald and his brother shared with their handsome father, Greg, while his sister favored his attractive mother.

"Are you enjoying yourself, Ms Hendricks?" Mrs. Williams asked.

"Yes, very much. Please call me Taylor. The NAACP always has lovely affairs," she said with a smile.

Carl frowned in concentration, wondering where he had heard the name before. He had a feeling Taylor was responsible for his brother's drastic mood swings of late.

"As you might have guessed we're thrilled by Donald's award and speech," his mother beamed with pride. "Detroit is our home, even though my husband and I now spend most of the year in Florida. Are you from the city, dear?"

"Yes. My parents also live in Florida . . . St. Petersburg. They were forced to relocate, due to my father's health, when my brother was still in high school. He's at University of Detroit now."

"Taylor and I met while I was here a few weeks ago on business. Her brother Scott is center on the University team. He's a very talented basketball player. We met at Edmund's Place while she was lunching with her brother," Donald explained, looking from one curious relative to another.

He knew how rare it was that he introduced a woman to his family. He'd never been crazy enough to do so while the woman was on a date with another man.

"Aw, I remember now. From what I've heard from Donald your brother is a gifted athlete. According to my brother he has a real future in the NBA."

"Until my brother met your brother he had a future in chemistry. You see, our family values education. Scott has a full athletic scholarship and he has worked hard to keep his grades high. Neither our parents nor I want Scott to give up his education to play professional basketball. It would be a drastic mistake that could destroy his future." She couldn't help looking at Donald accusingly.

"Don't you think you're being a bit dramatic?" Donald asked with a scowl.

"Not at all. I think I'm being realistic. There are no guarantees in life."

His parents exchanged a concerned look, as did his sister and brother. It didn't take a rocket scientist to figure out that Taylor and Donald had a serious difference of opinion. Her resentment of him was evident, as was his keen interest in her. Donald could not seem to look away from the beauty of her flawlessly smooth brown face.

"We can certainly understand how you feel. Did your brother finish high school in Florida?" Megan asked.

"No. He stayed with me during those years," Taylor said, carefully cognizant of Donald's look of surprise.

Her response certainly explained their closeness. She had been substitute parent/sister/friend all rolled into one. Donald had no idea that she had practically raised her younger brother.

"Has your brother decided to quit college?" Donald's mother asked kindly.

"Not yet, I'm afraid that he has been so overwhelmed by Donald's celebrity status and his interest in him that he still doesn't have his feet on solid ground."

"No one is denying the benefits of an education. My degree has served me well, both in basketball and in business. But it's the basketball that has allowed me to do things I never dreamed possible as a young black male in this country. I'd be lying if I said that I don't think Scott or any other talented youngster can ignore the tremendous potential and opportunities pro ball can offer them," Donald ended quietly.

"Taylor has a good point." Megan surprised her brother and husband by saying.

"Scott can't just ignore this opportunity. It could change his life," Carl said. "What if he gets hurt in college ball? There goes his pro ball career."

It was Margie who said, "He could be hurt badly during his first season in the pros. Then what? He would have no degree to fall back on."

Greg Williams nodded "It's not an easy decision. I remember reading about the young man who was trying to decide whether to go into professional golf. There was a lot of speculation on the news over what he should do, but when it comes to Olympic gymnasts or tennis players, age is not an issue."

It was more than an interesting discussion to Taylor. She had worked too long and too hard to keep Scott in school to accept Donald's views as gospel. Donald's name, his ability, his masculine appeal didn't have a thing to do with Scott's future. She had to safeguard it without being sidetracked by his masculinity.

For the first time in her life, she felt utterly feminine in a man's arms . . . Donald's arms as he moved her along the dance floor. It was as if she couldn't control her reaction to his closeness, his hard body. Taylor was intensely aware of him . . . his size, his scent, the richness of his deep teakwood coloring, the strength and character in his distinctively African features.

What woman with a heartbeat would not be attracted to him? Nonetheless, she was not about to let her hormones do her thinking for her. She had a brain. Wasn't it time she used it?

While Donald might be a man's man because of his openness and athletic ability, he was also a woman's sizzling-hot fantasy. Did he offer his lady sensual pleasure as effectively as he played his sport or conducted his business?

Goodness! Taylor suddenly realized she was in trouble. Despite a good dose of common sense and despite her animosity toward the man, it was Donald's kisses she longed to know, his arms she craved. Dear God, Donald should have been the last man on earth she would be attracted to. The very last!

She had a plan now and that was all she would concentrate on. She could convince him to help her. Her brother's future depended on her success.

"Donald, have you had a chance to talk to Bradford? What does he think of our plan? We should be able to break ground in April," Carl said, interrupting his thoughts.

"Yeah, I spoke to him on Friday. He seems to think . . ."

"Oh, no, you two don't. No business tonight. You promised, remember?" Margie said glaring at her husband.

Cart grinned, and openly caressed his wife with his gaze. His lips briefly touched hers, lingering for only a sweet instant while his eyes promised the world. "Okay, baby."

Donald sighed heavily, knowing that was what he wanted someday. That closeness, that deep love. He suddenly wondered if it were possible with Taylor. She alone had so effortlessly captured his thoughts.

What was happening to him? Her date was only several feet away, but he didn't care enough to take her back to her table. He wanted her here with him. He actually hated the idea of her being with another man even if they were not lovers. Taylor . . . When had he become so possessive . . . so single minded where she was concerned? Her continued resentment of him was really beginning to get to him. It gave her a legitimate excuse to keep him at a distance. Hell, no! He didn't like it one little bit. He knew that he had to woo her, change her mind about him. The trouble was, would she give him the opportunity?

Taylor chose that moment to remind him that she hadn't come with him. "It has been a pleasure meeting all of you, but I must be getting back to my friend."

Although his family quickly expressed the niceties,

Donald was not the least bit happy about escorting her back to her table and her date for the evening. He consoled himself with the reminder that the next time they were together he would be her date.

During the week, Taylor's thoughts returned time and time again to her conversation with her brother after church on Sunday. Scott had come by the house, even taken her to church without even a token amount of protest. Taylor scowled, realizing it had been a setup.

"Mmm, these potatoes are really good, Sis," he crooned.

Her fork hit the plate with a loud clank. "All right, spill it. What's going on?"

The enticing aroma of collard greens, scalloped potatoes, baked ham and homemade buttermilk biscuits were ignored as she stared suspiciously at him. He was up to something.

The two generally spent their Sundays together, ending the evenings with a long distance call to their parents. Often, Jenna joined them, but today she was working on an upcoming term paper.

"I talked to a couple more scouts from the NBA," he beamed, quite proud of himself.

"Are they supposed to bombard you like this?"

"Calm down, Sis. No one is forcing me into anything. This is a decision I have to make by myself. And as much as I love you, I have to do what I think is best for me and my future."

"You are going to say yes, aren't you? You're going to submit your name to the draft in the spring, aren't you?" she asked bluntly.

He nodded, his mouth suddenly tight with tension, while his deep set eyes pleaded with her to understand.

"I see," she said tightly, instantly furious. Donald's

face flashed through her thoughts. This was all his doing! Why couldn't he stay out of it! Why couldn't he see that what was good for him was not necessarily good for Scott?

"No, you don't see. Taylor, you haven't really given this a chance. Just because I want to postpone my classes until the off-season doesn't mean I'm not going to graduate. A lot of the NBA players go back and finish. Donald did."

She huffed. "I'd be willing to bet that most of them don't ever finish. There are no guarantees in this life, kid. None. Remember, a fool is easily parted from his money," she quipped.

"I'm going to get my degree, I promise you that," he insisted, not pleased at her implication that he couldn't take care of himself.

"Save your breath. You can't do it for me, you have to do it for yourself. You'll be giving up a full scholarship. How quickly you forget how hard you worked to get it. I remember."

"I won't be giving up a damn thing!" he snapped, then, realizing who he was speaking to, he said sheepishly, "Sorry, I didn't mean to swear. Sometimes, Sis, you make me plain crazy."

Taylor couldn't remain at the table a second longer. She jumped to her feet and moved to the living room, pacing in front of the picture window. No! This could not be happening. What could she say that she hadn't already said before? How could she convince him he was making a huge mistake . . . a mistake that might affect his entire life. Why was he so blind? So plain mule headed?

"Taylor, I know you are upset, but . . ."

"Scott, you don't know the half of it. What would happen if you were seriously injured on the floor? How would you take care of yourself? How long would the money last? A year? Maybe two? What would you have to fall back on?"

"I thought about it, decided it was worth the risk. The same thing could happen in my very next game. Then what would I have to fall back on?"

"You have your brain! An education! That is something no one can ever take away from you."

"Why do you keep saying that? I am not planning on giving up my education! I'm just postponing it."

"Why can't you see what's in front of your face? What if you are wrong? What then? It's not as if you can get your scholarship back. Once it's gone, there is no turning the clock back, kid." She longed to shake some sense into his hard head.

"A couple of million can help not just me, but all of us. I can help Mama pay off Daddy's medical bills. Get them a house of their own, then they can stop worrying about the rent in that apartment they have. I can help you so that you can stop working and can go to college full time. Don't you think I know why you take only one class of your graduate work at a time? Money! It can help us all, not just me."

Taylor's heart softened somewhat due to his generous nature, but she held fast to her convictions. "Do you even remember the hardships black folks have endured over the years for the opportunity to have an education? It wasn't uncommon for whole families to toil in the fields so that one person in that family could have an education. And everyone was so proud of that person. It means a lot to our people. It always has . . . it always will. Our people have given up their lives for the right to be educated. How can you turn your back on all that?

"If you don't want to remember the history, think of our own family. Mama and Daddy have made so many sacrifices for us. It was a struggle for them to help me until I finished my degree. Then it was your turn and

Daddy couldn't work on at the plant. I don't remember anyone in this family not willing to give you all the help you needed to get through. You, kiddo, are a joint effort. Mama and Daddy may not be here physically but they are still working to make sure you have all you need, knucklehead!" She said tightly, "Speaking of Mama and Daddy, let's see how they feel about your decision."

Their meal was forgotten on the dining room table. He grabbed her wrist before she could pick up the telephone on the side table in the living room.

"Wait!" he scowled, turning away from her too-sharp gaze.

"Why not? Haven't you told them?"

"No! I wanted to tell you first."

The two had always been close, able to talk to each other about anything. After sharing a house and having only themselves to depend on, they understood each other.

"And?"

"I need your help on this one. If you are on my side, they are bound to understand."

"I don't believe you said that," she said without hesitation. Although it hurt her to her heart for she had always supported him . . . been there for him . . . she said it anyway, "No, Scott. Not this time."

Scott was crushed. He looked away from her. She was the one who had been willing to care for him, thus allowing him to remain at home and finish school here in Detroit rather than having to follow their parents south. He wanted her approval, longed to have her in his corner.

"This has not been an easy decision for me or even a quick one. I've been thinking about it for some time, even before Coach mentioned it. Meeting Donald was the clincher for me. I've admired him for years. He's not only a strong player, but he's got his head on straight. I want to be like him."

Taylor didn't want to hear Donald's name, she didn't want to even think about Donald. She didn't want to recall how it felt to be in his arms. A couple of days had not diminished his appeal. She had a feeling that two weeks . . . two months . . . possibly two years would not change her intense reaction to the man. His virility and masculine charm had her thinking about him each and every night before she closed her eyes.

No matter how attractive she found him, he would be the one responsible for ruining her brother's life unless she could convince Donald that he was wrong. She didn't have to date him to do that. They just needed to talk.

"Why can't you take my side in this?"

"I think you are making a terrible mistake. I can't stand back and not try to stop you."

It would all work out. If anyone could talk some sense into her brother, it would be Donald. There was still time. He said he wanted to quit school. Then, let him face some of the ramifications for this rash decision. She picked up the telephone and started dialing. The receiver was picked up on the second ring.

"Hi, Mama. How are you and Daddy? Oh, he had a good week. Great! Hold on, Scott has something he wants to tell you." Taylor handed him the telephone refusing to be swayed by the mulish set of his face.

# Seven

She sank onto the sofa, crossing her legs and folding her arms beneath her breasts. Her entire body was taut with tension. She only half listened to her brother's side of the conversation. Her mind was on the man who was never far from her thoughts.

How could she have responded so naturally to his closeness? When they were on the dance floor she automatically followed his smooth easy movements. He was so at ease with his body. It felt as if they had been dancing together for years. Their bodies came together so effortlessly.

At five feet, ten inches, there weren't very many men she could look up to, especially in heels. Donald was such a man. What had been really disturbing was how wonderful it felt to be surrounded by his hard male length. She found herself closing her eyes, imagining the two of them were on a moonlit beach making love, her body open to his. She trembled with feminine need.

She'd only had one lover and he had betrayed her trust. She had learned her lesson well when it came to risking her heart. She'd heard about him. She would be foolish to jeopardize her happiness by becoming involved with another womanizer. Donald was a man who had unlimited females at his disposal. Whether he admitted it or not, he attracted women the way flowers attracted bees. He had a raw sexuality that was positively lethal to a woman's well being.

Thank goodness, he was not the man for her. The only reason he was attracted to her was because she hadn't fallen all over him. Women probably made fools of themselves over him on a daily basis. She, no doubt, was a refreshing change.

She would be making a serious mistake if she took his interest as more than casual curiosity. Surprisingly, the roses had not stopped coming even though she had agreed to see him again. Well, that would soon change. He would have no choice but to give up on her romantically once he realized that she really didn't want to date him, but was only interested in talking to him on her brother's behalf. Could she do it? Could she convince him to help?

"Here, Daddy wants to speak to you." Scott shoved the telephone at her. Before she could do more than lift it to her ear, he had slammed the front door behind him.

"Hi, Daddy."

"What has gotten into that boy?"

"I wish I knew. I've been trying to talk him out of this for weeks. I've run out of words. I don't know what to say to convince him."

"You keep trying, baby. He's making a mistake. He only has his family to make him see reason. Mama and I will call soon. You take care. Love you."

"Love you, too," Taylor whispered as she hung up the telephone.

She had been twenty-three and Scott fifteen when their parents had been forced to move to a climate conducive to their father's asthma. Although they both missed them terribly, Taylor hadn't been the least bit reluctant to take on the responsibility of a teenager. It had worked out well. As was their custom, they had driven down to spend the Christmas holidays with their folks.

It seemed to Taylor that the latest trend in the NBA was to take guys younger and younger. A few kids were given this difficult decision when they were fresh out of high school. What chance did they have of making a wise choice? Eighteen and nineteen-year-olds were trying to decide something that could negatively affect their entire life. Scott had such potential. He could easily become a brilliant research chemist, perhaps own his own pharmaceutical company some day. If becoming an NBA player was so important to him, then he could do that as well. All he needed was two years to get his undergraduate degree. Two years!

As Taylor cleared the dining room table, she decided that she had been wrong to agree to date Donald. At the very least, he deserved an explanation. She wasn't a coward. She simply would not go out with the man. Her first loyalty should belong to her family . . . not to a man she wasn't even sure she liked. They didn't really know each other and she didn't plan on giving him an opportunity.

Taylor tried time and time again to get her brother to change his mind. Nothing was working. She enlisted Jenna's help to persuade Scott. It didn't work. She was crushed when she learned that Scott went ahead and submitted his name into the NBA draft. But she hadn't given up. She told herself there was still time. Until the day he signed his contract, she would not give up.

The situation with Scott didn't help ease her resentment toward Donald one little bit. As the night of her so-called date with Donald approached, Taylor continued to hope that he would call and she could solve the matter over the telephone. It would be so much easier that way.

By Friday, she was on edge the entire day, her eyes constantly going to the clock. As the evening approached, she reassured herself over and over again that when he left, he would be leaving without her.

So why then couldn't she forget how he looked? Or how it felt to be in his arms? Or how she had become so easily lost in the depth of his dark eyes? His voice was deep, seductive. She could not deny her attraction to him, no matter how hard she tried. Nor could she prevent herself from imagining how deeply satisfying it would be to be on the receiving end of his kisses. Kisses!

What was her problem? How could she forget even for a minute that he was all wrong for her? She wanted a man who could provide a lifetime of stability and love. A man who was not afraid to make a commitment. Most important, a man she could trust with her heart . . . with her love. Any way she looked at it, Donald was not that man. She would ask for his help with her brother . . . nothing more.

If she were dressing for an evening out, Taylor would have chosen a cream silk sheath that clung lovingly in all the right places but left her torso exquisitely clothed. She would have chosen the pearl and diamond earrings her parents had given her for her college graduation. Her thick black hair would been styled to curl around her shoulders. She would have worn very little makeup: a touch of caramel foundation to smooth out her coloring . . . highlight the cheekbones with a deep rose blush. She would have chosen charcoal gray eyeshadow and a deep rose lipstick. Taylor had done none of these things.

She was dressed in jeans and a red turtleneck sweater she had changed into after work. When the doorbell sounded at seven she had to use the legs of her jeans to dry her clammy hands. There was nothing she could do about her stomach, it was a mass of butterflies.

"Hello. Come in, please." Taylor caught her breath at the sight of his long dark length. He was gorgeous in a three-piece dark blue, custom made Italian suit. His shirt was pristine white, his silk tie navy and white stripe. His warm manly scent was as provocative as he was.

"Hey, beautiful," he smiled easily. "Aw-oh, one of us is overdressed. I thought we'd eat at the Whitney. You prefer something less formal?" he asked casually, his eyes drinking in her soft, queen-size beauty. Would he ever get used to the way she affected him? One long glance and he was hard and ready . . . ready to make her his. Any way he looked at it, he craved her sweetness.

"I'd hoped we could stay here and talk. I had no way of contacting you in order to let you know," she said quickly, before she lost her nerve.

He shrugged. "I been on the road. Even if you had the number of the condo you wouldn't have been able to reach me. But I'd be happy to give you the number for my cellular phone," he said, warning himself not to get too close, not to touch her no matter how innocently. One kiss and he'd be lost.

"You don't mind?" She was surprised.

"Not at all. We can always order in. Pizza, Chinese, whatever you like." He was relieved. He wouldn't have been surprised if she had canceled. Nevertheless, he'd been looking forward to spending time with her. Where they were didn't matter to him. Besides, he had a good idea what she wanted to talk to him about. He hadn't fooled himself into thinking she'd done a complete about-face. She wanted something from him. That was nothing new. It was something he had come to expect from women.

"You're really accommodating," she said suspiciously. Donald laughed, a deep throatily sound that had nothing to do with humor, more to do with sarcasm. "Just realistic. What do you want?"

Taylor glared at him through the thickness of her lashes. She couldn't dispute his claim. What was the point? "Come on in. Have a seat."

Donald left his overcoat on a brass hook in the foyer before entering the living room. He casually unbuttoned his suit coat and vest, glanced around the living room before he made himself comfortable on the sofa, stretching his long legs out in front of him.

She stood in front of him, her hands on her hips. "I think it is only fair to be honest with you. I don't want a romantic involvement with you. But I do need your help."

"I don't believe that anymore than you do. I've seen the way you look at me when you don't think I am looking at you. You may not want to be interested, but you are."

"Didn't it even dawn on you that you could be wrong? There are a few of us not killing ourselves to go out with you!"

When he remained silent, but quirked a brow at her reminding her that she was the one asking for his help, Taylor sat down, crossing her legs and arms tightly.

"Mind if I order dinner?"

"No . . ."

"Preferences?"

She shook her head no, deciding to calm her temper and start using a little common sense. There was no point in antagonizing the man.

Spotting the yellow pages on the side table, he grabbed it and began flipping through the pages. Without another word, he took a cellular telephone from his inside jacket pocket and began punching numbers, all the while Taylor looked on with a frown marring her lovely face. "Yeah, please send over two large pepperoni and green pepper pizzas. Do you carry salad or pop? Great!" With his hand over the mouth piece, he said, "Taylor?"

"That's fine."

He went on to give her address. "Thanks," he ended, disconnected the call. His eyes leisurely traveled over her soft red-tinted mouth, with the upper lip fuller than the bottom, before he pulled his hungry gaze away. He reached inside his jacket pocket and pulled out a business card. On the back he wrote out his home and cellular numbers. He rose slowly from the sofa and dropped his jacket over the back of an armchair before he caught her hand and gently tugged her down with him to the sofa. He left his card on the coffee table.

Once they were seated side by side, he asked curiously, "So tell me what's wrong, Taylor? What's happened to upset you enough to ask for my help?" His voice deepened even more as he studied her small brown features.

Her eyes glinted with temper, while Taylor raised her chin indignantly. "I haven't asked yet." There was no point in pretending she wasn't furious. Besides, she did not believe in playacting. It was a waste of time. She blurted out, "My brother has entered the NBA draft. I'm sure you know all about it."

He shook his head. "I haven't spoken to Scott about it one way or the other. Why blame me, sweetness?"

"My name is Taylor."

"It should be sweetness," he crooned, softly, seductively, his dark eyes on her mouth. If he didn't get a taste of her soon . . . Donald swallowed with difficulty, his voice heavy with arousal, when he said, "I don't want to talk about your brother. I have other things on my mind."

Too stunned to move, Taylor's heart raced as his lips stroked over hers as lightly and gently as a breath of fresh air. He teased their soft fullness until her lips parted, opening under his.

Donald growled low in his throat, unable to resist the allure of the sweet interior. His tongue slid over her incredibly soft mouth, licking the top lip before returning to sponge the bottom, then slowly teasing the corner before dipping inside. He groaned his enjoyment, finally able to taste her sweet essence as he stroked her velvety soft tongue with his.

"Taylor . . ." he whispered, blood, hot and heavy rushing through his system. "So sweet . . ." he said, his voice thick with desire.

Taylor knew she was lost, lost to everything outside of the firm warmth of his masculine lips. "Mmm," he tasted good, too good. His wide deep chest was so appealing, she found herself pressing close against him, her soft full breasts flush against him as she inhaled his incredibly pleasing male scent.

"No!" Taylor said, suddenly pushing herself out of his arms. She was shaking all over. She told herself it was a result of anger, not feminine longing. Yet, the tips of her breasts had peaked, aching for his attention.

It took Donald longer to recover. His need was keen and unmistakable. He wanted her . . . wanted to make love to her. But then that was nothing new. He'd been hungry for Taylor since the instant he'd laid eyes on her in the restaurant.

For quite some time he had done without rather than dealing with the kind of women who threw themselves at him. He had sense enough to know it was not really him they wanted. They wanted the wealth and status he could easily provide. He was not willing to be a trophy for some selfish woman's mantel. Now, suddenly, all of that longing, all of that need that he had kept buried deep inside of him centered on this one special woman:

Taylor. It had not been planned. It had just happened. And there was nothing he could do about it.

She had scrambled to her feet, determined to put as much space as possible between them. "You had no right!"

"Perhaps I should apologize for rushing you. I don't feel the least bit sorry. The truth is, I find you extremely attractive."

"Look, I appreciate your . . ."

"The trouble is that we don't know each other. Give us a chance, Taylor. What can it hurt?"

"It could hurt me," she longed to shout at him. She would be the one with the broken heart if she were careless enough to get involved with a man like him. There was nothing ordinary about him. He commanded attention wherever he went. He could have any woman he wanted. He didn't even know her. She wasn't even certain that he wanted her in his life. Oh, she believed that he wanted her sexually. When the next tempting beauty came along, he would be on the prowl once again.

The only reason he wanted her was because she was unavailable. If she actually agreed to his terms, he would tire of her in no time. He might be able to have any woman he chose, but he could not have her.

"I know all I need to know about you. I'm not looking for Mr. Super-Jock. That's someone else's fantasy, not mine."

"Great. Because I am not Mr. Super-Jock. I'm a man, nothing more, nothing less. And you are the woman I want to get to know much better. All I ask is that you give me the opportunity."

"Look, I need your help to convince my brother he is making a mistake. I didn't invite your lovemaking."

He stared at her before he said, "I kissed you. I didn't

make love to you. Believe me when I say there is a difference."

Taylor swallowed with difficulty before she said, "Scott values your opinion. With your help he might decide to stay in school. You can't tell me every new rookie is successful. There have to be some that prove to be too young to handle professional ball."

"You're right. I can't say that. But Scott isn't immature. I think he can handle it. Taylor, this is his decision. He has to decide for himself. This choice is not mine or yours." He hated the hurt he saw in her eyes. "Taylor . . ."

"You didn't even consider what I said."

"Yes, I did. But, honey, he is a man. Let him stand on his own two feet. Don't baby him."

Before she could say more, the doorbell chimed, signaling the arrival of their meal. Within a very short time they were set up in the living room, each equipped with a plate and utensils.

She was determined to concentrate on her food, rather than her disappointment or the masculine charm that seem to radiate from the man beside her. She would look up and find his eyes on her as he quietly ate.

He had downed several slices of pizza and a large helping of salad before he asked, "Why have you decided to work at the University's computer lab rather than in the business? With your degree in Computer Science you have a lot of options."

At her arched brow, he merely smiled while waiting patiently for her answer, as if he had all the time in the world.

Taylor found she had to force herself to look away from the seductive warmth of his smile. Instead she concentrated on using her napkin to wipe her trembling fingers and hide her nervousness. She knew that he had gotten most of his information about her from her big mouth brother. The rest had come from meeting her boss and friends at the NAACP dinner.

"Some day, I hope to teach computer classes on the college level. Working in the lab is good experience for me."

"Are you in grad school?"

"Yes, I'm working on my master's."

He heard her small sigh and wondered about it. "Hard going?"

"Impatience. It's taking longer than I expected," she found herself confessing. "Not that I mind helping my brother—because I don't. Classes are so expensive these days. I can't afford more than one class each term."

"I thought Scott was on a full scholarship?"

"He is. But there are so many expenses that it takes the entire family's help in order to handle it. We are not an affluent family. My parents were able to put me through college. Unfortunately, my dad became ill and was no longer able to work."

She frowned, realizing how candid she had been with his family the other night. There was no way she could be so open about her personal life unless she felt comfortable with them . . . with him.

"I'm sorry to hear about your dad. How's he doing now?"

"Much better. The warmer weather agrees with him."

"You're very lucky to have come from such a loyal and supportive family," he said softly. "I think that is why so many kids get off to a bad start."

Taylor nodded. "I think you're right."

Donald smiled genuinely hopeful that, for the first time, she was seeing him as a man. "Was it a hardship for you taking on the responsibility of a teenage boy?"

She shook her head. "I was lucky. Scott has always been a hard-working, determined kid. Besides, even though our parents were no longer here in the city, we still had their emotional support to fall back on. There has never been any doubt of their love."

Donald nodded, leaning back against the back of the sofa. Now that one appetite was appeased, he recognized that he had others when it came to Taylor. She fascinated him. He found himself doing something he hadn't done in a long time. He relaxed in her company.

"I've been very fortunate. That's one of the reasons why I feel it's so important for someone in my position to give back to the community," he said candidly.

"Is it true you are working with Charles Randol and Dexter Washington to expand the Malcolm X Center throughout the city?"

"Yeah," he grinned. "Do you know of Charles and Dex's work?"

Taylor laughed, unaware of how enchanting she was to the man studying her. "Scott benefited from the center. I didn't want him getting in with the wrong crowd. The center was the answer. He had contact with kids who wanted more for themselves than what the streets had to offer. Tell me about your work in Chicago?"

"I started the sports camp during the summer while I was in New York. But by the time I moved to Chicago I realized that a few weeks in the summer was not enough. With the help of my teammates, we were able to implement a year-round sports camp."

Taylor found herself listening intently to his plans for expanding on the concept across the country including Detroit. He told her about his business dinner with Dexter and the Randols. His enthusiasm was evident. She liked the fact that, even though he was a very busy and highly successful man, he still found time to help others.

"How did you and Charles meet?"

"In Washington during the Million Man March. It is hard to believe that more than a year has passed since that momentous event." He went on to tell her why he felt it was so important that black men become involved in saving black boys by teaching them what it is to be a man. It had nothing to do with producing babies.

Donald was so enthused by her open, easy manner that he risked arousing her animosity by asking, "Why aren't you involved with someone? Do you resent all men or is it just me?"

Taylor stiffened. "Are you deliberately trying to antagonize me?"

"That's the last thing I'm hoping to do. What I would like to do is get to know you. The fastest way to do that is by being direct. When it comes to my personal life I don't believe in playing games."

"If you're asking if I date, the answer is yes. If the question is, am I serious about any one man the answer is no. Why did you . . ."

"I think you know the answer to that one." He didn't even try to hide the hint of possessiveness in his voice. "You're more than welcome to ask me anything you like. In fact, you don't even have to ask, I'll tell you. No, I'm not seeing anyone. I'm not engaged nor am I married," he volunteered.

"Why are you being so candid?" Her soft brown eyes focused on his generously shaped mouth.

He was in his shirt sleeves and those were rolled up, baring his muscular lower arms. They were seated side by side, their feet propped on the coffee table, stereo playing in the background.

He moved so fast she did not have time to prepare for the shock of finding herself seated across his thighs. His breath, warm on her neck, caused shivers of awareness to dance down her spine.

"I don't know what it is about you, Taylor, but I can't think of anything I want more than having you in my life."

She wiggled in his lap, trying to get up. He held her

still because she was driving him wild with sexual hunger and he did not need any help in that department. He was extremely aware of her closeness, her sweet magic.

"Let me up," she insisted.

"Why? Are you uncomfortable?"

"You know why," she whispered, cognizant of him in her every pore. She didn't like the feeling. No . . . that was not entirely true. She adored the feelings because she felt so feminine, so aware of his masculinity but it made her much too vulnerable. The vulnerability was something she was not interested in exploring.

"Relax," he said huskily, moving a soothing hand over her shoulders and down her back. He relished the feel of her in his arms. He couldn't imagine anything he would enjoy more than being in bed with her, his body deep inside of hers. Imagining being surrounded by her sweet, damp heat had him throbbing with desire. Donald swallowed a deep, husky groan.

"Why me?" she asked seriously, needing to know.

Donald chuckled, a deep throaty sound. "Surely you know the answer to that?"

She shook her head, causing her cottony soft hair to caress his throat. "I'd like to know."

"I find you extremely attractive. Don't you dare tell me you're surprised. I am not stupid. I've no doubts that you have your choice of men."

"You think so?"

"I know so. I count myself lucky that you're not involved at this time."

"Mmm," was all she was willing to say on the subject. She unwittingly relaxed against his chest. He was so solidly built and he smelled so good.

"That's your response?"

"That's it."

He chuckled. "Taylor, all I ask is that you give us a chance." When she would have spoken he pressed his fingertips against her soft pretty mouth. "Sleep on it. I'll call you tomorrow. Maybe we can go out for a late dinner after the game on Sunday?"

He eased her up so that he could rise, then caught her hand and pulled her loosely into his arms, only for a moment, before he picked up his vest and suit jacket, putting both on. From his pocket he pulled out three tickets. "I hope you and Scott, perhaps a friend of his, can make the game."

"Thank you. But . . ."

Donald pressed his lips briefly over hers and then gently stroked his thumb along the soft flesh along her jaw. "Until Sunday," he whispered, placing a lingering kiss on her mouth. He wanted so much, so much more than those few tender kisses. He was hungry for the taste of her.

He wisely pulled back, reminding himself he had to be patient. He had to give her time to get used to him, to believe in his sincerity. Taylor was more than worth the wait. He never let himself believe that he might not succeed. He was not prepared to let her walk out of his life, not without a fight.

# *Eight*

Taylor gave up trying to sleep and turned on the television. But the old Diana Ross movie didn't hold her attention. Her thoughts continuously returned to her evening with Donald. She'd been missing quite a bit of sleep lately because of him.

At her front door he had surprised her when he made no move to kiss her good night before he left. She was unexplainably disappointed. She had no idea why she craved his romantic attention. In all honesty, she wanted more than the few kisses he had given her. She longed to enjoy the deep thrust of his tongue inside her mouth, the firm pressure of his hard chest against her breasts.

She was asking for trouble! She knew better than to let her guard down. How could she trust a man with his depth of sensuality and blatant magnetism? He was too attractive.

Unfortunately, she had known how painful and crushing it was to experience betrayal. She had lived through that unique brand of heartache. She never wanted any part of falling in love, ever again. Why would she willingly open herself up to that kind of utter despair. No . . . never again.

Donald was an icon. He was well known all over the country—no, the world. Half the females in America would not consider telling him no if he came knocking at their doors. He was so wonderfully handsome and he was wealthy. How could he possibly be sincere? She would be silly not to think of herself as just another notch on his bedpost. There certainly wasn't any way of finding out without risking her heart.

No! She would not be used. She was not an empty-headed female whose most difficult decision of the day was what color of nail polish to wear with what dress. She was a hard working woman. She had been blessed with a loving family and above average intelligence. She did not need a man in her life to feel complete.

But she was all woman. She yearned for a man in her life. She longed to marry and share a home with a loving family. She yearned for a man able to make a long-term commitment and to share a love so deep and strong nothing could separate them. She strongly believed that that kind of love was built on nothing less than a solid foundation of friendship and trust.

How many relationship books had she read that dealt with the black woman's difficulty in trusting the black male? Too many to count. Was there a solution to that monumental problem?

She shivered, remembering the seductive allure of his mouth on hers. She still tingled from his deep sexuality. She had responded to him without thought, without conscious awareness. And she knew he had harnessed himself. He had been so gentle with her. She suspected that he hadn't given her even a glimpse of his erotic depths.

What was it about him that affected her so strongly? She knew her responses had nothing to do with who he was but the man he was. Something very female in her responded at the most elemental level to something very male in him. She couldn't even name it, yet nevertheless she knew it was there. His closeness had caused her heart to race with sexual excitement. Something as sim-ple as the stroke of his fingertips on her face had heightened her senses. If he had caressed her breasts she probably would have fainted. Taylor covered a giggle at the thought. Donald was dangerous to her peace of mind.

Seriously, what would she have done if he had deliberately set out to seduce her? Gone after her with both guns smoking, so to speak? Would she have been able to resist? Taylor moaned. She didn't honestly know. All she was certain of was that Donald was a clear threat to her equilibrium. She hadn't been angry when he insisted that Scott's decision should be his alone. She didn't agree with him, but it didn't upset her as much as it once had.

Saturday seemed to move at a snail's pace as she went about her household chores. Her heart pounded with excitement when she picked up the telephone that evening and he was on the line. Their chat was not long nor was it more than friendly, yet she hung up smiling. She couldn't decide if she should go to the game or not. In fact, she was unsure of herself until Sunday afternoon, when her brother and Jenna stopped by for her.

Scott was in great spirits. It wasn't until they were inside the Silver Dome that he asked, "These seats are great, behind the Bull's bench. Now how did you got these tickets so close to the action?"

Taylor ignored him, her eyes on the basketball court as she watched Donald and his teammates warm up. Donald's brother and brother-in-law were seated behind them. Taylor smiled, quickly introducing them to her brother and Jenna.

She had really tried not to come determined to give the tickets to Scott and let his friends and him enjoy the game between the Detroit Pistons and the Chicago Bulls. It hadn't worked. When they came by to pick up the tickets and see if she would go with them, she had been dressed and ready to go. She had done what she told herself over and over again she wasn't going to do.

As she sat watching Donald, her heart raced with excitement and her eyes sparkled. She had unexpectedly looked up to find his eyes on her. Her cheeks were hot when he smiled at her and waved.

Jenna had caught the exchange but Scott had missed it. Thank goodness, he had been busy studying Jordan's moves. Jenna squeezed Taylor's hand but she did not comment on it.

Neither Jenna nor Scott had any idea how difficult a decision it had been for Taylor to come. She'd been fighting her interest in him from the first. She was beginning to feel as if she were holding back a tidal wave. Her feelings were just that powerful, that unwelcome. She felt as if she were not only going against her better judgment but going against her parents. Unfortunately, it didn't stop how she felt about him nor did it stop her from wanting to spend time with him.

Her eyes never left him. He was so magnificent, so talented. At thirty-one, he was considered an old man on the court, but his long, strong body moved with such ease and expertise. His coordination was phenomenal, she decided as she watched him play. He knew how to use his powerfully muscled body to his advantage. He was a physical player, willing to take risks unmindful of possible injury to himself. He had her tight with fear on more than one occasion as he went down or took a hard hit.

When he received a vicious elbow in the windpipe that caused him to stay down, Taylor was on her feet calling his name. She was wringing her hands until she saw that he was on his feet again and okay. When he rested on the bench, so did she. This was worse than when she watched her brother play. She was a nervous wreck and was grateful for half-time so that she could relax. She was exhausted and the game was at mid-point.

Once Scott had gone for soft drinks, Jenna smiled

sympathetically. "Now you know how I feel when I watch Scott play. I worry about him almost every second he is on the floor. The trick is not to let him guess."

"I'm that transparent?" Taylor whispered, aware of his family close by.

"Don't worry about it."

"I don't want to care about him," she said in an angry whisper. It was already too late. She had feelings for him that she could not explain. When had it happened? More importantly, how? She had been so careful. She had worked hard to keep her resentment for him firmly in place. Her protective shield had not protected her. Something had gone horribly wrong.

"Do you think Scott noticed?"

Jenna laughed. "I seriously doubt it. He's into the game."

"I don't want him to know."

"But why?"

"I don't know. I suppose I need time to get used to it myself. It certainly wasn't planned. Just the opposite, in fact."

"Hey, guess who I ran into?" Scott announced enthusiastically. "John! John Moore. You remember him, don't you, Taylor?" At her blank look, he insisted, "You know. Daddy's friend. He used to come by and help when Daddy first took sick."

"Oh, yeah. I remember. How is he? His family?"

"Everyone is great. He invited us to come by the house any weekend. What do you think?"

"Sure, why not. Daddy will be thrilled when you tell him." He'd also be upset that his daughter was fraternizing with the enemy.

Taylor was grateful that Scott was busy entertaining Jenna with stories about the old friend of the family. She could no more explain why she wanted to keep her feelings for Donald to herself right now than she could fly.

The trouble was, she did not want to care about him . . . did not want to become involved with him. Despite her best efforts, she had not been able to resist his masculine charm. She wanted to scream her frustration! How could she care about him? She had essentially thrown her common sense out the blasted window.

What about tonight? He was coming by later for their late night dinner. Even though she knew she should turn him away, she could not help wondering if she were strong enough to do so.

"Taylor?" Scott nearly shouted. His sister hadn't said a word since Donald appeared on the court after halftime. She had not looked away from the guy as she followed his warm up. What in the hell was going on here? "Taylor!"

"What?"

"Is something going on between you and Williams?"

Taylor blushed, ready to cover her face, while praying his relatives hadn't overheard.

Jenna shushed him. "Must you tell everyone?"

"I don't care who hears me. This is important. I want to know what's going on." Thank goodness, his voice was modulated, Taylor prayed.

"Leave her alone. Can't you see you are upsetting her?"

Scott looked from his sister to his lady. Neither one of them seemed too pleased with him at the moment. He realized he didn't have much choice but to keep his mouth shut for now, unless he wanted to drive home in an uncomfortable silence and probably receive nothing warmer than a cold shoulder later from Jenna. With a frustrated sigh, he returned his attention to the action on the court. Detroit had Chicago fifty-five to fifty.

In spite of the fact that it was one of the most exciting games Taylor had ever seen, with icons like Rodman, Hill and Jordan right in front of her, she had a difficult time concentrating on anyone but Donald. She was so distracted that she couldn't even follow her brother's enthusiasm over the game on the way home. Chicago beat Detroit by two points.

They were in front of her home when Scott asked, "Are you all right, Sis?" When he'd encouraged her friendship with Williams, he had thought she'd enjoy dating a celebrity. He'd never considered that she might care deeply for him, possibly fall in love with the man. He didn't want her hurt. Nor did he want the man playing with her tender feelings.

"Yes. I'm fine. You two enjoy what's left of the evening. Night." She waved as she ran onto the porch. She hurried inside, knowing full well that her brother would not leave until she had locked the door and turned on the lights, signaling all was well. She stood in the foyer until she heard him drive away, only then did she collapse on the sofa.

Maybe she should have told him that Donald was coming by later? No, she needed time. For now she needed to sort out her feelings. She had still not quite accepted that, not only was he coming, but that she definitely wanted to see him again. No matter how confused he made her, Donald was good company. She enjoyed the time she had spent with him. He certainly wasn't like any of the men she was currently dating. They were nothing more than friends.

Glancing at the wall clock, Taylor hurried into her bedroom to shower and change into a pink silk shirt and pale ivory wool short skirt; ivory hose and high chunky heels completed the look. Glancing down, the knee-length skirt had her wondering if it was too short. Gold hoop earrings and her favorite ankle bracelet were her only jewelry. Her hair had been swept up into a French roll, leaving the long graceful lines of her neck exposed.

The doorbell sounded just as she was picking up a three quarter length ivory wool jacket from the bed. Her heart raced with anticipation as she made her way to the door.

"Hi," she said, nervously wetting deeply rose-tinted full lips as she stepped back to let him enter.

One look at each other sent them both into peals of laughter. Donald was wearing a navy blue sweatshirt and jeans and sneakers on his long feet. Once again they had gotten their signals crossed.

"You look gorgeous," he grinned, pressing a quick kiss against her soft, sweet smelling brown cheek. "Why did you change? You looked so cute in those tight jeans and white sweatshirt."

She blinked, shocked that he noticed. "You were supposed to keep your mind on the game, mister."

He chuckled. "I didn't do too badly. Scored twenty-four points."

"Congratulations on the win."

"Thanks. Did you enjoy yourself?"

His pulse raced from the adrenaline still pumping in his veins. It was always like that after a game. Yet tonight was different. His excitement came from being near Taylor. He must have built-in radar where she was concerned, because he could swear that despite the size of the arena, he had felt her presence, felt her cheering him on. She was so good to look at. It was all he could do not to focus on her but to concentrate on the game. He had never had that problem before. Never!

"Yes," she smiled. Her dark eyes traveled slowly over him, from his dark, rugged face, over broad shoulders down a wide chest to a lean middle and trim waist, heavy, muscled thighs and long, long legs.

She refused to allow her gaze to linger on the distinctly masculine bulge. She blushed at her interest in that part of his anatomy. What was wrong with her? She had no business wondering if she affected him in that very personal, private way.

Donald closed his eyes briefly to steady himself, for he had felt her feminine curiosity and found it extremely arousing. He could think of nothing he would like better than to let her explore his body with her soft, silky brown hands. The thought of her loving him, moving her hands along his shaft, had him so blasted hard he had to fight back a hungry groan. His entire body had heated with delicious expectation.

Determined to keep his hands to himself and his mind above his belt buckle, he asked as casually as he could manage around the lump in his throat, "Ready?" The last thing he needed was to let his hunger for her scare her off. He had the entire meal to get through and all he had done was kiss her cheek and he was already indulging himself in some serious fantasizing about her.

He had it bad for her. He was doing everything he could not to let his eyes linger on her wondrously full breasts or her long gorgeous legs. She took his breath away without lifting more than her thick-lashed brown eyes.

How had she managed it? One glance into her lovely eyes and he was rock hard, ready to give her the sweet loving they both deserved. Damn! He knew he wanted more, needed much more. This was not about s-e-x. He hungered to know everything there was to know about her: what she liked, what made her laugh, what made her heart race with joy?

Above all else, he needed her to know him and accept the man he was within. That took time. He had no choice but to wait and hope for the best.

If only he could control his impatience to have her. It felt as if he had waited forever to meet a woman who was not hung up on gaining his name and access to his bank balance. Taylor was real. She was so down-to-earth. There was nothing fake about her.

"Ready?"

"Mmm-hmm," she said, handing him her jacket. "Are you sure you are up to going out? Aren't you exhausted?" she said from over her shoulder, accepting his help with her coat.

Donald was shocked by her concern for him. His heart warmed with pleasure due to her interest. Once they were comfortably seated in his rented Lincoln, he said, "I won't keep you out late. You probably have to be up early?"

She asked, "What about you?" instead of answering and letting him know that she was an insomniac, thanks to him.

"I have a late flight out tonight. I see so many hotel rooms that whenever I'm this close to home I'd rather sleep in my own bed, no matter how late I get in," he found himself admitting.

He'd chosen a quiet, out-of-the way restaurant, so if anyone was aware of his celebrity status, they'd hopefully choose not to intrude on their privacy.

"Do you come here often?" she asked, looking up from the menu.

"It's not fancy, but the food is good. I hope you don't mind," he said softly, aware that he was not going to impress her here.

She looked surprised. "Not at all. How are the fried clams?"

He smiled. "Great. The fries are out of this world. Hope you're not on some silly diet? You're perfect just the way you are."

Taylor laughed, shaking her head. "No, but I appreciate the compliment."

They both ordered fries and clams and a large salad with plenty of thick-sliced French bread and wine.

"Good?"

"Delicious," she smiled. He was as self-assured and confident off the basketball court as he was on. "How long have you been in Chicago?"

"Seven years. I was drafted by the New York Knicks right out of college."

"Which city do you prefer?"

"Detroit," he said with a grin.

"Why? You've lived and traveled all over the country. Why not somewhere warm and sunny?"

"Detroit is my home. My family lives here. My roots are here. Why didn't you relocate to Florida with your family when your parents moved south?"

Taylor shrugged. "I would miss my home and my friends too much. I'm one of those people who enjoy the changes in the seasons. I especially love the spring. It's always so exciting. The fall is beautiful, also, especially when the trees turn golden." She smiled thoughtfully. "I don't particularly care for the winter."

"I agree." Leaning back in his seat, he was totally at ease listening to her, able to truly relax and enjoy. She was so refreshing.

He reached into his pocket and placed a well known jeweler's box on the table.

"What is this?"

He shrugged. "I saw it and thought of you."

"No," she said, not even opening the box. "I don't want it. I think you have confused me with someone else. I don't take expensive gifts from men."

He was surprised by her answer. It was not uncommon for a woman he had been seeing for even a short time to start asking him to buy her things. As time went on the gifts were more important than he was. He had learned the hard way to go slowly to determine whether the draw was him or his bank balance. All too often it was not him. He felt none of that concern when he was with Taylor. He longed to lavish her with beautiful things . . . things to make her smile. But he now realized he was very lucky she had not refused the roses.

"Okay," he said, slipping the unopened box into his pocket. He hadn't meant to upset her, but when he had seen the bracelet he had immediately thought of her. He wanted her to have it, but he wouldn't push. He hoped he hadn't unwittingly spoiled the evening.

He was relieved when he reached for her hand and she didn't pull away. "I'm sorry. I didn't mean to anger you. It was an impulse. I saw it and thought of you. It was nothing more than that. Okay?"

She looked at him then, and found herself smiling. "Okay. As long as you understand. I am not interested in what you can give me. I can take care of myself."

He smiled, desperate to touch his mouth to hers. Instead, he swallowed with difficulty. He found himself confessing, "When I retire from basketball, I plan on buying a home here in Detroit." he said watching her closely.

She blinked in surprise. "That's right. You have family here." Then she returned her attention to her meal. She didn't want to show him how disturbed she was by his announcement.

"Taylor?"

"I thought Detroit would be too square for you, especially given the kind of life you've lived. You have a knack for surprising me."

"I don't know. You certainly have thrown me off balance. You're nothing like the women I generally meet."

"Is that a compliment?"

"Absolutely. You're down to earth. I like that about you. No pretense."

Taylor found herself tongue-tied, uncertain what to say. She didn't know how to be any other way. She put down her fork, unable to eat another bite.

"Had enough?" he asked, making an effort not to caress the soft fingers toying with her wineglass.

"Yes, thank you."

"Dessert?"

"None for me."

Donald didn't want the evening to end, but all too soon they were back in the car heading for her home. He was quiet on the drive, considering her possible response to his desire to see her again, the following weekend.

She surprised him when she asked him in. He quickly agreed, not about to overlook her first open invitation to him. They had entered the foyer when Donald placed his hands on her shoulders and slowly turned her to face him.

"I enjoyed you tonight," he said softly. "Did you enjoy yourself?"

"Yes," she smiled, unable to look past his dark eyes.

"I'd like to get to know you much, much better."

"I'm not the one due out later tonight," she teased.

"True. I do a great deal of traveling. I can't get around that."

Taylor was aware of his eyes lingering on her lips before moving down to rest on her full breasts. His eyes were so hot that they felt as if they could burn through her clothing.

"Taylor, if we put our heads together we can find time to get to know each other. That's if you're so inclined. I don't mean to rush you." He knew he was lying. He wanted her firmly situated in his life, damn it. How long did he have to wait?

"Yes, you do. You're too mule-headed to take no for an answer for very long," Taylor said, thinking of her brother.

"Oh, no, you don't. Please, don't start putting up

those walls again. I thought we agreed to keep our differences concerning your brother out of it."

"I never agreed."

"Yes, you did. Why else are we together tonight?"

It was a good question but so help her, Taylor didn't have a clue. All she could seem to remember was that she did not want their evening to end.

"Give us a chance, Taylor," he said before he let himself out, leaving her staring after him.

Taylor was at the computer working on a complicated project for her boss. She was so lost in her work that she didn't look up from the keyboard until the man standing in the open cleared his throat loudly.

"Donald!"

He eased away from the doorframe he'd been propped against before he said, "Hi." His large frame seemed to fill the tiny cubicle she called an office. One entire wall was glass, where she could look into the computer lab where she spent much of her time.

"Sorry, I didn't mean to scare you."

"What are you doing here?" she whispered. As she expected nearly all the staff and students in the lab were indeed watching them.

Donald Williams's appearance wasn't exactly a daily occurrence. Even worse, she knew she was blushing and had to fight the urge not to cover her burning face. She had never been one eager to be the center of attention.

"Hoping you're free for lunch," he said matter-of-factly.

Taylor didn't know what to say. She had schooled herself not to react to the man's natural grace and charisma. She also wanted to keep their interest in each other private, constantly reminding herself it was nothing more than a passing thing.

Donald watched her closely. His gaze lingered on her simple blue denim jumper and pink long sleeve turtleneck blouse. But it was her eyes that caught and held his interest.

"What's wrong, Taylor?"

"Nothing. I just didn't expect to see you, especially not here." She looked away, her face hot with embarrassment. She had already fielded what seemed like a thousand and one questions after the NAACP dinner. She did not welcome more. Unfortunately, his appearance would only add fuel to a new wave of gossip.

"If I were not such a self-confident guy, I'd say you were embarrassed to be seen with me. Why? My fly open or something?"

"No! Oh, why would you say something like that?"

"Why are you embarrassed?"

"I told you. I'm a private person. I don't want the entire world to know my business."

"I'm asking you to eat not go to bed with me," he said smoothly.

At this point, Taylor would have agreed to dine with Attila the Hun in order to get away from so many frankly curious eyes. She grabbed her purse from the bottom drawer and her navy blazer from the hook behind the door.

"I'm ready."

"Where would you like to go?" he asked, lengthening his stride to keep up with her near run. They were practically running by the time they reached the sidewalk. He caught her arm. "Where's the fire?"

"Sorry," she mumbled. "I'm not that hungry."

"Then let's pick up a couple of sandwiches and eat them in the park. The car is over here," he said cupping her elbow and steering her through the parking lot.

"I didn't know you were planning a trip to the city."

They had spoken several times since their date, light casual conversations.

He shrugged. "Unexpected business meeting."

They stopped at the deli near the bookstore in the shopping center across from the college. What started as a simple errand quickly turned into a circus. Within minutes of entering the crowded deli, Donald was recognized and completely surrounded by autograph seeking patrons.

Taylor's mouth hung open as she was pushed aside by eager fans. She couldn't imagined living like he did with so little privacy. She was shocked at how bold one very beautiful woman was as she slipped a sheet of paper into his suit pocket while he was busy signing anything his fans shoved at him.

Taylor was the only one still in line for service. She stepped up to the counter and ordered two turkey sub sandwiches, pickles, chips and sodas. After picking up the order she waited near the door for Donald.

"Donald! Mr. Williams!" were being shouted as even more people entered the deli.

Taylor watched as he worked the crowd. Although smiling he slowly, but steadily moved in her direction. Before she could utter a word he grabbed her arm and led her out the door, racing for the car.

"Sorry about that," he said helping her inside and quickly making his way round to the driver's side. He drove away humming to himself as if nothing unusual had happened.

Taylor stared at him. "How can you get used to that? It could have turned into something very ugly . . . a mob." She trembled uneasily.

He shrugged. "Yes, it can happen but most of the time it's more an interruption than anything else. Nothing to be concerned about," he soothed, momentarily taking his eyes off the road to glance at her.

The weather had turned cold and began to rain in earnest, too much for an outdoor picnic. They stopped at the neighborhood park, but decided to eat in the car. They didn't exchange more than a half-dozen words during the meal.

"Are you okay?" he asked. "You were really worried, weren't you?" he said, caressing her soft cheek and angling her face so that he could see her clearly.

"Yes, I suppose I was." Suddenly, she realized she didn't want anything unpleasant to happen to him. He might be completely wrong for her as far as a relationship went; nevertheless, she cared about him.

"Thank you, Taylor." He suddenly realized that she had positive feelings for him and it left a warmth deep inside.

"You were lucky. It could have turned into a real nightmare."

"We haven't known each other very long, but I am afraid anonymity is rare in my line of work. More often than not, I'm recognized. I accept that as the price for being able to play the game I love. It's never seemed like a great sacrifice until lately. Yes, I have suffered some unpleasantness due to being recognized. But I've also gained financially, emotionally and intellectually. I wish you wouldn't look at it so negatively."

"I don't."

"But you do. You were embarrassed by the interest we attracted at your office."

"Do you have any idea how many questions I was forced to answer after that dance at the awards dinner? It wasn't pleasant."

"Naturally, you blame me."

When she didn't respond, he went on to say, "Yes, I've had to deal with some uncomfortable situations. Some people can be a little too eager to attract a celebrity's attention. It's part of the life I live. A small part."

"*Women* are a little too eager, you mean. I've only known you a short time. And I don't like being the center of gossip. I value my privacy." Taylor was studying her French manicured nails. She was also trembling. Why?

She had only gone out with him once and enjoyed herself. Their lunch together was unexpected and certainly not what she would call commonplace. Donald drew feminine eyes wherever he went. His height, his looks, his celebrity status, his income were all powerful forces that caused too many women to consider him an open invitation.

Oh, why had she agreed to see him again? Was she simply flattered by his interest in her? He certainly knew how to overwhelm her with his masculine appeal. Every time she saw him, she wanted to see more of him. No matter how hard she tried she couldn't seem to forget how wonderful it had been to be with him, to be in his arms and once again experience his dark, sweet kisses.

She found herself longing to see him, hoping to at least hear his heavy masculine voice on the telephone. Yet, she fought her interest, determined to keep her feet firmly planted on the mother earth. As often as she reminded herself of his negative influence on her brother, she remembered the huskiness of his voice or his easy going nature. He was not just a superstar, he was also a man. A man who was generous with his time and money. He was close to his family and valued others. She liked those things about him . . . liked them more than she was willing to admit.

"I'm no different than you are. I also enjoy my privacy. I refuse to consider the intrusion of the media as more than a distraction."

"It's like living in a fishbowl. How can you stand it? How can you encourage my brother to want the same?"

He swore mildly. "You know, I thought we might spend a little time together without talking about your brother."

She blushed, knowing she deliberately brought Scott into the conversation like a protective shield. She hadn't really been thinking of Scott but of the beautiful woman who had brazenly put her phone number into his pocket.

Glancing at her watch, she said, "It's getting late. I should be getting back."

He made no move to touch her but turned the key in the ignition. He had obviously chosen the Lincoln because it fit his long frame.

Neither spoke until they entered the University's gates and pulled to a stop near her building.

"Thanks, Donald. I enjoyed the outing."

"How about Friday evening? Dinner . . . dancing . . . whatever you like."

She shook her head. "Dinner, yes but at my place. My way of repaying you for the meals out."

He caressed her soft check. "You don't owe me anything. But I'm not about to turn away a home-cooked meal." His wide mouth formed a charming grin that set her heart racing.

"Good. See you around seven-thirty."

As badly as he wanted to hold her, kiss her, he was aware of their surroundings, so instead he gave her small hand a gentle squeeze. "Take care."

Before she hurried away, she called over her shoulder, "Don't bring anything. Not flowers or candy . . . nothing. Just you."

He blinked, shocked by her command. His heart beat wildly at the possibility that all she wanted was him. That

indeed was heady stuff that left him whistling to himself
as he headed for the airport.

"Well, he's punctual," Taylor said smoothing her navy
skirt. She had teamed it with a simple white, lacy blouse
nothing fancy. Although she didn't have the money to
go out and buy a pretty new outfit, she wanted to look
her best. She was nervous about having him in her
home. She wanted everything to be just right. Her navy
high heels clicked on the hard wood flooring as she
went to answer the doorbell. "Hello. Please come in."

"How are you?" Donald smiled, placing a kiss on her
cheek. His dark gaze caressed her mouth before dropping to linger where her soft brown skin was veiled beneath her lacy slip and sheer lace top. His blood heated
and he had to force his gaze away.

"I said no gifts," she scolded softly.

He was dressed casually in dark brown slacks and
cream pullover cable-knit sweater. "The wine is for our
meal," he explained, shrugging out of a tan leather
jacket and hanging it on one of the brass hooks in the
hall. He needed to bring something to insure a smile
on her beautiful face. He caught her hand and played
with her fingers. "You look nice," then he teased, "And
smell even better."

"Thank you." She smiled in spite of herself. "Have a
seat." She indicated the living room, then added
quickly, "I'll just check on dinner."

To her annoyance, he followed her into her small but
tidy pink and green kitchen. She was hoping for a few
minutes alone to settle her nerves. She'd been disappointed when he hadn't taken her into his arms and
kissed her.

"Something smells good."

"Nothing fancy, just pot roast, carrots and potatoes,

tossed salad, biscuits and lemon meringue pie for dessert."

"Oh, baby!" he exclaimed. "Sounds heavenly. I haven't had a home-cooked meal in some time. Lately, it's been mostly hotel and restaurant fare. Sometimes my sister or sister-in-law feels sorry for me and invites me over."

Taylor laughed. "Somehow, I doubt you're starving." He looked not only healthy, but fit, his body taut and muscular.

He shrugged. "I have a housekeeper and she's an excellent cook. But, I'm on the road so much it doesn't matter. Believe me, there's a difference."

"Why is it that most men don't feel cared about unless their women cook? This is the nineties, for goodness' sake. That attitude should have ended with my father's generation."

"There's something very loving about a woman willing to cook for her man. And it has nothing to do with the date on the calendar."

Taylor shook her finger at him. "You need to quit!"

Donald roared with laughter.

"Why don't you put on a CD?"

"Anything special?"

"Nope. You choose."

Taylor was bent over the stove basting the roast when Donald returned to the kitchen while Gladys Knight's voice soothed in the background. Suddenly conscious of his interested male gaze on her soft bottom, she blushed managing to straighten as naturally as possible.

Donald made no secret of how appealing he found her when he said, "You are a very lovely lady, Taylor."

"No gifts, Donald. Not even fancy compliments." She needed to do her thinking with her head and not allow her feminine hormones to take over. Right that minute it would be so easy to forget their reality. She hadn't forgotten his influence over her brother. Yet, she had invited him here and even cooked for him while know-ing they had absolutely nothing in common.

"Simple truth, Taylor." Deciding it was best to change the subject before they got into a serious discussion, he said, "I bet your folks are very proud of you."

She blinked in surprise, her eyes locked with his from where he stood leaning against the counter. His long arms comfortably crossed in front of him. "How did . . ." She stopped abruptly.

"How did I know?"

She nodded.

"You've done well for yourself. You own your own home, maintain a good job. And you're working toward your goals." He still couldn't believe his luck in finding such a grounded woman, who knew what she wanted in life and wasn't afraid to use her intellect to get it. There was a lot more on her mind than pretty clothes, fancy cars and what a rich man could do for her. He liked that about her.

Taylor was so flustered she nearly dropped the oven-mitt and hurried to the refrigerator. She saw herself as being quite ordinary. Sure, she worked hard to get ahead and stay ahead. But so did everyone she knew. Wait? Was this some new form of flattery designed to weaken her resolve? If that was his purpose, he was cor-rect. She was seeing things in him that she didn't want to see, didn't even want to know about.

She stared inside, having no idea what she was looking for. Then took out the salad to give herself something to do . . . anything to focus on other than Donald. He so easily overwhelmed her.

So what if he could be understanding? Kind? Even considerate? That didn't make him the man for her. She wanted a man who shared her views, who lived in the real world, rather than some kind of fantasy land. She was safe with him as long as she remembered that. She had allowed only one man to hurt her to the core. She was not about to let it happen again.

"Where do you hide them?"

"Hide what?"

"The roses." He laughed at her utter dismay.

"I don't hide them. I prefer to keep them in my bedroom."

"Aw. So your brother doesn't know about them, huh?"

"What does my brother have to do with us?"

He scowled, instantly recognizing he was about to open a can of worms that he would rather leave unopened. He hastily shrugged. "Not a thing." He knew he should be relieved that she hadn't thrown the flowers in the trash.

Taylor swallowed, reminding herself to stay calm and keep her temper under control. She needed all her wits about her. She must not let her attraction to him outweigh her common sense.

"Can I help?" he offered, watching her lift the salad bowl and bread basket.

"Yes." She smiled, handing him the covered vegetable dishes.

Once everything was arranged to her satisfaction on the dining room table and they were both seated, she looked at him. "Would you say grace?"

He nodded and did so with quiet reverence. "Potatoes?" he offered, handing her the dish.

The meal was comfortable and very enjoyable. Donald didn't hesitate to tell her so. Taylor couldn't help but feel pleased and was surprised when he casually helped with the clean up. As they worked together she had to remind herself that this was the super-star jock, who women idealized and men so admired, casually drying her dishes.

"Here, let me carry that." He brought the tray of

coffee and dessert into her cozy living room. He put it down on the low table in front of the sofa and watched as she sank down on the cushion beside him. As he found himself studying her sweetly curved mouth, he absently accepted the generous slice of pie she handed to him.

"Well?" she prompted.

Realizing she was waiting for him to taste the sweet treat when what he truly wanted was something much more tempting and satisfying. Recovering quickly, Donald sampled the pie. "Mmm, you're a great cook."

"I learned at my mother's side." She then shocked them both by asking, "Did you call her?"

He quirked a brow. "Who?"

"That beautiful, slim woman who put her telephone number in your pocket."

Swallowing quickly, he cleared his throat before asking, "The deli?"

"Yes," she whispered tightly. It was none of her business. She knew that. What she didn't know was why his answer mattered.

He carefully placed his plate on the tray before he looked into her lovely eyes. "No, I didn't call, although there was a time when I may have. If you must know there are very few days when I don't have several numbers in my pockets. They end up in the trash. I'm old-fashioned in some ways. I like to decide what woman I want to spend my time with. By the way, I was where I wanted to be then as I am now. I wanted to be with you."

Taylor couldn't look away from his gaze. When his eyes dipped to her mouth she quickly looked away, determined to ignore the hot need simmering inside of her.

"Taylor . . ." he said.

She interrupted with, "How long will you be in Detroit?"

He sighed, glancing at his watch. "Another hour or so. Why? Are you tired of my company already?"

"No. Are you saying you only came for the evening?"

"Exactly."

Taylor didn't know what to way . . . what to think. At times he seemed so ordinary; then suddenly she had to accept there was nothing commonplace about him. He was clearly out of her . . .

"Don't," he said softly.

"Don't what?"

"Don't put up barriers between us." He lifted her chin and dipped his head to sample her soft, sweet mouth. When her lips opened beneath his, he groaned his pleasure then slid his tongue inside to savor her sweetness.

"Spend the weekend with me."

"What?'

"I have to go down to South Carolina on business on Friday. Come with me. Let's fly down and relax and get to know each other."

"I'm not interested in sleeping with you," she insisted.

"I haven't asked you, yet. No pressure." He smiled that warm charming smile of his.

Her dark brown eyes searched his black eyes. Taylor was the first to look away.

"I thought it best to be honest," she said, her chin jutted forward.

"Will you come?"

"Yes . . ." she said in a whisper, but he heard.

"Great," Donald said, an instant before he pulled her against him. He intended to keep it light, but the instant his mouth covered hers his hunger intensified. He gave her a deep tongue-thrusting caress before he dropped his arms. "I'll be in touch." He closed the door softly behind him.

# Nine

When dawn lit the sky that next morning, Taylor was curled on her side unable to sleep. As she glanced at the clock, she realized she had seen every hour come and go during the long restless night.

The puzzle that she was determined to complete was how she had managed to get through dinner without showing Donald any sign of resentment. The only thing that had upset her was when he had offered her that jeweler's box. Imagine, she didn't want him to think badly of her.

Where had the outrage gone? It certainly was present now as she tossed and turned from one side of the bed to the other. All the clear reasons why she should not be involved with Donald were percolating in her brain . . . now. It had all rushed back in one big giant sweep. She should have followed her instincts. She should not have gone out with him. She certainly should not have agreed to go away with him for an entire weekend. She was not a naive teenager. Why hadn't she asked about the sleeping arrangement? She was quite literally asking for trouble.

What had she been thinking? That was the problem, she hadn't been thinking at all. She had been focused entirely on how he made her feel. She'd been lost in Donald's irresistible masculine charm. If she actually got on a plane with him she would be asking for some serious complications.

Donald had turned seduction into an art form. And he was the master of the game. Why else would so many women be so very interested in him at any given time? He was a heart-throb. She saw the way females had turned their heads when he entered a room. It happened without fail. It was more than his good looks, more than his wealth. She summed it up as pure male magnetism. Women couldn't help but respond to his raw masculinity.

It was evident in everything he did from the basketball court to the board room. It was most noticeable on the basketball court. He seemed to exude pure sexuality, his physical stamina unbelievable.

What kind of lover was he? Was he unselfish, putting his partner's needs above his own? How could any woman survive his unique brand of potent sexuality with her heart whole? Goodness! What was she thinking?

It had been years since she had allowed herself to be intimate with a man. She had been young and stupid, barely out of high school. At nineteen, she had been so sure of herself. Alex Adams was clearly the most handsome man on campus. She, like the other females in his class, was awed by his status as a single professor. She had been blind to the truth about him, focused on his looks.

It hadn't taken long for him to convince her that he cared about her. A couple of weeks of his smiles and the smoothness of his sex appeal and Taylor had fallen hard. She gave her love without assurance of any kind of commitment, certain that someday after her graduation they would marry. There was nothing she wanted more than to be his wife. Stupid! Stupid!

She almost laughed out loud, something she could now do easily. She could not have been more wrong about him. Alex was a player, after one thing . . . sex. One night of seduction was all it took. Alex was in love all right, but with himself.

Taylor learned from that heart-breaking mistake. She had become quite good at avoiding entanglements. Now she was wondering if she was about to make the same mistake. Was she poised to fall down the same rabbit hole yet again? Was she falling in love with Donald?

Tears slowly filled her dark eyes and slowly trickled down her face, soaking her pillow. She didn't try to stop the flow. She did not want to care about him. He was all wrong for her.

He was everything she hated in a man: rich, arrogant and egotistical. He was every bit as good looking as Alex, maybe even more so. How long would it be before he either gave up on her or got what he wanted?

She had no doubt that sex was his motive where women were concerned. Love them and leave them with perhaps a few pretty baubles to keep them silent. How else had he managed to stay single all these years? He could probably buy his way out of any difficulty.

There was no doubt in her mind that he was not interested in a commitment. The funny part of it was that she understood his attitude. Women literally threw themselves at him and his teammates on a regular basis. Most of them were willing to do anything to gain a pro ball player for their very own. She found the entire thing downright sickening.

What was she worrying about? As long as she remembered that Donald was not to be trusted, she would be fine. She knew the rules for this little game they were playing. The question that remained unanswered was whether she was smart enough not to fall into his trap.

She was no weak-minded ninny. She had been able to stand on her own two feet for many years now and take care of herself and her younger brother as well.

She had learned to depend on herself for all her needs. The difficulty came when she had to look outside herself for happiness.

When she was in his arms, all she could think about was how he made her feel. There was no comparison. She had never known such sweet magic, such sizzling hot desire. The memories of him could not be held at bay. Her breasts had ached for his touch. The trouble had been that she wanted him. She wanted the hot sweetness of his mouth caressing the ultrasensitive tips of her breasts. Her nipples were so sensitive, so achingly hard as she recalled the feel of his broad chest against them. And they both had been fully dressed. Their kisses were so wondrously erotic.

She almost lost it . . . almost lost control. For an instant at the door, she had nearly rubbed her aching nipples into the muscular pads of his chest, but had caught herself just in time, before she had made a fool of herself. She had no idea what he would have thought.

She had really tried not to take note of his body, but she knew he found her desirable. That knowledge was more potent than the aged wine they'd drunk during their meal.

What would he have done if she had given in to her aching need? if she had opened her thighs and pressed herself against his arousal? Taylor covered her face as if she could hide from her own thoughts. The unvarnished truth of the matter was that when she undressed, her panties were damp from her arousal. She wanted him, so badly. For the first time in almost a decade, she wanted to take a man inside her body and love him the way African women had been loving their men throughout time, giving them utmost pleasure. The problem was that she wasn't his woman and he was certainly not her man.

Maybe this trip would help? Maybe if she went ahead

and slept with him she could get him out of her system . . . out of her doggone head? It certainly worked for men. Why couldn't it work for her? She would make sure she was protected from unwanted pregnancy, insisting that he use a condom. She was no longer a girl. She was old enough to take care of herself.

They would make love. No. They would have mutually gratifying sex and then be done with it. Once the weekend was over, their involvement would be over. She would go into this with her eyes wide open. There was no chance of her getting hurt this time. They would have sex once, possibly twice. That should relieve both their sexual interests in each other. They would both walk away, ready to get on with their separate lives.

The alarm clock suddenly went off, startling her. Well, she had wasted enough time mooning over the man. Having sex was the quickest way possible of getting over her silly infatuation with him. Taylor was humming to herself as she showered, pleased that she had hit upon the solution to her dilemma.

"You can't do this," Scott yelled, yet again.

Taylor rolled her eyes and went back to her packing. He was pacing her bedroom, refusing to let the subject drop.

"You can't go away with him!"

"This has nothing to do with you, little brother. This is between Donald and myself. You are not involved."

"If it were not for me you wouldn't have even met the guy!" he practically shouted.

She went up on tiptoe and kissed his cheek. "Thank you."

"Taylor . . ."

"I thought you liked Donald."

"I did . . . I do. But that does not mean I want you

sleeping with the guy. You don't even know him, not really."

"That's why I'm going." She sighed, tossing in a swimsuit and a short toweling robe. She tried to hide the way her hands were shaking with nerves.

"There are other ways to get to know someone . . . without going away for a weekend, Sis."

"I'm not disputing that. Scott, this is my decision, not yours. I thought you approved of me dating him."

"I do. This is way beyond an innocent date. Think, girl. What do we really know about him? He is used to having women chasing after him."

"I've had enough of this. I stay out of your relationship with Jenna. Kindly extend to me the same courtesy."

Jenna had been sitting on the side of the bed, listening to the exchange between the siblings. "Scott, why don't you go see if the car is here?"

He was scowling, but he left.

"Thanks," Taylor sighed, zipping her garment bag closed.

"No problem. You're nervous enough. You don't need Scott acting like your father."

"I'm that obvious?" she asked as she turned around in a circle trying to remember what she might have forgotten. "Do you agree with Scott?"

"It doesn't matter what I think. You're going to have a wonderful time. When is the last time you've gone on a real vacation?"

Taylor shrugged. "Other than visiting the folks during the Christmas holidays, I haven't. I've been too busy for a vacation. Besides, there was always Scott to consider. I couldn't very well leave him at home alone."

"Well, it's way past time you did something strictly for yourself. Just have fun."

"Oh, Jenna. You are so kind. Where did Scott get the

good sense to hang on to you?" She worried that it was time she stop protecting Scott and let their parents know about his living arrangement. He claimed he was an adult. Was she treating him like a kid?

"He's no dummy."

Both women were laughing when Scott stuck his head inside the room to say, "Your limousine has arrived."

"Wow!" Jenna exclaimed, jumping to her feet. "Your man sure believes in traveling in style."

"We're meeting at the airport in Chicago." Taylor nervously reached for the jacket to her peach pantsuit.

Scott was scowling but he carried her luggage out to the car while Taylor locked up and walked arm and arm with Jenna down the drive.

"You be careful," her brother whispered, as he kissed her cheek and gave her a big bear hug. "Call me if you need me. I'll be on the next plane."

"Don't worry. I'll be fine."

Next was Jenna's turn, she gave her a hug. "Forget about Detroit. Enjoy yourself."

"Thanks, hon." Taylor waved from the backseat of the sleek gray car.

"Why did you tell her that?" Scott asked, tightly.

"Why not? Taylor deserves some happiness. This is not about you. This is about her. She needs to find out how she feels about him." Looking at her friend and lover, she reached up and kissed him. "Stop worrying. Trust Taylor. She knows what is best."

"I hope you're right." His troubled eyes followed the car until it was out of sight.


Taylor used the drive to the Metropolitan Airport and the plane ride to Chicago to calm herself. It was a short flight and she was thankful that no one could see her shaky knees when she walked off the plane. She was ushered into a VIP lounge. Donald was there, waiting for her.

"Hey, beautiful," he said, enfolding her into a warm hug. He had nearly paced a hole in the carpet. Finally, Taylor was here. He could relax. He had just gotten in from Toronto on business. It had been a hectic week. He was beat, but the feel of her in his arms was what he needed more than rest, more than anything else in the world.

"Hi!" she whispered, her face buried at the base of his throat. He smelled so good and felt even better. He was so solid, so real. Taylor suddenly realized that she had, indeed, missed him, even though they had talked several times during the week.

"I missed you." His voice was gruff with emotion. He'd been needing to kiss her, taste her—but not here, not in public. When they kissed he wanted absolute privacy so that he could show her how desperately he wanted her. Only an iron will kept his hunger at bay.

Taylor looked up into his beautiful eyes and recognized the longing lingering there. Suddenly, she knew that what she had been struggling against was her feelings for him. She wasn't sure how it had happened or even when. All she knew was that Donald had taken part of her heart while she hadn't been looking.

She was here because he wanted her here. She had come because she cared for him and could deny him nothing. Was it already too late? She knew she was vulnerable when it came to him. She was safe as long as she did not fall in love with him.

He saw the uncertainty in her eyes. "Taylor?"

"I'm sorry." She blushed, realizing that he had been talking to her. "What did you say?"

"Are you ready to leave?"

"Did they announce our flight?"

He smiled. "We're not traveling on a commercial

flight. We're taking my private plane. The resort we're traveling to is on one of the small sea islands off the coast of South Carolina."

His own plane! Goodness! "You didn't say anything about going to a resort."

"Is it a problem?"

"No . . ." She was simply overwhelmed. She wasn't used to limousines or private planes and resorts.

Donald lifted her cases in one hand and dropped the other to the center of her back. "Let's go." He led her directly out to the tarmac, where private planes were serviced and waited to be boarded.

As they approached the custom built jet the door opened and the staircase dropped. They were greeted by Jack Thomas, their pilot. The interior of the plane was lavishly furnished, looked more like an apartment than a plane. There was a comfortable sitting area with large burgundy leather armchairs, a roomy desk, a tiny kitchen area and a bedroom with a bathroom in the rear.

"Comfortable?" he asked, after stowing away the luggage. He took the armchair next to hers and clasped her seatbelt, as well as his.

"I'm fine." She smiled, her hands tightly laced in her lap.

"You're not afraid to fly, are you?" His hungry gaze caressed her dark peach-tinted mouth.

Taylor laughed, displaying even white teeth. "No, but I do believe in saying my prayers . . . make sure I'm all right with the Lord."

"Makes sense to me," he grinned. Donald could feel her tension and assumed it was due to the flight. Although the jet was fairly large it didn't compare to a jumbo-jet liner. He reached over and laced her fingers with his, making no effort to converse as the plane accelerated down the runway.

Taylor clung to his hand until they were airborne. When she loosened her fingers, he had to keep himself from not letting go. It had been too long. They spent too much time apart. He needed to be able to look at her . . . touch her. He closed his eyes knowing he needed so much more from her. He craved her love, but he was hungry for her sweetness. He had witnessed her devotion and love for her family. He wanted that kind of loyalty and love for himself.

"How was your week?" Taylor asked.

"Hectic. I feel every one of my thirty-one years. Or shouldn't I tell you that? Might spoil my image."

"That image is a facade. It's not real."

"How right you are. How was your week?"

"Busy," she laughed. "But I did make progress in planning the reception and reading for Dr. Van Sertima. I'm on the committee that is responsible for bringing him to the University. It is so important to know the history of our people."

"I agree. Van Sertima is a remarkable speaker. I attended one of his lectures in New York. His books really give you something to think about. We come from a strong, loving people."

Taylor stared at him, shocked by his insight, his Afrocentrality. No, she didn't really know this man. He was more than a basketball player. He was a strong black man who cared about his people. He worked long hours to provide career opportunities for small black entrepreneurs across the country.

"I enjoy his work also." She surprised herself by asking, "Did the March really change your life as so many brothers claim?"

"Yes," he said without hesitation. "It was a profound experience that I would not have missed for anything. I left motivated to try harder to make a difference to my folk. I'm not proud that Williams Enterprises was first developed ten years ago as an economic loophole."

She was shocked by his candor. "But you do so much to empower the black community."

"That is the result of years of growth, finding out who I was as a black man. It was only after I found myself that I was able to reach out to others. I have been blessed in many ways. Thank goodness I was raised by people with their feet firmly planted on this earth," he confessed.

Taylor recognized that she was seeing a part of this complicated man that very few people ever saw. "I feel very blessed that I'm also fortunate enough to have that same advantage."

They smiled at each other in understanding. As she looked into his eyes she wondered if she had only seen the superficial and not the caring man beneath the fame and glamour. He looked smooth and sophisticated in his custom-made deep wine and beige tweed sport coat that he wore with dark brown slacks and cashmere sweater.

"How close are you to finishing your degree?"

"Years and years. I need to finish my master's. And I don't plan to stop there. I won't be satisfied until I finish my doctorate."

"Have you ever regretted the demands your family has placed on your shoulders? You've taken on a great deal of responsibility at an early age."

"Sometimes, when I first finished college, I felt that way, but thank heaven, the feeling didn't last."

"You're a very special person, Taylor," he said softly. "I can't believe we both grew up in the same city."

She blushed in spite of her efforts not to. "We got off to a very rocky start. I'm still not sure . . ."

"Shush," he whispered, pressing his finger against

her soft mouth. "Can't we leave our problems in Detroit?"

"I don't know."

"Sure, we can. All we have to do is want it. When is the last time you've seen your folks?"

"A few weeks. We drove down for the Christmas holidays. Folks had a chance to meet Jenna, Scott's girlfriend."

He winced as he shifted his long legs.

"What's wrong?"

"I aggravated an old injury during practice this week." He was warmed by her look of concern. "There is nothing to worry about. I'll be in top shape by next weekend when we play Seattle."

"You push yourself too hard," Taylor scolded. "You're constantly on the go. Do you ever just rest?"

"I plan to rest all weekend. Do nothing more strenuous than swim and admire your beautiful legs in a swimsuit. You did bring one, didn't you?"

She teased. "I got the impression it was a requirement."

Donald grinned, his dark eyes twinkling. "Absolutely."

He could think of nothing he would have enjoyed more than to be able to openly admire her beauty. Well, that was not exactly true. He wanted her. His desire for her had gotten to the point that he doubted he would be easily satisfied. His keen interest in her was new for him. Yet it had started the very instant they met.

This trip would be good for both of them. They needed time alone. He was grateful that she had given them this opportunity. He had worried each time they talked that she would change her mind and not let him have her to himself. Even as he waited for her at the airport he'd paced the waiting room uncertain that she would come. He'd never been more relieved than when

he'd seen her walk into the lounge. He wanted to grab
her and never let go.

"Tell me about the island."

# Ten

With a long fingered hand, he traced down the length of her silky brown throat. "It's quiet, restful. No hassles." No family, no business, no NBA.

Taylor shivered from the brief contact. She suddenly dropped her gaze. She studied her unvarnished nails as her thoughts flew. She had not expected to be on a private plane. But then she hadn't known what to expect. She had convinced herself that what she needed was to get him out of her system.

Once the sex was over, so would the relationship. She wanted her life back to normal. She wanted what she had before they had met. He had managed to tilt her world on its axis. She needed to be on solid ground once again . . . which meant she wanted it over. Only then could she focus on her own goals and dreams. It seemed so simple, until she realized that she cared for him, but she could do this. She could.

"Taylor," he said quietly, tilting her face until he could see her lovely eyes. "Talk to me, sweetness."

She fortified herself with a deep breath designed to calm the butterflies in her stomach. "I'm a little nervous."

"Don't be." His voice was deep, so husky with unmistakable yearning. "I'll keep you safe."

Donald's mouth settled on hers and he sponged the fleshy bottom lip with his tongue, causing her to gasp—thus allowing him access to the honeyed interior. He moaned throatily.

"Oh . . ." she whimpered, melting against him, eager for the firmness of his arms, hating the barrier of the armrest. Her entire body was trembling when he drew away, depriving her of his tongue, of his heat.

Her breath came in quick pants. His hungry gaze dropped to the sweet bounty of her breasts. The nipples were clearly evident, pressing against the soft cloth of her cream blouse, twin points of desire asking for the warmth of his mouth.

"No . . ." she protested, unwittingly tightening her arms around his neck. Her mouth caressing the side of his throat.

"You expect too much," his voice gruff with desire.

"A kiss?"

He could tell by her eyes that she had no idea what she was asking. She went straight to his head, more potent than one-hundred-year-old brandy, directly into his bloodstream.

"No . . ." he snapped impatiently, unable to stop himself from taking her hand, guiding it along his cashmere-covered chest, then slipping it beneath his sweater against the heat of his dark skin.

When she paused for an instant near the nipple, he closed his eyes as he guided her soft fingers over the tiny ebony disc. He showed her how to use the tip of her nail, circling the nipple, then moaned from the pleasure.

He whispered heavily, "Sweetness, you have me trembling with need. I want you." He licked her lips. "I want your soft hand touching me . . . stroking me." He lifted her hand away from his hot flesh and pressed a kiss into the center of her palm. "I've shocked you, haven't I?"

There was no way for her to deny the truth, so she merely nodded.

He smiled charmed by her innocence. He suspected she wasn't a virgin, but he believed her involvement with men had been very limited. He said softly, "If you want me, you're going to have to get used to the way I am. I tend to speak my mind. I'm a big man, with a man's desires. I want you, Taylor," he said huskily rubbing his fingertip along her soft mouth. "But I want you to want me as much as I want you. Tell me . . . tell me what you're thinking."

He dropped his head to press his lips to the silky brown skin of her throat, ever so briefly tonguing the base of her throat, filling his lungs with her exquisitely sweet woman's scent. He couldn't help wishing he could tongue her sweet heat. He was trembling with the need to know all her feminine secrets.

"I can't." She blushed, wanting his hands on her breasts, caressing her the way she had caressed him.

"Do you want me?"

"Donald . . ." Taylor whispered, pressing kiss after kiss against his generous lips. He opened for her as she slid her tongue inside and gave him the deep sizzling hot caress he craved.

He moaned heavily, loving the feel of her mouth, relishing her taste. She was so sweet, so wildly seductive. He had a point to make and now was not the time to be sidetracked.

"Answer me, baby. Do you want me as much as I want you?"

Taylor longed to press her breasts into his chest. She shivered with sweet expectation.

"Yes."

"Good," he said with satisfaction, yet he was the one to break the seal of their mouths. He forced himself to move away. He would not take her like this, aboard his plane, although he was shaking with need.

He wouldn't cheat her of a beautiful romantic night

of sweet seduction. She deserved the candlelight, roses, champagne, the moonlit stroll along the beach and silk sheets. She deserved that and more. Taylor was special and he intended to treat her that way.

Donald walked over to the tiny built in refrigerator behind the bar and pulled out two cans of cola. He tried to concentrate on nothing more than filling two glasses with soda. His hands were shaking badly as he fought to contain his desire, but he promised himself that the wait would be worth it. He wanted more than a weekend fling with her. He wanted a relationship. It had been such an uphill battle to gain her trust. He still was unsure if he had it.

He was not only fighting her, he was also fighting himself. His healthy male body reminded him exactly how long it had been since he had been inside a woman. He sighed heavily. Over the years he had grown so disgusted with the type of women he met due to his high visibility and wealth. He had been propositioned and been stalked in efforts to compromise him. He had finally gotten to the point where he said the hell with it and had embraced celibacy for well over a year and a half.

He knew he was more vulnerable than he had ever expected to be. His acute hunger for Taylor left him so damn needy, but he refused to let his penis do his thinking for him. He would wait—but he was convinced that once they became lovers, things would settle down nicely.

He had never met a woman like Taylor. She challenged him intellectually, thoroughly intrigued him. Yet she easily aroused him to the point of madness. While his mind told him it was too soon even to consider intimacy, his body told him it couldn't happen soon enough. He almost laughed aloud at his choice of words. He warned himself not to rush things, give them the time they needed.

When Donald returned, he carried the cool drinks. He would have preferred something stronger, but he was already tired. The booze would relax him too much. He didn't want to miss a second of their time together. He would love the evening to end with her in his bed, even if it was too soon for them to make love. He pacified himself with the thought that maybe she would allow him to sleep beside her. He longed to hold her all night long.

"I had a chance to meet one of my heroes last summer during the Olympics."

Taylor jumped, having been caught up in the magic of his touch. She felt as if she had been floating on a cloud. His kisses left her weak with yearning. She had to force herself to concentrate on what he was saying rather than the warm magic his touch and kisses aroused within her.

"Who?"

"Bishop Desmond Tutu," he said proudly.

"Donald! Oh! How exciting. Tell me about it."

He told her about the summer Olympics in Atlanta. He had been part of the Dream Team. He found himself enjoying her easy companionship as he related the experience.

"Have you been to South Africa?"

He smiled. "Not yet. But I'd love to someday. What about you?"

"Yes. I always had Scott to think of." She wasn't even aware of the sigh of longing. She realized what she had almost told him. She was becoming too comfortable with him. Now all that might have changed. If Scott . . . No, she wouldn't think about her brother or his plans for the future. For this single weekend she wanted to be selfish and concentrate only on herself. This weekend could very well be all the time she would have with Donald.

"Someday," he acknowledged, praying that she wouldn't let the old argument come between them.

Donald accepted how much she had come to mean to him. She was so rare, one of a kind. With her, he could be himself. He needed this chance with her. He wanted her to see not Donald Williams the businessman or the NBA athlete, but the man.

"I'll take you, if you like," he found himself saying and meaning it. He was thrilled by the possibility.

Taylor shook her head. "Nice thought."

They were smiling at each other when the seatbelt sign came on.

"Need this?" He offered his hand.

"Yes." She did not even pretend that she liked take-offs and landings, but simply laced her fingers with his. As she closed her eyes she realized that she was allowing herself to lean on him. It felt surprisingly good.

It was early evening. Once they were safely on the ground, Donald whisked her off the plane into the waiting limousine.

"Comfortable?" he asked, his fingers playing with hers. His heated gaze stroked her lips as he wondered if he would ever get his fill of her. He suspected that making love with her would only be the tip of the iceberg. Would he need more and more of her sweetness?

Taylor smiled. She was having a wonderful time, her excited gaze moving time and time again from the lush green scenery back to the man beside her. "It's beautiful here. How often do you manage to come?"

"Not as often as I would like. I'm usually here on business."

"Don't you vacation during the off-season? By the way, who owns the resort?"

Donald reluctantly admitted, "It's a family owned enterprise. I'm the major stockholder, although both my brother, Carl, and my brother-in-law, Jess, own equal shares. The island has been in my father's family for generations. It's only been since land developers became interested in building a resort here that we decided to keep it in the family. The uncles, aunts, cousins all own a piece of it. I've shocked you."

Taylor's eyes had gone wide with disbelief. "I don't know too many people who own their own island or plane for that matter."

He was studying her as she averted his face, looking out the window at the passing greenery rather than at him. He could sense her withdrawal, a quiet distancing. Something he was not about to stand for.

"What's wrong?"

"Nothing."

"Taylor?"

"I guess I was just thinking how little we have in common. We live in two very different worlds."

"Why do you say that? Because I am wealthy?"

"Partly."

"Totally," he snapped. "Most women find my bank balance more intriguing than my personality."

"I don't believe that." Her eyes were on her clasped hands in her lap.

"Believe it," he said bitterly. He cradled her soft jaw, turning her face toward his. "It's taken forever to find a woman who isn't impressed with my income," he revealed. "Unfortunately, you seem to be distancing yourself because of it."

"That's not true."

"It is. I was reluctant to even tell you that I own my own plane. But I travel constantly. It was a necessity."

"You're not being fair," she said unhappily.

"The resort is only a small part of my business, Taylor. I own property all over the world. That's one reason I'm forced to travel so much."

"I see."

"No, you don't. Rather than accepting it as part of my life, you seem to be using it against me. Why?"

"I'm not used to any one person having so much wealth. It throws me, that's all."

"It scares you," he said softly. Stroking her soft chin, he said, "I have no intention of taking advantage of you in any way. I only want what you want."

"How can you possibly know what I want?" It was true she had agreed to go away with him, but in the hope that being with him, sleeping with him would solve her dilemma.

She wanted to get him out of her system. She was convinced that his love-making would end his fascination with her and her desire for him. She must not weaken now. A romantic weekend was enough for her. She didn't need or want more. As long as she remembered that no one would be hurt.

Deciding it was wise to change the subject, Taylor said, "Tell me more about the island." She subtly moved away from him. "It's very lovely."

She might not have wanted him to notice, but he did and he didn't like it one little bit. "My father's family have lived here and farmed the land and raised their families on this island for years," he answered as patiently as he could. "Rice was the major crop before we decided to develop a portion of the property into a resort. We're very close to St. Helena, where the Penn Center is located."

"Really?"

"You heard of it?"

"Yes, hasn't everyone?" she laughed. Looking out the window, she thought the land was lush and green, even in the early spring. They passed a quaint shopping area, small boutiques and an open air market. Then they left the village behind and the two lane road curved through the countryside.

"It was my sister's idea. Turn part of the island into more than a haven for the family. The entire family is involved with the resort in some way, although many of the younger members of the family are more interested in what the big city has to offer."

"How can anyone not like it here? It's beautiful."

"Yes," he agreed, but he was not looking out of the window but at her. "Opening the Sea Island Resort has been an interesting mixture of business and pleasure. It has a great golf course. It has proven to be a highly successful business venture for all of us. We've all benefited."

"I'm glad." She smiled. Her eyes told him she was sincere. "How can you own something so lovely and not want to spend time here?"

"During the off season I try to make a special effort to get down here."

"It must be wonderful to get away during the cold months," she said dreamily.

"That could be arranged, if you like."

"What?"

"A suite can be made available for you during whatever month or weekend you choose. In fact, I would be pleased to do that for you."

Taylor's eyes collided with his. She didn't hesitate to say, "No, thank you. I'm not interested in becoming a kept woman."

"A man in my position is used to assisting others. It would give me pleasure to do this for you."

"I don't want your money."

"What are you interested in, Taylor?"

"From you? I don't know," she answered candidly.

"A friend? A lover?" His eyes glinted.

"I'm not sure. But whatever it is, it won't involve money."

"Money can provide pleasure," he persisted.

"No! I'm not for sale!" she shot back.

"I know that. I'm not trying to buy you, but I would be lying if I didn't admit that I want you, Taylor Hendricks."

Taylor's eyes flashed with temper. He was so blasted arrogant. She knew he wanted her sexually. He was pulling out all the stops in order to get her, willing to say whatever he thought she wanted to hear. Well, he would have her, only on her terms not his. She planned to walk away from him unscarred, unhurt and heart-whole.

When she looked away, Donald sighed, amazed at his own level of disappointment. Had he offended her with his bluntness? Damn it! How else was he going to find out what she was thinking? Maybe he was just in too much of a hurry. He cautioned himself that they had the entire weekend to get to know each other.

"Are you angry?"

When she lifted the thick heavy veil of black lashes her cheeks flushed with heat. She knew if she wanted to be with this man, even for a short time, she had to accept his frankness.

"No. Why should I be? You have been very straightforward."

He nodded, suddenly thrilled that Taylor was the first woman he'd met in a very long time who was not interested in what he could do for her. If anything, she was too independent. The only thing she had been willing to accept from him were flowers.

"What are winters like here?"

He roared with laughter. "I have no idea. I've spent every season for the last ten years on the basketball court."

Taylor blinked in embarrassment, then giggled. "Sorry, I forgot."

Donald was enchanted. She touched his inner core

and stroked his heart. Her smile caused his breath to catch in his throat.

"Don't be sorry." All he could seem to think about was whether she would be willing to sleep in his arms, her long beautiful legs tangled with his.

The car eased to a stop in front of a sprawling U-shaped hotel. There was still enough light for her to see that it was surrounded on two sides by the sea. There was an inner court, swimming pools and tennis courts, as well as lavish gardens.

"Oh, Donald!" she exclaimed, not waiting for him to help her out. Her eyes sparkled like a child's on Christmas morning, filled with delight.

Donald couldn't stop himself from wondering how she would look when he made slow, deep love to her. He ached to hold her, taste her, love her from the top of her dark thick curls to the tips of her pretty toes.

They had barely entered the busy yet spacious lobby when the hotel manager, Ron Williams, came forward to greet them.

Donald had barely made the introductions when Ron, his cousin, began rattling off a long list of problems that required Donald's immediate attention.

Running his hand over his close-cut natural, Donald turned to Taylor with an apology. "I'm sorry. Hopefully, I can straighten this out before long. Why don't you go on around to the suite and relax."

Taylor smiled, determined to hide her disappointment. "That will be fine. See you later." She followed the bellman past the bank of elevators.

They had this weekend and that was all. She would focus on nothing more than enjoying their time together and not worry about the future.

As she looked around the resort, she realized that much attention had been paid to every detail. She smiled and listened while the bellman talked about their fine weather with a Gullah accent. She reassured herself that she could handle this situation and she had no reason to be nervous.

The bellman let her into a large suite that was unexpectedly not empty.

Two lovely women seated side by side on a plush sofa were laughing at the tall man sitting across from them in matching armchairs. A wide-screen television built into the wall unit was on while two pretty little girls played on the huge area rug with their dolls.

All heads turned toward the open door.

The bellman urged Taylor inside, as if she were expected.

"I'm sorry. I must have the wrong room?" she said, quickly backing out of the door.

"Taylor?"

"Yes."

"Hi. I'm Megan, Donald's sister. Come on in."

She smiled, recognizing the petite beauty she had met the night of the NAACP dinner-dance. It seemed as if the whole Williams's family was here. "Yes of course. How are you?"

"Fine. Please, come in. Do you remember my husband, Jess, and my brother, Carl, and his wife, Margie? The two little ones on the rug are my daughters."

Carl rose from his chair to instruct the bellman where to put the luggage and tip the man. "Where is that brother of mine?"

"He was delayed by the hotel manager," she said, having recovered somewhat. No one seemed the least bit surprised to find her here with Donald.

Taylor glanced around the beautifully appointed suite. It was huge, made up of four bedrooms with baths, large living and dining rooms, as well as a kitchen. A patio opened onto a private pool area and deck.

"Please sit down. Make yourself at home. Would you like some ice tea, lemonade?"

"Tea, please," Taylor said taking a seat on one of the sectional sofas.

"I didn't know Donald was headed this way," Carl laughed, exchanging a look with his wife.

"This should be interesting," Megan giggled.

"We have evidently gotten our wires crossed. We weren't expecting him and he, no doubt, was not expecting us," Jess surmised with a grin.

No one seem the least put out by her arrival, but they were all openly amused. Taylor could guess why, everyone assumed that she and Donald were lovers and had come to the resort for a romantic weekend. Well, they were partly correct, she admitted. Taylor wondered how Donald would react to finding his entire family here ahead of him. She couldn't help feeling an odd mixture of disappointment and a bit of relief. Maybe she wasn't quite ready for them to become lovers? Maybe they were rushing things? Or maybe she was just getting cold feet? She had been so certain when she boarded the plane in Detroit. Now that she was here, she was having second thoughts. Well, whatever happened she couldn't very well stay in the same suite with him and his family. She need her privacy.

"How was the weather when you left home?"

"Chilly," Taylor smiled, sipping her tea. "How are your parents? Are they here as well?"

Carl laughed. "No, the folks are in Florida. How is your family?"

"Well, thank you."

"And the flight down?"

"Great. How long have you been enjoying the sunshine?"

"We flew in on Monday. Decided to take the week off.

Oh, this is going to be interesting." Margie said to no one in particular.

Everyone seemed to agree. Their laughter was contagious, for everyone joined in. Everyone but Taylor. She was thoroughly embarrassed.

"Now look what we've done. We didn't meant to upset you, Taylor. We're being tactless," Megan said, scolding the others.

Taylor blushed, thoroughly embarrassed.

# *Eleven*

Donald was impatient to get back to Taylor. Ron had said something about the family get-together, but he had been so self-absorbed that he hadn't asked for clarification.

Donald was stopped several times before he cleared the lobby. Normally, when he was stopped and asked for an autograph by a fan he didn't mind. In fact, he took pride in his work on the court and was pleased by the interest in the sport it garnered. Today was different. All he could think about was Taylor.

Nevertheless, he effectively hid his annoyance at the continued delay and took the time needed to sign his name and answer the questions put to him. As he walked away, he vowed not to let business intrude on their time together. They were here to relax and enjoy themselves.

Perhaps, he should seriously consider building that house on the island. He had considered it before, but was generally so comfortable in the family quarters that he didn't see the need. Yet, if he built that house, he would have the total privacy he craved. He knew that even if he quit the game tomorrow, he would still be recognized and stopped.

He had so many ideas on expanding his businesses. Then there was practice and the games. What he did not have was time for himself. Right now, he needed time to be alone with Taylor. He was fed up with all the things keeping them apart . . . distance, her brother, his work. Just forget Ron, forget the resort, forget it all but her. He yearned to concentrate only on her. Now was not the time to be concerned about the weeks ahead involving completing the regular season or the upcoming play-offs and finals.

While his long legs eliminated the distance from the lobby to the family suite, he let his mind wander. Finally, they could be alone and enjoy being with each other. Tonight they could relax in the moonlight. Tomorrow he could take her swimming and dancing and out to dinner. They would walk in the moonlight. They had two wildly romantic nights alone together. He smiled to himself, accepting that he had planned to enjoy every second of their time. It had taken some major engineering but finally he had Taylor all to himself.

When Donald let himself into the suite, the first face he saw was his brother's. "What the hell!" He had barely gotten the words out before his nieces screamed, "Uncle Don," and threw their small bodies at him. He caught them without thinking, automatically giving and receiving kisses and hugs.

"Hey, Donut and Cupcake."

"You know my name is not Donut! I'm Sissy!"

"No," he said, seriously looking into dancing dark eyes. "Your name is Donut. All pretty sweet chocolate and I'm going to eat you." He started blowing on her chubby little neck. "Mmm, taste like chocolate, must be chocolate."

"Mommy! Tell Uncle Don my name!"

"And what about you?" Donald asked the other little girl.

"My name is not Cupcake!"

"It isn't?"

"No." She shook her ponytail little head. "My name is Kimmy!"

"But you look like a strawberry cupcake. Give me your arm so I can bite it." As Donald carried out his ritual teasing with his little nieces, his eyes focused on Taylor. She was comfortably seated on the sofa between his sister and sister-in-law. Damn! The whole gang was here!

"What are you guys doing here?" he asked, finally putting his nieces back on their feet.

"We're on vacation, bro. How about you?" Carl said with a wicked grin. He didn't dare glance over to Jess or they both would break out laughing at Donald's flashing eyes He evidently was not pleased to see them.

The only thing that kept Donald from venting his frustration was Taylor. Not that he wasn't thrilled to be with his family—just not this weekend.

"Do you guys communicate?" his sister-in-law put in playfully.

"Evidently not!" Donald snapped. His family often used the resort. The guys generally took advantage of the eighteen hole golf course, while the gals enjoyed the boutique shopping in town and the swimming pool and tennis courts that were also available. They had all the amenities they wished. The hotel had no less than two four-star restaurants, plus a nightclub with a live jazz band.

For the life of him, Donald couldn't remember if they had told him they were coming or if he had been so caught up in his thoughts of Taylor that he had not been paying close attention. Either way, they had a problem.

His bedroom was the only vacant bedroom in the suite. He wasn't egotistical enough to think that Taylor would consider sharing it with him. Damn! He didn't want her in another part of the hotel. He wanted to wake up with her in his bed and if that was not possible, then wake with her being no more than on the other side of the wall.

"If you two don't have plans for tonight, you are more

than welcome to join us for dinner. We're grilling steaks on the patio." Megan's eyes were frankly curious as she looked from one to the other.

"Thanks, short stuff, but we have plans."

Taylor glanced up at him in surprise. That was the first she had heard of it, but kept quiet. She was suddenly very tense, worried about the impression she was making on his family. She saw his frown. Had he noticed that she hadn't really looked at him since he walked into the suite?

"If you'll excuse me, it seems as if we need another room." Donald didn't even look at her then, he couldn't. He already wanted her so badly that he was on edge. He didn't need to make a complete fool of himself in front of his family by begging her to let him sleep with her. They had come all this way for some much needed privacy. He intended to see to it that they got it.

Taylor was blushing, knowing that his family was curious as to how Donald was going to solve this one. The only ones not obviously interested in Donald's telephone call were his two nieces. Taylor suspected that although a man like Donald was never without a woman, it was not his practice to bring his women around his family. Should she feel honored that he had already introduced her to them?

"All set. You'll be right next door, if that is all right with you?"

"Fine." Taylor smiled her appreciation at him.

For a moment, Donald couldn't look past Taylor's soft brown features. She had no idea how beautiful he found her or how much he wanted her. He had tried to put it into words on the plane, but knew he had failed. He would do whatever he had to do to have her. It wasn't her fault that his family had popped up out of the blue. He almost expected his parents here as well.

"Is this your first trip to South Carolina, Taylor?" Megan asked, interrupting the couple's gaze into each other's eyes.

"Yes, although I'm familiar with the Penn Center and the Gullah people who live on the island. I've been fascinated by their close ties to the motherland."

"Although none of us speak the dialect, we've come here all our lives. Our father's side of the family is from the Sea Islands."

"Donald mentioned that. I'm surprised that your parents didn't retire here," Taylor said.

Megan laughed. "That would have been Daddy's choice, but my mother's from Florida. They divide their time between the two places."

"We love it here," Jess added. "Our family's little business venture has turned into a gold mine. Carl here is an architect and I'm a contractor. The three of us put our heads together and have been in business together for six years now."

"Although we saw the resort as strictly business, our wives had other ideas," Carl laughed.

Donald could not believe it. His normally close-mouthed brother-in-law and brother had both apparently been won over by Taylor's sweet smiles.

"That's right," Margie said. "We all enjoy it here and come as often as we can."

As Taylor asked a few more questions, Donald put a niece on each knee, bouncing them as they told him about their progress in the pool. Both girls complained they never saw enough of Uncle Don.

The knock on the door was the bellman with the key to the room next door.

"Ready?" he asked. He had dismissed the bellman and collected her luggage himself.

"Yes," Taylor said coming to her feet. She smiled, saying, "It's been good seeing you again."

"We'll get to visit again before you leave on Sunday. Won't we, brother, dear?" Megan said pointedly.

"Yeah," he answered impatiently. Holding the door open, his chin was angled stubbornly. He ushered Taylor to her room.

Impressed by the sheer opulence of the suite next door, Taylor slowly looked around. This one was smaller than the Williams's family suite but just as beautiful decorated in shades of pink.

Donald pushed the door closed with his foot and placed her things beside the luggage rack in the bedroom. "What do you think?"

"It's beautiful," she whispered. A satin-covered king-sized bed seemed to be the focal point of the bedroom. Her feet sank into lush burgundy carpet as she retraced her steps back into the sitting room where a pale pink armchair and sofa were positioned in front of a floor to ceiling glass doorwall that overlooked a private patio area while oak dining table and chairs were placed near the side wall.

Donald's dark hungry gaze followed her as she explored the room. What he wanted her to explore was him, every pulsating inch. He was so damn needy he was not sure how much longer he could wait to have her. When her brown eyes finally swung to him, he was leaning against the door frame. He didn't trust himself. His control was dwindling.

Taylor understood the naked hunger in his eyes, for she also felt it. Her pulse was hammering in her chest as she came to him. She surprised them both when she slipped her arms under his sport coat and around his lean waist. Lifting up on tiptoes, she raised her face to his.

"I'm sorry about the family. I don't know how I messed up like this, but I did," he said. Although his eyes seemed locked on her pretty mouth, he made no effort to kiss her. The feel of her lush breasts against his chest alone was driving him wild. "Can you be ready at nine for dinner and perhaps a show or dancing?"

"Yes . . ."

"Good." He gave her a quick hug before he moved away. "See you later."

Donald closed the door quietly behind him, leaving Taylor thoroughly confused. What had she done wrong? She stood staring after him, her heart pounding with disappointment.

Had he changed his mind? Had he suddenly decided she wasn't as desirable as he had first thought? Or did this have something to do with his family being here? He had been as surprised as she was to find them in residence. Perhaps he was embarrassed by her.

She certainly was not wearing a designer suit like his sister or a silk dress like his sister-in-law. She had not had her hair professionally styled in years.

What was she doing at this expensive resort with a celebrity like Donald? she scolded herself. Why couldn't she see that she was in way over her head? If she wasn't extremely careful, she would end up falling in love with him. Hadn't her involvement with Alex taught her anything?

She had come knowing exactly what she wanted. She was ready to make love with him, even though she knew that was all he was interested in. No, she was not going to back down. After they made love, she would be the one walking away with her head held high. She wanted to be with him. But only for two nights.

They would both get what they craved . . . enjoyment of each other's body without the emotional complications of a love affair. When it was over she would have put the past behind her. That whole experience with Alex would be replaced by memories with Donald. It would be enough.

Taylor was grateful that she had packed her black dress. He had seen it before because she had worn it to the NAACP dinner. She told herself it didn't matter. What was important was that she looked and felt good when she wore it.

She took her time, enjoying the sunken tub in the huge bathroom. She indulged herself, letting the hot water soothe her tight muscles. She used her favorite scented body lotion, smoothing it into her skin until she was as soft as silk. She left her hair softly curled on her shoulders, held in place by a gold comb. She wore the small gold hoop earrings and her favorite gold heart charm ankle bracelet.

Taylor was ready and her heart was racing when Donald knocked on the door.

"You look good, girl. I'm glad you decided to wear that dress tonight. I like it." Donald was dressed in a navy suit and pristine white shirt opened at the throat. He left off the tie and socks but wore Italian loafers on his long feet. He was not just attractive. He was very sexy.

"Thank you. You also look nice," she said, taking his arm.

The restaurant was as tastefully decorated as the rest of the hotel. Although the dining room was crowded and their entrance was noted, he escorted her first to the kitchen to meet the head chef, his aunt Charlotte Williams and her assistants, his cousins Deanna and Darlene. Taylor was impressed by the spotlessly clean kitchen, with delicious smelling pots on the stove.

She would have liked to stay and learn more about the authentic low country cuisine served in the restaurant, but Donald hurried her away to a somewhat secluded corner surrounded on two sides by floor to ceiling windows overlooking the garden and sea beyond.

Donald was pleased that they were not disturbed by

# WE HAVE 4 FREE BOOKS FOR YOU!

**ARABESQUE**

(If the certificate is missing below, write to: Zebra Home Subscription Service, Inc., 120 Brighton Road, P.O. Box 5214, Clifton, New Jersey 07015-5214)

## FREE BOOK CERTIFICATE

**Yes!** Please send me 4 *Arabesque* Contemporary Romances without cost or obligation, billing me just $1 to help cover postage and handling. I understand that each month, I will be able to preview 4 brand-new *Arabesque* Contemporary Romances FREE for 10 days. Then, if I decide to keep them, I will pay the money-saving preferred subscriber's price of just $16.00 for all 4...that's a savings of almost $4 off the publisher's price with no additional charge for shipping and handling. I may return any shipment within 10 days and owe nothing, and I may cancel this subscription at any time. My 4 FREE books will be mine to keep in any case.

Name _____

Address _____ Apt. _____

City _____ State_____ Zip _____

Telephone ( ) _____

Signature _____ AR1097
(If under 18, parent or guardian must sign.)

autograph seekers. He wanted her to try a little of everything and ordered portions of nearly the entire menu.
They started with a watermelon soup, black-eyed pea
salad, saltfish fritter, shrimp and sausage gumbo, jam-
balaya, Gullah vegetable paella and Hoppin' John. Taylor was holding her stomach when she finished her
meal.

"Ready for dessert?" he asked with a grin.

She was busy shaking her head. "No, thank you. I
can't do it. Although I am tempted to have one small
taste of huckleberry honey cobbler."

When he lifted his arm to signal their waiter, she
grabbed it and held on. "Don't you dare. I was only
kidding."

"You sure?"

"Positive. Thank you. Everything was fabulous."

Donald ordered coffee even though he didn't really
want it. He was concentrating on keeping himself in
check. He had very nearly lost control in her room earlier when he held her close. He wanted so much more.
The time was not right.

"Are you on a special diet during the basketball season?"

"Sure, anything that lies down on my plate, I eat it,"
he quipped, enjoying the way her eyes sparkled.

Taylor was giggling so hard she had to inhale quickly
in order to catch her breath. "Stop! You are terrible!"

Donald leaned back in his chair, a wide grin on his
handsome face.

"Answer the question."

"I eat pretty much what I want. I try to stay away from
processed foods and white sugar. I eat a lot of fresh fruits
and vegetables. I love chocolate brownies with lots and
lots of pecans." He shrugged, "When I indulge, I add
a couple of miles to the morning run and put in more
time at the gym."

"Have you ever been seriously injured?"

"I've had my share of injuries."

She nodded, thinking of her brother and his high hopes for the future.

"Don't," he said. His hand covered hers. "We're suppose to leave the worries at home, remember?" He did not want her worrying about her brother and he certainly didn't want her blaming him for Scott's decision. "No serious topics. Okay?"

Taylor nodded, conscious of the way he caressed her hand "The play-offs are going to start soon, aren't they? Are the Bulls going to win the championship again?"

"Absolutely! Who told you?" he teased, then went on to tell her about the upcoming games.

"What has been your most exciting game?"

"That's a hard one," he said thoughtfully. "I guess it was playing on the Dream Team for the Olympics. I'm used to playing against the top players in the NBA. This was different—spending time with and playing with guys like Grant Hill, David Robinson, Charles Barkley. It was so exciting when they gave us the Gold Medal. Standing there watching our flag being raised was like nothing I've ever experienced. I've never been prouder to be an American."

"I saw it on television. But I can only imagine how exciting it was being there." Taylor was touched, pleased that he shared it with her. "Thank you for sharing."

"Thanks for listening. Hey, ready for dancing? Work off some of this food?"

"Would you be disappointed if I say no? I prefer a quiet walk on the beach . . . away from everything but you and the moonlight."

"As long as I can hold your hand, I assure you I'll get over it." He was smiling, but he was serious. The number one appeal of dancing was having her in his arms close to his body.

The stars were high in the sky, bright and luminous, Taylor decided with a smile, inhaling the smell of the sea. She'd kicked off her shoes enjoying the coolness of the sand beneath her stockinged feet.

"You're so quiet," she said looking over at him. Her hand was firmly laced through his. "Is this all commonplace for you?"

He shrugged. "Not quite."

"A penny for your thoughts."

"It will cost you more than that."

"How much? A dime?"

"A kiss. . . ."

"No, I don't think so. I offered you one earlier. You didn't seem interested then. You're out of luck, my friend."

"I was interested," he corrected, pleased by her candor. "Did you think I was rejecting you?"

She shrugged and would have let his hand go, but he held on tight.

He was not about to let her go. His voice was rough with desire. "You ask too much."

She shook her head. "No, you're confusing me with one of your other women."

He roared with laughter.

"Did I say something funny?"

"Why would I even want another woman? Girl, you keep me so hard I can't think straight." He grabbed her around the waist. "What's wrong? Can't take the truth?"

She was staring up at him, half furious, half crazy with desire for his hot deep kisses. "I . . ."

Whatever she would have said was left unsaid as Donald crushed her mouth beneath his. He didn't ask for entrance into the honeyed interior of her mouth. He took what he wanted . . . what he needed, deep tongue-stroking kisses that left her limp in his arms.

He was forced to pull back, away from the sweet softness of her breasts and the seductive allure of her hips, in hopes of gaining control of himself. He literally ached to have her. There was nothing he wanted more than to make love to her.

The intrusive sound of voices nearby broke into the dark magic of the night. Donald swore softly, catching her hand and dragging her with him.

"Slow down. My legs aren't as long as yours."

Donald slowed but he didn't speak until they were inside her room. Before she could even reach for the light, he backed her up against the closed door. His long, aroused body pressed into hers. There was no way she could fail to notice his erection.

"What is there about you that makes me so hungry for you? It happens every time I touch you. I had hoped . . ." he stopped.

"Donald . . ."

His lips were warm and tender over hers then he nibbled down the length of her neck, his tongue sponging the sensitive hollow at the base. She was a trembling mass of raw nerves.

"Oh, baby . . ." he whispered into her ear, sponging it before tenderly scraping it with his teeth then sponging the lobe yet again as if to soothe the small hurt.

Donald felt her trembling in his arms, knew she was not unaffected by his touch. There was no way he could hide his own feelings. They had gotten off to such a shaky start. He didn't want to disturb the precious trust they had managed on this trip. First there had been his family and now she seemed upset with him.

"How can you doubt how much I want you?" His voice was thick with his arousal. He lifted her chin until he had full access to her mouth. He held none of his feelings back. "I want you . . . only you." His hands lifted to cup and caress the softness of her breasts. He kissed her over and over again while he rubbed his fingertips against her aroused nipples. "Let me stay with you to-night, sweetness. Let me make love to you."

# Twelve

Taylor had been so sure of her decision, sure she was doing the right thing. So why was she suddenly shaking like a leaf in a windstorm? She stared at her image in the bathroom mirror after she had showered and perfumed her skin with body lotion. She braced herself against the sink.

This was ridiculous. It wasn't her first time with a man. She was no virgin. She had been around this block once before, so why was she practically frozen stiff with fear?

As she examined herself, she wondered how she could possibly please a man like Donald. Her breasts were too large, her waist too blatantly narrow for such full generous hips, even her size nine-medium feet displeased her. She was being silly and she knew it. She was more than hips and breasts and thighs. She didn't have a clue when it came to pleasing a man because she was a woman with very limited experience.

Donald had been straightforward about his desire for her. Her generous figure was not a problem for him. The problem rested inside of Taylor. It was the result of another man's callousness.

Alex Adams had taught her a painful lesson and taught it well. After tonight she would never have to worry about Donald's attraction to her. It would finally be over and done with. She reminded herself that that was the way she wanted it. She had gone into this with her eyes wide open. She would be the one doing the stepping, this time. She wouldn't look back and have to feel as if she were less desirable than other women. One night with him would be enough. And she wouldn't go to her grave having loved and lost only one man . . . a real snake like Alex Adams. With Donald it was bound to be better.

Taking a deep, fortifying breath, Taylor slipped a dusty rose nightgown over her head. Her full breasts were veiled by scalloped lace. The gown was slit high on both sides, exposing the smooth length of her long legs. She turned and the tiny gold heart charms shimmered on a fine chain around her ankle. Her hair was combed back and pinned into a knot at her crown. Soft curls framed her face. Her only makeup was a touch of deep rose tint on her lips.

"Tonight is forever, tomorrow doesn't matter," Taylor told herself as she slowly opened the bathroom door.

Donald turned at the sound of the bedroom door opening. His breath lodged in his throat because he couldn't breathe, couldn't make a sound as she moved to within scant inches of where he stood at the patio doors. He'd been looking out into the night, trying to harness his impatience.

"It's beautiful," she whispered, as her eyes moved slowly around the candlelit room. They were on every flat surface, on the end tables, the coffee table, the dining table. Their low light flickered softly in small glass globes. "Oh!" she exclaimed, going over to the large oak desk in the corner of the room, where a large crystal vase was filled with more than a dozen long-stemmed pink roses. Her hands were trembling when she lifted the card. She didn't need to read the name to know they were from him. Their scent perfumed the air.

She looked at him in wonder. "Thank you, Donald. They're lovely. In fact, everything is so perfect." Everything except her. She was a quivering mass of nerves. She smiled in hopes of hiding her uneasiness.

"No. You're what's beautiful," he said hoarsely, unable to get past the lump in his throat. He made no move to touch her. Instead he handed her a glass of perfectly chilled champagne. "To us," he said, touching his glass to hers.

She echoed him, taking a small sip.

Her eyes dropped briefly to his heavily muscled torso. He still wore his evening clothes. Only his jacket had been removed and was tossed over the back of an armchair. His dress shirt was unbuttoned to the middle of his chest and the sleeves rolled to his elbows.

He put his glass and hers down, asking "What's wrong, sweetness? Have you changed your mind?" It hurt him even to say the words but he had no alternative. Her reluctance was evident. She had looked everywhere but at him.

Taylor shook her head. "I'm fine."

"No, you're not. Taylor, if this is not what you want . . . just tell me now." His hands were balled at his sides, but he was still very much in control of himself.

"Donald . . ."

"I can stop now, sweetness. But later, after I've seen you, tasted you . . ." Donald sighed, his body taut with tension.

"I'm ready. I only ask that you use something."

"A condom?"

She nodded, dropping her gaze, then realized that she was focusing on the blatant fullness between his muscled thighs. She blushed, averting her gaze.

"Come here," he commanded, his voice gruff with sexual need. He did not move, he couldn't. His heart was racing with excitement as he waited for what seemed like an eternity.

"You didn't answer. Will you . . ."

"Yes." He grabbed her when she was a hair's breadth away, pulling her into his empty arms. Her lush softness enflamed his already flaming senses. He dropped his head, pressing his mouth against her cheek, her sweet smelling throat.

He groaned, gathering her as close to his aroused body as he could. "Taylor, you're so sweet. Take the gown off. I want to look at you." He made no effort to help her. He couldn't. He was hanging on to his self-control by a single thread.

She wasn't sure she could do it. She was no seductress. There was nothing provocative about her.

"I'm . . ." She hesitated. She'd almost told him she was afraid, afraid of him and the way he made her feel. She didn't want to care too deeply, didn't want to love him, nor did she want his love, because she didn't want the hurt and heartache that came along with it. They had one night in time. After this night, it would be over. She would go back to her life in Detroit and he would go back to his in Chicago. They didn't have a future, but there would be no regrets.

Donald dropped his head to her shoulder, smoothing his tongue along the sleek lines. He nudged the straps away. Taylor gasped, managing just in time to catch the slippery material before it dropped to the floor. She held it clasped against her breasts.

Donald lifted her chin so he could study her face, her eyes. He was floored by the beauty and uncertainty he saw. He closed his eyes against the stark fear he found in their brown depths. She was terrified.

It took all his strength to drop his hands and move away from her. His arousal was unrelenting, so painful that he clenched his teeth, forcing back every male instinct to claim her as his own that he possessed.

"Do me a favor? Put this on." He tossed her his suit coat before he walked through the bedroom into the bathroom and slammed the door so forcefully behind him that the glass in the mirrored dresser vibrated.

Taylor dropped down on the large sofa, tears of shame ran unchecked down her cheeks as she listened to the sound of the shower being switched on. She wasn't sure what she had done wrong, but she knew she had messed up royally. He obviously was disappointed. He was used to sophisticated women. Women who knew how to arouse and satisfy a man. She was twenty-eight years old. How could she possibly be so old and so stupid?

Determined not to have him find her crying like a baby, she quickly dried her face and pulled her gown into place, putting on his coat as requested. What could she say? How was she going to explain her reluctance to him?

When Donald reentered the room, a towel was slung around his neck, and his upper torso was still damp from his shower. He wore only his dress slacks, and carried his shirt.

Embarrassed, Taylor averted her head, wishing she had somewhere to go, to hide. It had been bad enough before, now it was much, much worse. She certainly wasn't like those women who flung themselves at him, so desperate for a man. She still had her pride.

He went over and picked up the glass he'd been holding earlier and carried it, along with the bottle, to where she sat on the sofa. He sat down beside her.

"Here—take a sip of this. It will make you feel better."

"Nothing will make me feel better." She was furious with herself. "Perhaps it would be better if you left."

"Taylor, we need to talk this out."

"There is nothing to talk about."

"I disagree."

"Look, my coming here was a mistake. I should not have agreed." She had been using him to forget Alex. It was wrong. "I'm not ready."

"Sweetheart, all we need is a little time. Time for us to get to know each other better. There's still so much we don't know about each other."

"It's been wrong from the beginning. I was attracted to you and forgot everything else . . . my brother . . . how we met . . . I told myself none of that matters. But it's not true."

"We agreed to leave all that behind in Detroit."

"I can't," she whispered.

"Your brother isn't in this room with us. There is only the two of us." He swore bitterly, "Something happened to make you freeze up on me. I want to know what it was."

Taylor covered her face with her hands. "I can't talk about it."

"You don't trust me."

Taylor stared at him, lost for words.

"Tell me."

"I can't. It's too painful to talk about."

"Baby, you're trembling with fear." He came over to her and took her into his arms. He stroked her back until her trembling eased.

"Better?"

"Yes." She looked at him, knowing that if she lost her nerve nothing would change for her. She wanted that change. "I'm ready," she finally managed to say.

"Like hell," he grumbled, low in his throat before he moved away. He began pacing in brooding silence.

Taylor nervously crossed her legs, swinging her foot back and forth. "Why don't you believe me?"

Her comment brought his eyes to the lovely length of her brown legs. The gold diamond-cut hearts encircling her slim ankle shimmered in the candlelight. His burning gaze caressed the tender flesh of the inside of her ankle and her awareness of him rushed forward like a dam breaking: a tidal wave of emotion rushed over them both.

Donald was the first to turn away, moving over to the patio door. The cooling air of the ceiling fan overhead was not doing much to cool his overheated body. He reminded himself that he was a thinking individual. He would not let his body overshadow his common sense. He reassured himself that he would have her, just not tonight.

"What's this about, Taylor?"

"I don't know what you mean?"

"It's not about me. It's not about you. It's certainly not about your brother. Who then?"

Taylor stared, horrified by how close he was to the truth.

"Are you a virgin?"

Her mouth dropped open at his frankness. She shook her head; in spite of her best efforts, her eyes filled. She blinked as quickly as she could not to let them drop.

Suddenly, Donald was there and she was back in his arms, her head on his wide shoulder. He had lifted her as if she weighed no more than a child. He held her as the floodgates gave way and she cried. He rocked her, crooning until she eventually quieted. He handed her a linen napkin from the tray on the sofa table.

"Dry your face," he said softly. He waited until she was calm before he said, "Tell me about it."

"I was Scott's age when I fell in love for the first time. It was with one of my college instructors." It hurt to even talk about it, but she forced herself to go on. "I had no business getting involved with him. But he was so attractive, so handsome. All his female students were half in love with him. I thought I was so special because he asked me out." Taylor swallowed with difficulty, wanting to hide her face in shame. When she moved to get up, he tightened his hold.

"Let me hold you," he said, needing her closeness.

Taylor sighed. "I was so stupid!"

"You were young. Every one of us has done something we regret at one time or another. It's called growing up."

Taylor found herself laughing as she looked into his eyes. "You're a very nice man."

"Nice guys finish last."

"Not you," she said, caressing his cheek.

"What's his name?"

"Alex Adams. He taught World History."

"Is he still at U. of D.?"

She shook her head. "I was at Wayne State."

"No wonder I didn't know you." He chuckled. "I'm not that much older than you are."

"Are you saying that if we were at the same university that we would have dated?"

"I hope not. At that age, I lived and breathed nothing but basketball. I didn't take females seriously. I was a big kid," he admitted frankly. "Tell me about Adams."

"You actually think I'm going to tell you what a fool I made of myself? I don't think so."

"It's not idle curiosity, Taylor. What happened is between us just as much as the man who created this problem is keeping us apart."

Taylor knew he was right. Nevertheless it was not easy for her to say, "He was interested in one thing. Getting me into bed. When he succeeded it was over. He had done what he set out to do. End of story."

But it wasn't over for her. It had colored all her relationships with men for years. "And since him?" he persisted.

She dropped her head. "I haven't wanted to be with anyone else after that. I'm twenty-eight, but my experience with men is limited. I'm sorry."

"You have nothing to apologize for." He wanted to

punch someone, preferably Adams. He said, "I'm sorry he hurt you that way."

"I'm over it."

"No. He made it nearly impossible for you to give your trust to another man." He kissed her gently. "Thanks for telling me."

Taylor nodded, then yawned. Quickly covering her face with her hands, she said, "Sorry, it's not the company." She snuggled even closer to him. She was just so comfortable and it had been a long day.

He smiled. "I'm not offended. It's late. Let's go to bed." He felt her relaxed body instantly stiffen. "I'm not suggesting that we do anything more than sleep."

Taylor stared into his eyes, slowly recognizing that if he had wanted to take advantage of the situation, he could have done so when she invited his attention. He had been nothing but thoughtful.

"Okay." She tried to smile but failed. She had butterflies in her stomach when she slid off his lap and reached back to take his hand.

"That's it?" he asked, easily coming to his full height.

"Mmm," she murmured intent on pulling him along.

"I'll get the lights," he said. He blew all the candles out, but he waited until she had crossed the room and had begun folding back the spread and blankets before he switched off the lights. He'd kept his focus on what he was doing and not on the movement of her soft voluptuous body. "Would you like the patio doors open to let in some fresh air?"

She shrugged. "Doesn't matter. You decide."

Donald left them open. He couldn't have what he preferred. And it didn't have a thing to do with fresh air. When he crossed to the bed, Taylor was there the covers nearly up to her chin.

He turned out the bedside lamp before he unzipped his slacks and pulled them down his long legs. He did not remove his black silk bikini briefs. He was grateful for the darkness. He was not trying to hide his body from her, but trying to hide hers from him. It would be enough to feel her softness against him, for he refused to be denied that small pleasure.

"Comfortable?" she whispered from her side of the bed.

"Not quite. But I'll live," he grumbled.

"What's wrong?"

"Besides the bed being too short?" He knew perfectly well that his oversized bed in the family's suite next door had been designed for his body. None of that mattered because Taylor was here and that was where he wanted to be. "You're too far away."

He let out a long sigh when she moved until her head was cushioned on his shoulder and her soft breasts pillowed on his chest. One of her thighs rested against his.

"Mmm, that's much better. Are you okay?"

Her racing heart gradually slowed as she closed her eyes concentrating on the warmth of his large male body. She relaxed even more as his stroking hand smoothed over her back.

"Sweetness?"

"Yes," she murmured, sleepily. Taylor wiggled until she was just where she wanted to be, her body cushioned perfectly by his. Gradually, as the breeze fluttered gently over them, she slept.

Donald wasn't quite so lucky. His relentless need rode him hard. Yet, he was so relieved that she was exactly where he wanted her, he was not about to complain. Suddenly, he recognized that he wanted her like this each and every night. Slowly, he let that realization sink inside his being. He closed his eyes savoring the comforting warmth of her being in his arms.

But the aching need did not ease, it kept him wide wake. After a time he gave up trying. He quietly eased out of the bed, careful not to wake her. As much as he hated it he knew if he didn't eliminate the pulsating desire, he would be up all night. Turning on the shower full blast he let the cold spray soak his hair, his long frame. He groaned, not from the discomfort, but the persistence. He stayed where he was until when he finally left the shower his teeth were chattering—but his hunger had eased so that he could sleep with her in his arms.

# Thirteen

When Taylor woke the next morning, the bedroom was bright with sunshine. She stretched, well-rested, then looked expectantly to the pillow beside hers. It was empty, but there was a note on it. She picked it up, but hugged the pillow to herself, inhaling deeply before she flushed as she realized that she was searching for his smell. She had no idea how long he'd been gone, but she missed him.

Had she ever spent a more exciting night? She blushed, realizing how much she enjoyed sleeping in his arms. She adored everything about him from his smell, to the feel of his supple dark-brown skin, to his muscular strength. He was so beautifully male. She laughed. She had no idea she would enjoy sleeping with him so much.

Curious, she read that he hadn't wanted to wake her, but he asked her to join him and his family for breakfast when she was ready. Taylor smoothed the note out, then hurried out of bed.

She dressed in navy slacks and a peach short sleeved shell. After curling her hair, she added a touch of bronze lipstick to her mouth and a touch of mascara, before she left the suite. She didn't allow herself to question why she was so eager to see Donald.

Her knock was answered by one of his nieces. "Hi,

come on in. Everyone is in the kitchen." Sissy showed her the way.

Taylor was surprised to find Donald manning the breakfast grill with spatula in hand. "Morning," she smiled, somewhat nervously.

He grinned when she entered the kitchen. "Hey, sleepyhead. Hungry?" His dark eyes moved slowly over her. He forced his eyes away from her lush breasts and pretty mouth.

Everyone was seated around the breakfast table and exchanged greetings, making room for her.

"Something smells good. You look like you know what you're doing."

The others looked at her as if she dropped a bomb. Taylor blushed.

Donald chuckled, coming over to place a full plate in front of her. It was filled with pancakes, sausages and scrambled eggs. He didn't leave until he had also placed a soft kiss on her lips.

"Donald's the cook in the family," Megan volunteered, holding up her plate for another helping of pancakes.

"Yeah. Uncle Don makes the best ribs," Kimmy said around a mouth full of food.

"Kimmy. You know better than to talk with food in your mouth," her mother reminded.

"I like his potato salad," Sissy added, refusing to be left out of the conversation.

Taylor's eyes went wide. "Aren't you something." Her twinkling eyes locked with his.

Carl was watching his brother. He shook his head. Donald had it bad.

The brothers didn't have a chance to talk until the afternoon. The ladies had gone into town to shop and the guys indulged themselves in a few rounds of golf.

"Are you sure about this, bro?"

Donald looked sharply at Carl, recognizing the note of concern. He didn't have to explain; Donald knew what he was getting at.

"Yeah. I'm sure. Why?"

"You haven't known her long. Why don't you give it some time? There's no rush, is there? Hell, man, she didn't even know you cook."

Donald shrugged. "She knows now."

"Seems to me that you're already in over your head. Give it time. Time to decide her motives. Don't let the sex blind you."

"It's more than sex," he said bluntly. They could be good together. No, better than good, if she gave them a chance. "I care about her."

Carl didn't want to see his baby brother hurt. He knew how the fame, the wealth, left Donald vulnerable to all kinds of scavengers, especially the sleek, beautiful variety. "How do you know you can trust her?"

Donald knew his brother spoke out of concern, but also knew he was wrong. Taylor didn't expect anything from him. She was reluctant to get deeply involved with him.

"Carl, I know what I'm doing. Taylor isn't asking for anything. I've been pursuing her, not the other way around. She's not even sure she can trust me. I want her more than she wants me."

Carl wasn't sure about the truth of that statement, but he was wise enough not to point it out.

"Hey, what's the hold up?" Jess asked eyeing them from the green.

Later that day, as Carl watched Donald approach Taylor, he knew that his brother had no idea the kind of heartache that could very well come his way if things with her did not go his way. He was vulnerable and didn't even realize it. Women considered him fair game. They more often than not saw the income not the man. Carl could only hope that Taylor was different.

"Enjoying yourself?" Donald said into her ear as he joined her in the shallow end of the pool where she was playing volleyball with his nieces and sister and sister-in-law.

"Oh, yes. The weather is simply wonderful and so is your family." She especially liked Megan. She was so easy to talk to.

Her smile had him thoroughly enchanted, hating every second of the day that they had been apart. This weekend was not working out as he had planned. He had hoped to have her all to himself.

"What you need is a little height on your team," he boasted, knowing what he needed was a taste of her sweet mouth. His keen gaze devoured her generous curves in a black one-piece suit, cut high at the thigh.

"Oh no! That is not fair!" Megan complained, yelling for her husband to come and join them. He had been comfortably relaxing beside the pool.

"That will never do. Carl!" Margie called.

Soon it became apparent that the grownups were having more fun than the kids. Shouts and laughter and giggles filled the air. Taylor was exhausted by the time they called a halt and went to change for dinner. It turned out to be a real family affair, with aunts, uncles and cousins included as they grilled salmon steaks beside the pool.

"Get enough to eat?" he asked quietly, close to her ear.

Taylor laughed. "I'd say."

Although Donald had not been far away all evening, she couldn't help wishing that she didn't have to share him with the others.

He laced his hand with hers. "Come on. Let's go walk off some of this food."

"Where are you two off to?" his sister asked. Her husband and older brother both looked at her in disbelief. "What?" she demanded.

Jess eyed his wife's soft mouth. He gave her a hard kiss, asking, "Has it been that long, baby?"

Megan could not help the blush that rose in her pretty brown cheeks.

"Later . . ." Donald called after them. He pulled her along with him.

"Hey. What is the rush?"

"Sorry, sweetheart. I love my family, but I'm about ready to toss all of them in the pool."

"Why is that?" she giggled.

"You know why," he said impatiently. His idea of a walk was around the outside of the hotel, through the lobby, and straight toward the door of her suite.

"Donald!"

His eyes were on her mouth. "Open the door, Taylor."

She was laughing so much she could hardly turn the key in the lock. Donald took over. His patience was non-existent.

"What are you doing?" He was right behind her. "Stop!" she shrieked as he was stalking her. "Donald!" She raced across the room. "Will you stop!" She was laughing so hard, her side was beginning to hurt.

Donald had no intention of stopping until he had her where he wanted her. He grabbed her by the waist and lifted her off her feet. They came down on the over-stuffed sofa together with Taylor on top of him. She was giggling so much that he still couldn't kiss her. But it didn't matter, nothing mattered but finally having her in his arms.

"You are terrible. Some walk!"

Chuckling, he said, "I'd had it with sharing you. I'm all for you getting to know the family, later. This was supposed to be our time. We've barely had two minutes alone all day. One tiny good morning kiss was all I got."

Taylor crooned in her throat. "You poor neglected baby." She placed a soft kiss on his throat. "I'm so sorry."

"And well you should be," he scoffed, angling himself so that he could cuddle her cheek. His eyes lingered on her tantalizing lips. He licked her mouth, before pulling her fleshy bottom lip into his mouth to suckle. "I need you," he admitted in a gruff whisper.

She sighed, loving the feel of him and wanting nothing more than to be right where she was, against his wide chest. She, too, had been unable to think of little else but Donald and the wonderful night they had shared. She was as eager to be alone with him as he was to be with her.

"Mmm, you are so sweet, so sweet . . ." he whispered. She was so warm and incredibly soft. She fit perfectly in his arms. "Adams didn't have the brains God gave a toad. He had no idea what a treasure he lost."

Having always considered it the other way around, Taylor decided she liked his interpretation better. "Donald . . ." she whispered his name with longing, shivering in response to the heat of his forging tongue.

Taylor was all woman and she belonged to him. He had no intention of letting her go. When she opened her mouth, giving him full access, he groaned deep in his throat. He gathered her as close as he could. Her lush breasts were cushioned on the wide expanse of his chest. There was too damn much material separating them. He wanted her bare, open to his hands . . . to his mouth, to his throbbing shaft.

Taylor was dazed by the heat of his kisses, each deeper and wetter than the last one. She moaned in protest when his mouth left hers. She'd pulled his shirt free of his jeans in order to caress his back and shoulders. His skin was supple, like velvet over steel.

Donald unbuttoned her blouse and didn't pause until he had unclasped her bra and her softness filled his hands. He nearly lost his head. She was so exquisitely lush.

"Taylor . . . baby, I knew you would be like this, wonderfully soft, beautiful." He dropped his head, licking his way across a brown, full globe until he reached the dark brown nipple. He laved the aching peak until it stood out hard and sweet as a plump raisin, only then did he suck it.

She nearly screamed from the attention as the red hot flames of desire flared along her nerve endings pooling in that womanly center between her legs. She whimpered deep in her throat causing quivers to race down his spine and he intensified the suction as his caressing hand squeezed her other breast.

She managed to gasp his name, unwittingly rubbing her aching mound against the hard muscle of his thigh.

"Is it good, sweetness?" he asked, his voice hoarse with desire.

He took his time ignoring his body's demands that he hurry, the clemental relentless urge to bury himself inside her sweet heat. He had waited too long to have her . . . to taste her. Taylor was a shivering mass of raw pleasure when he turned his hot mouth to her other breast. He laved the pebble-hard tip before applying the intense suction they both enjoyed.

She said his name, crossing her legs and squeezing her thighs in an attempt to ease the emptiness deep inside. It hadn't been like this before. That time with Alex could not compare to being with Donald. She had never known that a man could relish a woman's breasts the way Donald was enjoying hers. When she was close to sobbing her enjoyment, he lifted his head and looked deep into her eyes.

"Tell me. Tell me if you want me as much as I want you." When she would have nodded her agreement to whatever he asked, he clarified. "I'm asking if you are ready to take me inside your body?" He couldn't make himself any clearer. He didn't think he could turn back once he had felt her wet heat.

Taylor caressed his cheek, her mouth sweet against his. "I want you."

She would not have believed it if she hadn't witnessed it. She let out a whoop quickly covering her mouth with her hand as he lifted her into his arms and held her against his chest.

"Have you lost your mind? Put me down before you hurt something."

Donald ignored her protest as he crossed to the bedroom. Closing the door with his foot, he said, "Sweetness, I bench press 250 to 300 pounds. You're a lightweight."

When they came down on the bed together, his weight pressing her into the mattress, his mouth claimed hers over and over again. When she recovered her senses she was as bare as the day she was born. He had systematically stripped her. Some of her clothes were on the bed, some on the floor, some even on the chair. He was still fully dressed.

"No," he said when she would have covered herself with the sheet. His hungry gaze stroked her entire caramel-colored length. "You're beautiful."

Taylor blushed, her eyes on him. "Hurry . . . I need you."

He stood beside the bed and began to undress. He handled his clothes with as little regard as he had handled hers. She watched his every movement, mesmerized by the beauty of his body. When he unzipped his jeans and shoved them down his hips and legs, then kicked them away, she swallowed a gasp. His briefs were next. She did gasp aloud then. His sex jutted powerfully as he approached the bed.

At his knowing smile she blushed again. He knew she was fascinated by that very male part of him. His long body was an endless play of finely tuned muscle over a teakwood brown frame.

He was a warrior. For tonight he was her warrior. His tremendous power tempered by tenderness. His rich ebony eyes drank in the lush beauty of her long curvy body.

"Tell me. Tell me how much you want me." He growled the demand deep in his throat, his voice as heavy as his sex with need. The flare of his wide African nostrils and the set of his generous mouth spoke of an unyielding intent.

"I want you . . . now."

Donald smiled, sure that she didn't know what she was asking him to speed along. He shook his head as he sat down near the foot of the bed. He kissed each rose-lacquered toenail in turn, his heated eyes never leaving hers. He lifted her right ankle and leaned down to lick the ankle were the gold heart shaped charms glimmered against her soft skin.

"Donald . . ." she said impatiently, longing for his mouth on hers, his hands squeezing her breasts. But she didn't ask . . . she was too embarrassed to ask for what she wanted.

As he tongued her delicate ankle, his gaze was on the long expanse of her gorgeous legs. She had breathtaking thighs . . . so soft. His shaft pulsed with urgency. He watched the way she quickly looked away.

There was no need for modesty between them. Soon they would be lovers. There was no place for secrets in this room . . . in this bed. She had no idea what she was in for. But he knew how he planned to pleasure her.

There would be no urgency. This was no mad dash to the finish line.

"Relax, sweetness. Close your eyes. Close them and concentrate on how you feel." His warm hot mouth moved steadily up her shapely calf to the bounty of her petal soft inner thigh.

When she instinctively tried to keep them tight together, his hands cupped her outer thighs, stroking her, soothing her.

"Baby, we have no secrets. Nothing to keep hidden from each other."

"I-I-I'm not trying to hide from you."

"Good," he crooned, caressing up her inner thighs, relishing the softness of her skin. "Open for me, Taylor . . . give me your sweetness." His breath warm on her flesh caused goose pimples to rise.

"Why would you want to . . ." her voice broke off. She couldn't say it.

Donald read the uncertainty. Caressing her cheek, he said, "I want you, every delectable inch of you."

"But . . ."

Moving up her curvy length, he settled himself at her side. He offered her one deep hungry kiss after another until she was a-trembling all over with need. He caressed her, sliding his long fingered hands over her shoulders, down her back. Lifting and cupping her soft behind before he slowly began caressing her neck, his large strong hands, were gentle . . . arousing.

"You feel so good, so good," he whispered huskily as he stroked her tongue with his. "It's all about pleasure. You give me pleasure by letting me hold you, caress you, tongue you, baby."

Taylor trembled, "Mmm," she moaned, stroking down his arms to the thick wall of his chest. "It gives me pleasure to touch you," she whispered, her face pressed into the place where his shoulder and neck joined.

He shivered, loving her caresses. He gently cupped and squeezed her sex. He whispered, "Let me touch you."

Taylor trembled; her lips caressed his neck as she gradually relaxed her thighs. He didn't rush her. He concentrated on his caressing fingertips stroking the cottony soft thick hairs covering her mound. He let his fingers play, alternating gentle squeezes and teasing the plump folds, while his forefinger gently worried the tiny nub at the top of her womanhood.

Her sexy moans were driving him wild with longing, but he controlled his need. Her enjoyment accelerated his own pleasure as he continued his short, shallow strokes. His eyes were on hers. He watched the way her lids fluttered and closed as the maddeningly sweet caresses continued on and on. Her breath was coming in quick uneven pants.

"Relax . . . enjoy," he crooned close to her ear. His fingers slid over and around that feminine bud until she was slick from her own juices. His own breath quickened as he trembled in delicious anticipation. He wanted to drown his senses in her sweet scent and taste. But he held back, knowing she wasn't ready for that degree of intimacy.

As his questing fingertip moved deeper and deeper, Taylor gradually opened herself like the petal of a dew-kissed rose. He did not consider stopping until she was gloriously wet and inviting. His stroking fingers told him that she was not only incredibly responsive but incredibly tight. He didn't want to cause her pain yet as wet as she was, she still would not be able to accommodate him easily.

Donald dipped his head concentrating on the marble

hard tip of one breast, his stroking finger continuing to caress her clitoris.

Taylor was whimpering as the pleasure flared and sparked almost out of control. Her whimpers of pleasure built until he covered his mouth with hers as she climaxed, shivering and shuddering in his arms.

Donald knew he couldn't wait. He had to be inside her now. He slipped on a condom before he slid between her thighs and eased himself to the entrance of her body. Her moistness on the broad crest of his sex caused him to tremble with raw pleasure. Slowly moving against her, he pressed forward into her tight passage. He could feel her tightening around him . . . tightening against him. He knew he hurt her. He dropped his head whispering to her, soothing her but he didn't slow nor did he stop. He couldn't. He was only half way in and felt as if he were dying. He closed his eyes, saying her name as he plunged deep into her wondrous tight heat.

"Oh, baby . . ." he marveled. "You're so sweet, so sweet." He struggled to stay still . . . not to hurt her more . . . give her time to adjust to his size.

Taylor, having barely recovered from the incredible pleasure, was overwhelmed by the unyielding pressure. She tried to relax, to accept, but intrusive memories from the past caused her body to tighten with fear.

Donald sensed the change in her, knew that, as prepared as she was physically, mentally she was not. His voice was deep and reassuring as he whispered words of encouragement. Telling her how sweet she was, how perfect for him. His hands and mouth were never still as he caressed her, loved her. He did everything he could to keep himself still, allowing her time to adjust to his size.

There was nothing small about him and he had no choice but to accept that. But the hot sweetness of her body was quickly eroding his self control.

Taylor's eyes were liquid brown as she clung to him. She was unprepared for the rush of raw need flooding her as his questing fingertips returned to the tiny center of her femininity. While the pressure didn't ease, wave after wave of unrelenting pleasure caused her to move against him needing his hardness deep inside, instinctively tightening her inner muscles.

Donald cried out at the exquisite erotic caress that tantalized his entire length, causing him to increase his movements. His upper body was off the bed as he used the powerful muscles in his hips and thighs to plunge again and again deep inside her moist heat.

Over and over again he reveled in her sweet heat while Taylor clung to him, calling his name, begging for something she couldn't even name. Donald knew what she wanted and he gave her one hard thrust after another, until he felt the fluttering strokes of her body as she climaxed. He was a stroke behind her. He called out her name as he gave himself over to the sheer pleasure of his own powerful release.

Donald collapsed on top of her before he recovered himself enough to roll to his back and pull her into his arms. Taylor offered no protest. Her long feminine body intertwined with his as she rested her head on his shoulder.

Donald was the first to speak as he nestled against her throat. "How are you?"

"Good. How are you?" she teased, snuggling even closer to him.

Donald was not in a playful mood. "Don't pretend with me, Taylor. I know I hurt you."

She started to shake her head, then stopped, touched by his concern. "I'm a little sore. I'm just not used to making love." She flushed, in spite of her best effort not to. She felt as if she were in over her head. She had never had such an intimate discussion with a man.

"You're small. I tried to go slow, give you time to accommodate me." Donald repressed a groan. She had not only been small, but unbelievably tight. She fit him like a wet, slick glove. The thought had him erect, ready for more. He had a high sex drive. And, quite frankly, it had been a long dry spell. What had happened between them had not been about sex. He had made love to her. The difference involved how he felt about her. He cared for her, more deeply than he had even imagined.

She was so warm and caring . . . special. She had been more than worth the wait. He didn't want her sore to the point of discomfort. That was what would happen if he took her again and again the way he longed to do.

She may have been inexperienced, but she had pleased him thoroughly. He could not remember experiencing such an explosive climax. There was no comparison. But then he had never felt so strongly about any woman before.

"What's wrong?"

He looked surprised. "Nothing."

"You looked so serious. You were frowning," she whispered, as unspoken fear rose inside of her. She hadn't pleased him.

Disturbed by his intense reaction to her, Donald didn't know how best to answer. He sighed, uncertain what to say.

"Thank you for being so patient with me. You were so gentle."

Gentle was not an adjective he could accept. He had been horny as hell and he'd lost control at the end. Damn it! He'd enjoyed her so completely that he couldn't think past the magic of having her in his arms.

He snorted. He was furious at his loss of control. "I lost control. I could have really hurt you, sweetheart." He was not proud of the way he had rammed himself to the hilt, not easing up even as his body erupted and emptied inside of her. No, he had nothing to be proud of. Yet he had never been so sated in his life. He felt the release down to his toes.

Taylor shook her head, her soft hand stroking over his chest. "No, you were wonderful. I had no idea it could be so exciting."

His kiss was warm and tender, causing her eyes to fill from the tenderness of the caress. As he cradled her against him, he wondered if he could ever get enough of her sweet magic. He had fought the battle with her resentment and won. Could he win it all?

Her hand rested on his flat concave stomach, bare inches away from the crown of his shaft. He closed his eyes as his body ached for the warmth of her caress. He reminded himself that it was much too soon for her. If she touched him there he would be rock hard in an instant. It would not take long, not with Taylor.

She leaned over and kissed him softly, then snuggled even closer, closing her eyes too, feeling secure in the shelter of his arms. Although she knew he was aroused and longed to touch him . . . feel his steely hard length, she was still so unsure of her own sexual appeal. She would leave the choice to him.

Unwelcome thoughts of the next day being their last together managed to intrude, no matter how strongly she fought against it. How difficult would it be tomorrow when they separated? No, she would not worry about that now. For now she would enjoy what they had. Tonight would have to last forever, providing a lifetime of memories. Her sigh was barely audible as she slipped into sleep. Donald hid his disappointment as he, too, slept.

# *Fourteen*

It was early evening when Donald and Taylor said their goodbyes to his family. Taylor was pleased that Megan and Margie invited her for lunch the following week in Detroit. She genuinely liked both women and looked forward to seeing them again.

"Happy?" Donald asked as their plane lifted toward the sky. His strong fingers cradled hers. His dark gaze moved over her soft features to linger on her mouth.

They had had very little time to themselves over the weekend. This was the first time they'd really talked since he'd left her sleeping early that morning. He had reluctantly returned to the family suite to shower and taken an early morning run. He needed the time alone to clear his head, sort out his feelings. When they were together all he could think about was her.

"Yes. I really enjoyed myself. Thank you," she smiled. She had selected a red blouse to wear with a navy blue pantsuit.

"Should I apologize for my family?"

"Absolutely not. You have a wonderful family. They are so warm and generous."

"Money only enhances what's already there, sweetness." He looked so comfortable in jeans and a pale blue knit pullover. He moved his thumb soothingly over the back of her hand. "Don't," he said, when she tried to pull back but he held on.

"Scott and Jenna are picking me up at the airport," she said, searching for a harmless topic.

He sighed. "I suppose it's time we talked about Scott." He hated the way her pretty mouth tightened. While caressing her cheek, he said, "We've put it off long enough."

"You're wrong. We don't have to discuss him." She reminded herself that, once the weekend was over, their relationship would also end. Scott had nothing to do with what had happened between them.

"Taylor?"

"I don't want to get into an argument. We have very little time as it is. Soon you'll be on your way back to Chicago and I'll be back home in Detroit."

"I don't want to argue either." His kiss was warm and seeking as he parted her lips to receive the hungry thrust of his tongue. The telephone chose that moment to ring. Both were disappointed by the delay when he grumbled then said, "Excuse me."

The call was business and he put his hand over the mouth piece, saying, "Sorry. I have to take this one."

She nodded. "Take your time."

He squeezed her hand before he walked over to the desk where he'd left his laptop.

Taylor pulled a fashion magazine out of her tote and began flipping through the pages. Determined not to let her disappointment show, she scolded herself for caring. Yet their time together was so short. Even though she had known that, going into this trip, the reality of how rapidly their time together was dwindling was just beginning to sink in. Their weekend was over the minute the plane touched down in Detroit.

They had shared a wonderful weekend. It was only natural for her not to want it to end. She knew they were not right for each other. They were too different. They had nothing in common. While his life was glamorous and exciting, hers was neither of those things. Yet, she told herself it was only natural for her not to want it to end.

No, she wouldn't complain when they parted. There would be no room or reason for regret. She certainly would not cling or try to change what could not be. In fact, she was convinced that, in the long run, it was better this way. She could go on with her life, happier now that the degrading experience with Alex was finally behind her.

Being with Donald had changed how she felt about men and how she felt about herself. She was confident that her new attitude was a much healthier one. She might be plump, even a bit hippy, but that didn't mean she was not desirable. Or that she could not attract a man. Yes, her time with Donald had given her much to reconsider.

Taylor trembled when she felt the warm pressure of his open mouth on the side of her throat. He gave her a playful nip, then soothed the tiny hurt with his tongue. "Hi."

Trembling in reaction, she said, "Hi." She couldn't help smiling at him, angling her head toward him. "All done?"

He sank into the chair beside hers. Whatever he had been about to say was forgotten. Suddenly all he could think about was the enticement of her sweet mouth. Slowly he lowered his head and completely covered her mouth with his own. He licked her mouth, first concentrating on the pouty fullness of her upper lip, before moving on to suckle the bottom one. He licked her lips as if she were an ice cream cone and savored her with much enjoyment before he slid his tongue between her lips and ravished the sweetness inside.

Taylor moaned with pleasure, allowing herself to sink even deeper into his arms. No one had ever touched her the way he had. No one had made her feel cherished.

Donald took his time, enjoying her thoroughly The kisses went on and on, one right after the other, deepening until they were forced to stop in order to breathe.

His caressing hand cradled her cheek. "I wish I could stay the night with you, sweetness. But I have a meeting in the morning and practice in the afternoon. Even though the season is winding down, my schedule won't ease up. We're going into the play-offs soon, which means I'll have very little time to call my own."

"I understand," she smiled, determined to let him see that she was not like the other women who chased after him. She did not expect their weekend to mean they were engaged. Now was all they had. It would be enough. It had to be. She didn't want to try and hold a man who didn't understand the word commitment.

"I'm glad you do because I'm not feeling so understanding. I want to be with you." His voice was thick with desire.

Taylor looked away, fighting back unexpected tears. Deep in her heart she knew she wanted that also. Yes, he knew how to charm a woman. He was a master at it. As long as she remembered it was all perfectly normal for him, no one would be hurt.

"Taylor . . ."

When she didn't meet his gaze, he frowned and cupped her chin, raising her face until he could study her eyes. She dropped her lids but not before he saw the sadness she could not conceal.

"Don't look away from me like that. We're not talking about forever. Why don't you come to me next weekend? Fly to Chicago on Friday, stay until early Monday. I'll send the plane for you."

"I can't do that."

"Why not? We need to see each other. What could be more important than that?"

"You don't have to pretend with me, Donald. I'm all grown up. In fact, I prefer honesty."

"Pretend? What are you talking about?"

"After the plane lands, I know it will be over between us. I can accept that. You don't have to worry. I don't intend to chase you down or make your life uncomfortable." Taylor held herself erect, her head held high. "You will go on with your life and I will go on with mine."

Donald stared at her for a long moment before he asked, "What did you say?"

"I said . . ."

"No, damn it. Don't repeat it. You got kicked in the face by that jackass in college so . . ." he stopped abruptly, then took a deep calming breath before demanding, "What in the hell made you think that all I wanted was one time with you? Was it something I said?"

"No!"

"Well?"

"I woke up alone this morning. We did not make love before you left and then we spent the day with your family. So naturally, I assumed it meant . . ." She stopped, then said, "It confirmed what I'd been thinking."

"I didn't want to wake you. You were sleeping so peacefully. I went for a run, to clear out the cobwebs."

"I thought . . ."

"Look," he said, pointing a finger at her. "I'm not Alex Adams. I will never be him! Understand!"

"Stop shouting at me. It was an honest mistake!"

"Like hell!"

To say he was livid would be putting it mildly. He went over to the bar and poured himself a drink. He lifted it, then thought better of it. He couldn't remember the last time he'd been so angry. He found her view of him alarmingly hurtful. For the first time in a long time, it really mattered what a woman thought of him. He suddenly realized that he hadn't even begun to explore his feelings for Taylor.

"You don't trust men in general, do you? You especially don't trust me." Deep down he knew he felt more than outrage. It hurt.

"I don't think you're being fair," she insisted. She cared about him. She cared about him more than she had ever dreamed it possible for her to care about a man. She couldn't have made love with him if she didn't have deep feelings for him.

It was true that she'd started their relationship thinking the worst of him, she couldn't deny that. It had taken time, but she had finally seen what a wonderful, caring man he was. What she could not believe was that he also cared about her. From the first, she had considered herself a temporary diversion.

"That's the way it looks to me." A muscle jumped in his cheek as if he were grinding his strong white teeth.

"You're wrong. I trust my father, my brother."

"You're not sleeping with either one of them," he grated bitterly.

"It takes time, Donald. Trust doesn't happens overnight." Taylor got up and went over to where he sat at that bar with his long legs braced apart. "I'm sorry. I didn't realize I was judging you by Alex's yardstick. It won't happen again."

Donald, busy studying the liquor in the glass, didn't move. Eventually, he looked at her. She stood between his thighs; close, but not close enough. It was the softness in her brown eyes, pleading for his understanding and the sexy pout of her sweet red tinted mouth that eased the disappointment inside of him.

"Honey, please don't be mad" she whispered, her breath warm on his throat.

"Does it matter?" he asked tightly, his eyes on her mouth.

"To me, yes. I care about you." Her gaze locked with his.

"I don't want to lose you," he barely stopped himself from saying it, realizing that it was true. He not only wanted her sweet, sexy body, but he wanted her to care about him. They been together such a short time. It wasn't enough. He realized she mattered to him. He could not let her go.

If he hadn't been sitting down he definitely would have fallen. He had no idea where the knowledge came from . . . it was just there, right in his face. He couldn't ignore it or pretend it wasn't true. What in the hell was he supposed to do about it? Was he falling in love with her?

"Donald?" She reached out and stroked his throat, near the base, in the sensitive hollow.

He sighed heavily, pulling her deep into the vee between his thighs and up against his chest. Black eyes locked with deep brown ones. He held her close, stroking down her back to her waist. The flare of her hips was as tempting as was the softness of her breasts and the sweetness of her lips. His blood heated as he recalled the softness of her sexy behind, the sheer opulence of her breasts, the sweet bounty of her mouth and the tight sheath within her womanly core.

He had nearly gone out of his mind with pleasure last night when he was deep inside of her. He had never experienced such tight, wet heat. It was as if she had been made just for him. She blew his mind. It wasn't sex. He recognized that he had made love for the very first time in his life. It had been better than anything

he had ever experienced with anyone else. Would he
ever get his fill of her?

Donald didn't bother to ask for what he needed, he
took it. A sizzling hot, tongue-stroking kiss. One was not
enough, so he helped himself to another and yet another.

"I want you in my life," he whispered between kisses.

She moaned when it was over, leaning her head on
his shoulder, her arms locked around his neck.

He nodded. "I'm sorry I lost my temper."

She smiled, grateful that it was finally over.

"I'm not sure where we're going, baby. Please, let's
give it a chance. Give each other a chance."

"Yes," she sighed, pressing a tender kiss on his cheek.
"Let's." She refused to focus on her doubts, her fears
or even her disagreement with him concerning her
brother. For good or bad, she concentrated on how she
felt about him. She might not have planned on caring
about him nor had she wanted a relationship with him,
nevertheless, she acknowledged that she cared very
deeply.

There were so many things to consider. Would she be
able to cope with him living in Chicago and on the road
a good percentage of the time? He was not the average
Joe Blow. He was a celebrity whose name was practically
a household word. He was news. While he might fit easily
into her uncomplicated world, where did she fit in his?

"Come back with me tonight, sweetness," he said
softly. His heart raced at the thought. He knew he was
rushing things, but he couldn't help it. He needed her
with him.

"Chicago?" she stammered, uncertain if she had
heard him correctly.

"Yes."

"Donald! How can I?"

He placed his fingertips over her generous lips. "Humor me, will ya? Please, give it half-a-minute's worth of thought." The last thing he wanted to do was leave her in Detroit thinking he wanted less than a full-fledged relationship. They were connected now.

"How can I? I have a career and a family waiting for me at the airport in Detroit." He was asking too much. Yet, surprisingly, she wished she could forget about everything but how much she wanted to be with him.

"Somehow I knew you'd say that," he said impatiently.

"Don't you think you're being a tiny bit selfish? I went away for an entire weekend with you, didn't I? Isn't that enough for now?"

"Not hardly," he acknowledged to himself but thought better of saying it out loud. He flatly refused to offer an apology for wanting to be with her.

She sighed heavily. "We're fighting again."

"No. We are negotiating."

"Who's winning?" she teased, pleading with her eyes for him not to be upset with her. She was discovering that she hated his anger . . . adored his smiles. When he put his mind to it, the man could charm . . .

"We both are," he said huskily, his mouth lingering at that ultra sensitive point at the base of her neck. As badly as he needed to be in Chicago tonight, he needed to be with Taylor more. "Kiss me."

She didn't even consider resisting. She gave him her mouth without hesitation. Each new kiss was sweeter and hotter than the last.

She was pleasantly surprised when they flew into Metropolitan Airport and Donald got off with her. With her luggage over one powerful shoulder, while her hand was clasped firmly in his, they made their way to the passenger terminal.

Scott and Jenna were waiting for them inside. The hug that Taylor gave her brother was reassuring. Yet it was evident to her that he was on edge.

"What's wrong?" Taylor whispered. He had barely spoken to Donald.

"Nothin'. Just wanted to make sure you were okay."

Taylor chose that moment to introduce Jenna and Donald.

"It's a pleasure," Jenna said, shaking hands.

"The pleasure is mine," Donald said pleasantly but to Scott he said quietly, "Taylor is fine."

"Let her answer, please," Scott said through his teeth.

"What's going on?" Donald asked Scott directly. He was puzzled by Scott's hostility. He'd been all for them dating at first. What had caused the change?

"Nothing!" Taylor interjected.

Something was not quite right and Donald intended to get to the bottom of it. Taylor was his woman now. Nothing or no one could change that. Scott had no choice but to get used to the idea.

"I arranged to have a car waiting for us." Donald said.

Taylor nodded, recalling the quick telephone call he made before they landed. Glancing up at him, she accepted that the last thing she wanted to do was to say a hasty good-bye. And she was grateful for being spared a public display. She said for his ears alone, "I can go with my brother so you won't be delayed."

Donald shook his head. "I brought you to the party. I'm taking you home."

Taylor flushed, feeling almost singed by the heat in his possessive gaze. He wanted her and didn't care who knew it. She nodded, then turned to the others to say, "Thank you for coming for me. I'm sorry to inconvenience you this way."

"You're not an inconvenience. I'll meet you at the house," Scott said, tightly catching Jenna's hand in his. "See ya in a few."

"What's with him?" Donald asked, watching them depart before the two of them also started heading for the outside doors.

Taylor shrugged. "I have no idea. He was a little upset when I left. I thought he would be over it by now."

"Apparently not," he said dryly. It was a cool, clear night. The temperature a marked difference from the warm weather they'd left behind. Donald handed the luggage to the uniformed chauffeur before helping Taylor into the limousine. "He's overdoing it."

"A bit."

"You're his sister. I can appreciate that he doesn't want you hurt."

"This is crazy. He was the one pushing me into a relationship with you. Remember?"

"Apparently the idea of us sleeping together has gotten his back up. Cold?" He said, with her cuddled close. They had both donned jackets once they left the plane.

Taylor relaxed in his arms, relishing their closeness. "Yes. Honey, you really didn't have to go to the trouble of seeing me home. I know how busy you are."

"Yes, I did." He took the hand that was resting in her lap into his warm wide palm. He played with her fingers. "It was absolutely necessary."

She took advantage of his presence and rested her head on his shoulder. She only had to close her eyes to recall the pleasure of sleeping in his arms, surrounded by his male heat.

"Sleepy?"

"Getting there."

"We've done a lot of traveling in a very short time." He lifted his arm so that her cheek rested on his chest, certain he would never get tired of having her in his arms.

"It doesn't seem to be affecting you."

"I'm used to it. Rest; we'll have you home before you know it."

Taylor closed her eyes but she didn't sleep, she couldn't. She did not want to miss a moment of their brief time together. Where had the time gone? It seemed like it had vanished into a puff of smoke.

Scott was there to open the front door for them. He'd checked the house before he came back to the living room and sat down, crossing his arms over his chest.

Donald was amused, although he hid it well.

"How was the trip?" Jenna asked.

"Wonderful," Taylor interjected. "We were on one of South Carolina's privately owned sea islands. The weather was wonderful. Warm enough to go swimming. I didn't know what to expect when we reached home. Certainly not five feet of snow."

"It's nearly April," Jenna said with a laugh.

"It's also Michigan," Taylor teased.

Scott didn't even crack a smile. Even though she wasn't thrilled by her brother's attitude, she understood where it was coming from. They had always been close, but when it came to this he was clearly being unreasonable. He had no choice but to accept Donald. Besides, she desperately wanted to spend what was left of their time together alone in Donald's arms.

She said, "It's late, Scott. Shouldn't you be going?"

He blinked in surprise, but he didn't move from the armchair. "I'm in no hurry." His chin jutted mulishly, just like their father's. Taylor would have giggled, but unfortunately now she did not see anything amusing about it.

Donald could see that he intended to wait them out. He wasn't about to give up the little time they had left entertaining her brother. Their time was precious, all too fleeting.

"I'm not leaving, Scott. At last, not until dawn." He didn't bother mincing words. There was no way he could be misunderstood.

A muscle jumped in her brother's jaw. He was furious. "Now look, Williams." He was on his feet, his hands tight at his side.

Taylor jumped to hers and confronted him. "No, you look, Scott Hendricks. Donald and I don't have to explain our relationship." As much as she adored her younger brother, she was not about to let him spoil what she had with Donald. Wearily, she went on to say, "Scott, what has gotten into you? I know you like Donald."

"He's worried about you getting hurt," Jenna put in.

"Jenna!" he barked.

"Let her speak. You're not the only one with an opinion," Taylor scolded impatiently.

Donald stayed where he was on the sofa, but his tone was commanding enough to gain everyone's attention. "Scott, I care about Taylor. You have nothing to be concerned about. I won't hurt her."

Scott met the other man's frank scrutiny. Whether he was satisfied with Donald's comment was left unsaid. He kissed his sister's cheek. "Love you."

"I love you, too," she whispered, giving him a big hug.

Scott turned to Jenna. "Ready?"

She nodded. After hugging Taylor she said to Donald, "It's been great meeting you. I admire your work on the court."

"Thanks," Donald smiled, rising to his feet to shake hands "Take care."

At the door Scott looked Donald in the eye, then said, "I'm holding you to your word."

Donald nodded, admiring the other younger man's concern for his sister and his unwillingness to back down. "Night."

The door had barely closed behind them when Taylor walked straight into his arms, placing her arms around his trim waist. "I thought you needed to be back tonight?"

"What I need is to be with you. I have a point to make," he said softly, his cheek against the top of her head.

"What point?"

Donald didn't respond verbally, instead he took her hand and led her back into the living room. He dropped down to the sofa and pulled her down onto his lap.

"Taylor . . ." he moaned as he helped himself to the sweetness of her mouth. He did not stop until his tongue was stroking hers in a delicious erotic caress.

"You didn't answer my question." Her voice held tremors from the sizzling hot shivers running up and down her spine. She arched her neck even more, offering it to him.

Donald didn't disappoint her. He trailed warm kisses down her throat, laving the sweet scented spot behind her ear.

"Honey?"

"What?" he mumbled, tracing the small shell of her ear with his tongue.

"The point you . . . need to . . . m-make." She could barely get the words out as his large hands squeezed her breasts, worrying the nipples with his thumbs. Her head rested on his shoulder. She moaned, so hungry for his hands on her bare flesh that she unbuttoned her blouse and unhooked the front clasp of her bra impatiently.

Donald dropped his head until he could lave each brown peak in turn before he applied the exact suction she adored. He pleased her while he pleased himself. He loved the taste and smell of her soft caramel-colored skin. Taylor was whimpering in delight, eager for each hot stroke of his tongue. Her eyes were tightly closed and she was breathing heavily as sensations pooled in her womanly core.

"Donald . . ." she gasped his name. "Oh, please . . ." She wiggled in his lap, her bottom against his heavy shaft.

He groaned heavily, closing his eyes as she tantalized him. "Please, what?" He lifted his head until he could look into her lovely eyes but they were closed, the thick lashes resting on her cheeks. "Open your eyes, sweetness. Look at me. I don't ever want you to confuse my lovemaking with anyone else's."

"What!" Outraged, she knew she should pull free, but his stroking thumbs and forefingers were sweetly worrying her nipples. She could feel the wondrous sensation deep inside her womb, causing her to ache for him to ease the emptiness.

"You're mine." The possessive thrust of his tongue moved deep inside to caress the soft tissue of her mouth. There could be no misunderstanding. Alex Adams was her past, Donald intended to see to it that he stayed that way. The man must have been out of his mind to walk away from an involvement with Taylor.

She was sinking down even deeper against his chest, and she did not have the wherewithall to argue the point. She was weak with longing from the fiery pleasure he so easily gave her. She was trembling all over, a hair's breadth away from climaxing.

"Please . . ." she begged, taking his hand and placing it where she needed it most, cupping her emptiness. She squeezed her thighs against his fingers. Unfortunately, she was still fully clothed below the waist and could not feel him the way she ached to. "Donald . . ."

"Tell me what do you want, sweetness?" His voice was rough with increasing desire as he returned to laving the engorged nipple. "Tell me . . ."

Taylor lifted her lips to his ear and bit his lobe before tonguing it, causing quivers of desire to race down his spine and his manhood to throb with need. "Touch me . . ." She pressed his hand against her softness, hungry for the friction of his knowledgeable fingers.

"Tell me," he persisted, needing to touch her, long-

ing to feel her flesh wet and swollen, so fleshy and soft.
Even her feminine scent drove him mad with hunger.
He also craved the words, needed to hear her tell him
explicitly how she wanted him to give her the pleasure
she needed.

"There is no room for shyness between lovers. And
sweetness, we are definitely lovers." His hands moved
to the generous flare of her hips. He pulled off her
slacks and her pretty red lace panties. He couldn't help
giving her one seductive squeeze of her delightfully full
bottom.

His mouth returned to hers time and time again before dipping lower to give each elongated peak a hot
lick.

Impatient for him, she brought his long blunt-fingered
hand to the tiny center of her desire and applied pressure
she needed there.

"Good, sweetness . . ." his voice trembled with excitement. He gritted his teeth against the throbbing
strength of his erection. He had reached his full length
and he was cramped inside his jeans. He unsnapped the
waist to ease the pressure. "You feel so good, so wet. You
want me, sweetness?"

"Oh . . . yes. Touch me. Honey, I ache so badly."

He rubbed his fingers along the puffy folds, parting,
titillating. "You make me want you so badly," he
crooned deep in his throat loving the feel of her.

Taylor gasped out her delight when he caressed her
clitoris, unable to control her response. Each brush of
his fingertips brought her closer and closer to the edge
as he laved her entire breast, then focused on the sensitive tip, gently worrying it with his teeth, then sucking
deeply. Her climax was so strong that she cried out, unable to control her trembling. It came in a powerful
swell of incomparable pleasure.

Donald held her close, cradled against his heart. His

eyes were closed as he marveled over her womanliness. She did not have to do anything but be in order to drive him nearly insane with desire. Had he ever been this hard, this much in need? Somehow he doubted it.

"Oh, honey," was all she could manage, encircling his neck and giving him a soft, sweet kiss.

He was wildly responsive as she rubbed her breasts against his chest. "Don't stop," he whispered.

Taylor's hands were on his sweater, pulling it over his head. She slid from his lap, her hands going to his waist. He caught her slender hands, then kissed the soft palms.

"Let me. I'm too hard to get the zipper down easily."

"I'm sorry . . ." she whispered, feeling terribly selfish.

"For what?" he asked, stripping while she watched—then he grinned at her blush when his heavy sex jutted forward.

"Look at you."

He chuckled. "As long as I have enough to please you, then it doesn't matter."

Taylor covered her cheeks, not believing this conversation. It was far from normal for her.

"Why are you apologizing?"

"I was concentrating only on my own enjoyment."

"It's thrilling to watch your pleasure, baby," he said throatily.

He grabbed her around the waist and eased her down to the carpet beside him, unmindful of their clothes scattered about. He felt as if he had to get inside of her soon . . . he couldn't wait. He spread her thighs wide and high, her long legs over each powerful shoulder.

His penetration was as slow and easy as he could manage. She was so wonderfully wet and deliciously tight that his entire body shuddered from the burning pleasure of being inside of her. She cried out, unable to control the way her inner muscles caressed him in sweet welcome. Donald cried out his acute enjoyment as he began to thrust, long continuous thrusts designed to give them both the utmost pleasure.

"Honey . . . oh . . ." Taylor panted, kissing the base of his throat, his chest, whatever she could reach.

He increased his thrusts, his hands cupped her bottom, squeezing her fleshy softness. "Come with me, sweetness. Come with me."

Taylor had no idea how to accomplish such a thing. Suddenly, when she felt his fingertips caressing the highly sensitive heart of her passion as he drove his penis with such powerful force deep inside of her heat, they came apart in each other's arms, sharing a heart-stopping release.

Donald rolled so that Taylor could rest on his deep chest. Her body still throbbed from the aftermath of their lovemaking. Her small hand was silky soft on his chest as she caressed him. She was drowsy with sleep, certain she would never be able to move again.

Donald, having finally recovered his breath, chuckled.

"What's so funny?" she mumbled, her face against his throat.

"You. You're the least selfish person I know," he said, his hand caressing down her back. She had never accepted more from him than a few flowers. He smiled, wondering if she even heard him. One good loving and his lady was out like a light.

As he held her, he knew he would do whatever it took to keep her, whether that involved dealing with her brother's hostility or anyone foolish enough to get in his way. She was his heart.

She stirred somewhat when he lifted her and carried her into the bedroom. "What are you doing?" she mumbled.

He chuckled, standing her on her feet so he could pull back the comforter, as she swayed, he placed a supporting arm around her waist. "This is your bedroom, isn't it?" he asked, crawling in beside her on the queen-sized bed.

Taylor, curled up against him, murmured with eyes closed, "What color?"

"Pink."

"Rose . . . yes." Her lids were so heavy, she tried but failed to lift them.

She woke a few hours later to the warmth of his mouth on her breasts. She came awake as he fondled her. When she was thoroughly saturated with feminine dew he slowly slid inside of her. Donald's slow, steady movements caused her to moan, wrapping her arms around his neck and her legs around his waist.

Their loving was slow and drowsy with tenderness. They clung to each other not wanting the pleasure to end. He reached completion seconds before she did. Her cry of fulfillment was swallowed as he covered her mouth with his in a deep soul-claiming kiss.

The sky was streaked with soft color when he kissed her gently and told her he had to leave.

"Do you need me to take you to the airport? Remember, you sent the driver home." She covered a yawn, hating that he was dressed. Even though she did not want him to leave, she was not about to make a fuss.

He smiled, warmed by her generosity. It was so much a part of her that it touched every part of her world. "I called. He's on the way. Now give me a good-bye kiss."

She did with such warmth that his arms tightened around her. She tried to rise but couldn't. "Honey, let me up. I want to walk you to the door."

"No. I want to think of you just the way you are," he said, caressing her from her shoulder to the base of her spine. "I'll call tonight, okay?" Unable to resist one more lingering kiss, he eventually said, "Take care of yourself."

They needed to talk. There was still so much left unsaid between them. Despite her best effort, she found herself clinging to him for a long moment before she kissed him yet again.

"Be careful," she whispered.

"Bye."

# Fifteen

"Hey, sweet stuff," Donald crooned softly into the telephone.

"Hey, yourself," she laughed. "How are you?" Even though it was late she knew she would not have been able to sleep until she spoke to him. They hadn't seen each other in close to ten days. She'd been unable to go to him because she had a paper due and he'd been unable to get away.

"So . . . do ya miss me?" he whispered, closing his eyes and savoring the feminine appeal of her voice. So sexy, so sweet, just like her. Dear God in heaven, he missed her.

"Yes . . ." her breath held. "How was your day?"

"Hectic. You haven't asked but I'll tell you anyway. I miss you, sweetness." Between the basketball season coming to an end and the demands of the business he had little time for what really counted . . . Taylor.

She felt herself weakening, melting at the masculine warmth in his voice. She had been trying so hard to cement her defenses against him. Determined to keep herself grounded, she reminded herself that it was only a matter of time before he grew bored with their arrangement. He wanted her now. But her life did not compare in excitement to his.

When she was with him, her common sense flew out the nearest window. Around him, she functioned on pure emotions. She had even managed to push aside her resentment of his influence over her brother. Nothing mattered but how he made her feel. She had left herself vulnerable to him.

"Taylor?"

"I'm here." She could not stop herself from asking, "How much longer? How long before I see you?"

"Our last regular season game is on Sunday. Come to me, baby. Come and spend the weekend with me." When she delayed in answering, he urged "I'll send a car to take you to the airport. All you have to do is get on the plane. Don't even pack. I'll buy you whatever you need." Donald couldn't believe his own degree of need. He needed her . . . longed to see her, hold her.

"I thought we reached an understanding about you giving me things. I don't want you to buy my clothes or give me jewelry. I'm not like that."

He sighed heavily. "There is nothing wrong with me giving you things. You're still my lady, aren't you?"

"Yes, but . . ."

"Humor me once in a while."

"Not on this." She could not bear for him to think she was materialistic.

"Okay, baby. Will you come?" There was no point in arguing. She could dig her toes in when the mood suited her.

"Yes," she said around a sigh. "But I don't need you to send the plane."

"But . . ."

"No. I'll call the airport and let you know my flight number and arrival time."

"Friday?"

"Yes."

His voice had lost some of its tension when he said, "Have you thought about us? What we've shared?"

Her heart accelerated at an alarming rate. She couldn't

forget their lovemaking. She had never experienced anything so deeply gratifying or purely romantic.

"Yes, I thought about it," she said, grateful he couldn't see her blush. He was able to speak of it so openly while she was just the opposite. "We shouldn't talk about this," she whispered into the receiver.

"Oh, but we should," he persisted. "Tell me."

"It was unlike anything I've ever experienced," she confessed.

"Good. I hope to make it even better for you this weekend."

"That's not possible."

"Oh, but it is."

Curiosity got the better of her and she couldn't prevent herself from asking, "How?" She had never discussed sex with a man and never so intimately. Yet, Donald wasn't just a man. He was her lover. "No! Don't answer," she said, her voice laced with embarrassment.

Thoroughly charmed, he chuckled. "Don't be embarrassed, baby. We're lovers. We've seen each other, touched each other . . . loved each other. It's a little late for modesty, don't you think?"

"It's all so new," she tried to explain.

"We should be able to talk about anything including how we pleasure each other."

"Oh, honey . . ." finally she whispered. "I don't think it could be any better."

He swallowed a moan as his body prepared itself to love hers. "I was too impatient to be inside of you."

Taylor said, "You were wonderful. I didn't know what to expect."

"And now . . ."

"I know you'll make it special for me," she surprised herself by her candor. "I . . . well . . . I've never received such enjoyment before."

Donald could imagine how difficult it was for her to

share this with him. Oh course, he expected that was the case. She seemed shocked by her climax . . . her eyes had gone wide with incredulousness.

"Are you saying you never climaxed before?"

"Yes." Her voice was barely above a whisper, but he heard her.

"Oh, baby. It gave me a great deal of enjoyment. You were wonderful to watch. Your face is so expressive." He heard her gasp.

"You watched me?"

"Absolutely."

"We shouldn't be talking like this."

"Why not? This is a private line. No one can hear. Tell me what you are wearing?"

"I'm in bed."

"Do you have anything on?"

"I don't sleep in the nude."

"Yes, you do. You slept that way with me."

"I . . ."

"Yes?"

"Nothing."

"What are you wearing? A gown . . . a T-shirt?"

"Pink nightshirt."

"Mmm. What do you have on under it, sweet stuff?" he sighed heavily. "Come on, baby. I'm wishing you were here with me. If we were together, I'd see to it that you wore absolutely nothing to bed every night. I miss you."

Taylor found her breath quickening, seduced by his deep vibrant voice. "Donald, I miss you, too."

He was pleasantly surprised when she whispered, "It's been so long since we've been able to see each other."

"Think of me."

"Yes."

"Night, sweetness.

"Night."

Donald was not the only one who didn't get much

sleep that night. As the week progressed, their nightly calls became something of a ritual.

He was waiting at the airport with time to spare. He was grateful that he was not recognized or if he was, they were thoughtful enough not to approach him. It had taken all his energy to stay focused on his game. His timing wasn't exactly right but he was hitting the mark every time. He knew it was because he couldn't think beyond how much he wanted and needed to be with Taylor.

When she walked off the plane she was so nervous she was shaking. She didn't have a clue why she was so anxious. She'd been looking forward to it since the moment she agreed. She didn't know what to expect. She was unsure if he would meet her himself or send a driver.

Scott had not been thrilled by her weekend away, but he accepted it with a certain amount of protectiveness. He had at least wished her good luck when he'd kissed her good-bye at the Metro.

Just the prospect of seeing him had her heart racing like a schoolgirl's. She warned herself to be careful. She had to make certain she did not get her feelings anymore involved than they already were. The very last thing she wanted to do was fall in love with him. As long as she kept her head, it would be all right.

She didn't have any trouble spotting him. All she had to do was look up. He was head and shoulders above the crowd. Before she could do much more than smile, he had weaved his way to her side. He pulled her close for an all too brief hug. He placed a quick kiss on her lips, refusing to give into the urge to deepen the caress.

"Hey. How was your flight?"

"Good," Taylor said, somewhat out of breath. The

smile she gave him was radiant, so much so that Donald was unable to pull his eyes away.

She looked fabulously dressed in a black wool slack suit, a black blouse striped with white. The mandarin collar peeked above her scooped-neck jacket. Tiny jet and gold earrings and a velvet-strapped wristwatch were her only jewelry.

"Let me take that," he said, lifting the garment bag and the small case she carried. "Anything more?"

"Nope," she laughed. "I'm traveling light."

He laced his free hand with hers. "How was the flight?"

"Bumpy. We ran into a bit of turbulence."

"You didn't get scared, did you?"

"A little nervous. But it was a short flight."

Donald was stopped several times for an autograph, mainly by young male fans. He was pleasant, but each time a crowd began to form he took Taylor's hand and eased her out of the press. No matter how people tried to separate them, he made a point to keep her at his side. Each time they were stopped he took off at an even faster pace. Taylor was out of breath by the time they reached the car.

"Are you all right?" he asked, once he had her tucked safely inside the sleek burgundy Lincoln.

"I'm fine. Is it always so hectic?"

"No. But we're going into the play-offs. A great deal of attention has been focused on the team."

"Would you hate it if all the fame was suddenly taken away?"

He chuckled. "Not at all. It would be a refreshing change. I love the challenge and intricacy of the game, not the notoriety. Kids should not look to celebrities to be their heroes, but their fathers, brothers, uncles and grandfathers."

Taylor liked his strong, straightforward, honest approach to life. He honestly did not consider himself to be a hero. It was easy to see why others disagreed with him. He was not only a very accomplished and talented man. He was genuine.

"I disagree. I think you are very special."

"Thanks," Donald said, choking back emotions. Her positive opinion of him meant so much, more than he could comfortably express. "I think you're very special, too. You are more than just beautiful to look at."

She swallowed a gasp. It wouldn't take much more before all her defenses had vanished. And he had done no more than brush his lips against hers. Taylor smiled, hoping a change to a less personal topic would restore her equilibrium. "I like the car. No driver or limo?" she teased.

He grinned. "I prefer to drive myself, unless I'm traveling in an unfamiliar city or in a hurry. Then I'll use a service." He cupped her chin, turning her face toward his, deciding he had waited long enough. Finally, they were alone. He pressed his lips against hers, tenderly sponging their softness with his tongue before he slipped inside for an all-too-brief, but heart-stopping, caress.

Taylor was quivering from head to toe by the time he released her. Her eyes were dark and sparkling as she looked at him. "I missed you." It came out of nowhere. She had not been prepared to reveal so much but was suddenly glad that she had, for his eyes glowed with pleasure.

"I'm so glad you're here," he whispered, before turning his attention to the road. Chicago's streets were unbelievably busy even in the early evening. The spring night was clear and surprisingly mild.

"After dark the city comes alive. Hungry?"

"Yes," she readily agreed. "I'm starving."

"I know this tiny little restaurant where there is no

atmosphere but the food is fabulous. Interested in sharing a plate of pasta and thick slices of melt-in-your-mouth garlic bread?''

"Sound great. Let's go.''

Tony's was crowded. The popular Italian restaurant, located in the Northend near downtown, often had long lines, especially on the weekends. The tables were covered with red checkered tablecloths. Red candles adorned the tabletops. There was no mood music in the background. No fresh cut flowers, but the smells coming from the small kitchen in the rear were fantastic. The special of the night was a three cheese lasagna.

They were given a table right away, but were seated in the center of the room, where diners couldn't fail to notice the celebrity in their midst. No one bothered them and no one asked for an autograph.

"Oh, my," Taylor laughed when the meal was brought out. The servings were huge and the wine was rich and fruity. "No wonder you like this place," she said, enjoying a crisp green salad with homemade house dressing.

He chuckled. "I never leave here hungry." He grinned, loving the way she enjoyed her food. She didn't pick nor did she pretend she was not hungry. She laughed and teased him about the place while moving from one course to the next with relish.

She looked up to find him studying her. She lifted an inquiring brow. "Do I have tomato sauce on my cheek?"

"Nope. But you sure are beautiful. Ready for dessert?''

"I can't eat another bite.''

"You're going to miss a delicious apple crumb tart.''

"No, thanks.''

"It is fabulous.''

"You aren't going to let me taste yours?" she teased. Instead of laughing that wonderful hearty laugh of his, he stared at the soft generous curve of her mouth. The hunger in his gaze was unmistakable.

"Let's get out of here," he said gruffly. His voice was raw with need. He couldn't help it. He was fed up with people. He needed to be alone with her. In fact, his need was so urgent that he had no choice but to leave before he did something to embarrass them both in a public restaurant.

"What about the tart?"

"All I'm interested in tasting is you. Don't ask me to wait, baby."

He watched embarrassment wash over her face. She was still so inexperienced, unused to his male hunger. There was nothing refined about it. It was raw, it was unrelenting and it was blatantly sexual. It was something he had no control over. Oh, he could control whether he acted on that need but he could not alter the potency or the urgency of that desire.

He, too, was often surprised by the ruthlessness of it. He had never wanted anyone or anything more. And that was saying something because he had a warrior's heart. At first, it disturbed him because he didn't understand himself. As he came to accept his feelings for her, he began to comprehend the depth of his passion. He longed for her to return an emotion that he couldn't yet name. Nevertheless, he wanted her to fall in love with him.

Love was not something you asked for, it was a priceless gift that had no value unless given freely. Patience had never been his long suit. It was something that he had to work at. Somehow he knew that Taylor's love was worth waiting for, even if it took years to acquire.

Dropping a large bill on the table and with Taylor's hand clasped in his, he ushered her out of the restaurant. He didn't speak until they were alone in his four bedroom condo overlooking Lake Michigan.

"Oh, Donald," she said moving around his huge burgundy and navy living room. "It's beautiful. Did you have it professionally done?"

"Yes." He had settled for large, traditional pieces from the burgundy three-piece leather sofa to the large navy leather armchairs with ottomans. One entire wall was floor-to-ceiling windows with a spectacular view of the lake. The hardwood floor was covered with a huge Aubusson navy rug embroidered with a burgundy and cream floral border trim.

In the dining room was a large mahogany table, with highbacked chairs cushioned in burgundy and navy print, that was positioned in the center of an identical Aubusson rug.

"My sister oversaw the project under my mother's direction. They didn't trust me to decide on more than the colors I liked and the size of the pieces. They were not about to leave it all to a decorator. What do you think?"

Although it lacked the warmth of green plants and uniquely feminine touches, his family photographs gave it a homey feel. The oils on the wall were spectacular. He explained that they were done by a local black artist.

"I like it."

He laughed. "Didn't expect to, did ya?"

She giggled, "I'll take the fifth on that one."

"Come see the rest."

The den was done in shades of blue, clearly a home office with a large desk, computer and wall-to-wall bookshelves. Next door was the recreational room with a huge television screen, and the latest in stereo and video equipment. A pool table dominated one corner of the room, while huge loungers were positioned in front of the television.

Donald had placed her luggage on the rack in his bedroom at the foot of his huge custom-made bed. She focused on the navy velvet comforter and large, pristine-white tailored pillowcases bordered in navy. The room looked like him, from the burgundy carpet underfoot to the bold African art on the walls.

In the living room, she asked as she sat on one of the sofas and crossed long shapely legs "Do you have live-in help?" The place was spotless and smelled of lemon cleaner.

"Live in, no. But I do have a housekeeper, a maid and a personal secretary."

"Your view of the lake is wonderful."

"Care for something to drink? Juice, soda, wine?" he offered unaware that he stroked her with his gaze. What he wanted was not in a bottle.

"No, thanks." She patted the cushion beside her. "Join me."

Donald didn't need another invitation. "How did Scott handle your trip?"

"A little better than last time. I think he's getting used to the idea of us seeing each other," she said, drinking in the sight of him.

"Seeing each other. Is that how you think of us?"

"You prefer another term?"

"Yes, I do," he sighed, toying with her fingers before he looked directly into her eyes. "I know we've only known each other a few short weeks. We've been lovers for even less than that. I've never known a woman quite like you, Taylor. You're not out to impress me by pretending to be what you think I want. I like that about you. You're sincere and you're direct. I've always known, even from the first, where I stand with you. Believe me, it hasn't always been easy to take." Caressing her cheek, he said, "The fact that you gave me a chance to get to know you, when you didn't agree with me, has come to mean a great deal to me."

"Donald . . ."

"No, let me finish. I want to know you well, Taylor. I want you to know me." He stared down into her lovely eyes.

"I don't know what to say," she murmured.

"Say you'll give us a chance. Say you want a relationship with me as much as I want one with you." He had waited a long time to find someone he could care about. He suspected that Taylor was that woman. Now all he had to do was move a mountain as he struggled to get her to let go of the circumstances in which they met and see the man he was.

Taylor couldn't help wondering if he was asking for her reassurance that she was just as emotionally involved with him as he was with her?

"I've been hurt before. I don't want to be hurt again."

"It will be different this time. You won't be in this alone, Taylor. We'll be in this together. Trust me not to hurt you. Can you do that?"

The kiss she placed on his generous mouth was warm and giving. His response was utterly male and immediate.

Donald eased back against the cushions until her softness was pillowed on his chest, his thighs spread wide so that her hips rested against his. "Sweetness . . ." he groaned heavily as he licked her lips over and over again before he parted them to fully receive the thrust of his tongue. He lifted her until her mound nestled against his rock hard manhood. There was no way he could fail to feel her tremors.

"I need you. Make love with me, Taylor."

She moaned from his possessiveness as his tongue caressed hers. She trembled with desire, unwittingly moving along his aroused length, craving the steely hard feel of him.

"Taylor?"

She was shaking so badly she barely could handle a thought let alone answer a question.

"Yes," she whispered.

Donald smiled then. There were still so many questions between them that had no answers. Yet, one thing was clear and they both understood was that they cared for each other. For now it had to be enough because it was all that they had.

"Oh, baby." He quickly unbuttoned her suit jacket and the blouse beneath. He didn't stop until he had pushed both down her arms and unsnapped her bra. He couldn't seem to breathe until his hands were filled with her lush breasts.

"Do you want me?"

"Yes . . ." she moaned in anticipation. She knew the incomparable pleasure he was so capable of giving her. She could hardly wait to once again experience his strong male body, loving her beyond reason. She accepted the risks involved, for she could not turn back now. She was in this for the duration.

# Sixteen

Donald shook from need. He hadn't been thinking at all when they had made love at her place. All he had done was feel, lost himself in her sweet magic.

"Not here." He sat up, bringing her with him. They walked hand and hand into his bedroom. He closed the door behind them. "Taylor," he whispered before brushing her soft mouth over and over again with his.

But he didn't deepen the kiss as she longed for him to do. She was grateful for his support. She was suddenly so nervous, afraid she would not be able to please him. She felt as unsure of herself as she had that first time they had made love and she had no idea why.

His hands weren't steady as he undressed her. Taylor's were no better. Her breathing was quick and uneven as she undressed him. They didn't stop until they were both nude, nothing between them but their hot passion for one another.

Taylor's caressing fingertips worried the tiny flat pebbles of his nipples, then smoothed over the broad lines of his muscular chest. She dropped her head until she could lave him the way he had tantalized her. His response was powerful, his chest heaved from his sexual excitement and his sex flexed heavily against her.

"No more," he whispered, thrusting his tongue into her mouth as he angled her mouth to fully receive the deep thrust he craved. She was sweet . . . so sweet. He couldn't wait a moment longer, he cupped her sex, cradling her sweetness. Using the tips of his fingers, he caressed the damp cottony soft curls before he slid between the fleshy folds to luxuriate in the dewy moisture. He felt her trembling as he fingered the tiny feminine bud at the top of her mound. He lingered until she cried out and her unsteady legs gave out and he had to support her weight.

"Now . . . honey, now. I need you now." Her sexy sweet cries were his undoing. With her back against the door, Donald bent his knees, guiding himself as carefully as he could manage, slowly penetrating her. He didn't stop until he filled her to the hilt.

Taylor wondered how much longer it would be before her legs completely gave out on her. Her eyes were closed—trying to catch her breath while she relished the exquisite pressure of his body. Her feminine muscles stroked along his pulsating length.

Donald moaned at her pleasure for it shattered his control. "Put your arms around my neck, baby," he said, an instant before he lifted her until, although she rested against the door, it was his strong arms and legs that supported her. As he moved, increasing his thrusts, her cries grew louder and her inner muscles fluttered like the caresses of a thousand tiny butterflies. One powerful thrust after another and her climax came quickly just before his own. He shuddered in her arms, flooding her with his masculine offering.

They breathlessly clung to each other. When Donald's legs began to quiver he slowly let Taylor's slide down. Although she stood on her own two feet, her legs were also trembling. Donald held her close.

"Come on, sweetness. I think we both could use the whirlpool."

While they rested in the swirling hot water, Taylor with her back against his chest, her hips nestled between his thighs, he asked, "Are you all right?" His mouth brushed her temple.

"Mmm," she crooned.

"I can hardly believe I finally have you all to myself."

"I'm not the one with the crazy schedule. Don't you ever get tired of the travel?"

"Not until recently," he admitted. "Unfortunately there are times when I have no choice but to go."

"You love the work, don't you?" she asked.

He smiled, "I enjoy being able to give small businesses a helping hand, especially when there are few banks out there willing to take a risk with minorities."

"Have you ever been wrong?"

He chuckled, "Oh, yeah. I've been taken but it happens very rarely. Very few people are looking for a handout. Most of them are in desperate need of a helping hand."

"Oh, Donald," she said, turning in order to caress his cheek. "I like what you do. You are a very special man."

He swallowed with difficulty, her praise meant the world to him. He caught her hand and kissed it. "Trouble is I have very little time to call my own."

"Have you ever been in love?"

"Where did that come from?"

"Just curious," she shrugged, wanting to know but uncertain if he would answer.

"At the time, I thought so. But I was only seventeen. It was with my high school sweetheart. It wasn't until I was in college that I realized it was a bad case of lust."

"So you were the one to break it off with her?"

"No. She ended it because I wouldn't quit college and marry her. I wanted to wait until I could take care of us. I couldn't afford a car, let alone a wife."

"You were so young."

"I've wondered for a long time if I'd lost my chance for an honest, open relationship."

"Why would you think that? You were only a kid."

He rose from the tub and reached for a bathsheet to wrap around his waist. "Don't want you to turn into a prune," he said when he reached down and helped her up. He quickly wrapped her in a bathsheet.

"Why did you think that?"

He shrugged. "The women I've met from college on seem to want something from me. They don't really want me but something from me. Probably wouldn't matter except I can always tell the difference."

"How? How can you tell? Surely, everyone of them was not sincere."

"I'm lucky. I have a down to earth mother and sister. Oh, don't get me wrong, for a time I enjoyed the seduction game. Somewhere around twenty-eight I started taking a hard look at what my folks shared and what my brother and sister have in their marriages. I realized I didn't have a prayer at the rate I was going."

Suddenly, Taylor realized they had a lot in common. Difficulty in trusting was a problem they shared. "It's hard to believe . . ." Taylor forgot what she was about to say when Donald pressed his lips to her throat.

"What?" he whispered licking the silky flesh of her throat, lingering on the scented hollow.

Taylor moved her hand to caress his muscular chest. "What?"

"You were saying?" he teased, his eyes danced with mischief.

"I have no idea," she giggled. She'd completely lost her train of thought.

Following her into the bedroom, he watched as she presented her back to him and handed him a bottle of scented body lotion. "Please?"

Accepting the bottle, he sat beside her on the bed. He smoothed lotion down her back. He moved to her feet, stroking her heels and soft soles then moved toward her calves to the long expanse of her creamy brown thighs.

"You are so beautiful." His hands were replaced by his mouth and he kissed his way down her back, the towel that had once covered her bottom was sliding lower and lower.

"Donald . . ." she managed to say, breathlessly.

He paused to kiss the nape of her neck. "Sweetness . . ." he said as he laved the smooth expanse of her back. Slowly, he caressed her spine and cupped then squeezed her sweetly dimpled bottom before he moved down to part her thighs.

"Taylor . . ." he whispered huskily as he kissed, then licked, her sweet lips.

Embers of desire seem to burn her skin as she waited with wicked anticipation as he rolled her over and began the sensual assault on her senses all over again down the front of her body, starting at the base of her throat. He did not leave a single inch of her soft caramel skin untouched, from her full breasts to her flat stomach and the thick ebony curls between her thighs.

"Look at me." When her heavy lids lifted, her dreamy brown eyes locked with his rich ebony eyes. He saw a passion that she couldn't deny, no matter how reluctant she was to admit it. His dark hands stroked over her legs, caressing the outer curves before moving to the baby softness of her inner thighs.

"Baby, let me taste your sweetness. If you don't enjoy it, I promise I'll stop. And I won't ask again." His eyes never left hers.

Taylor bit her lip, but she nodded. She wanted to please him, give him pleasure more than anything else in the world.

Donald groaned, moving to her soft lips, placing one kiss after another until she opened for him. He held her tight, loving the feel of her velvety soft tongue against his. He slowly moved down her soft frame, leaving sweet lingering kisses behind. Taylor was trembling from head to toe when he smoothed his hands over her thighs lifting them until they rested over his shoulders.

He pressed kiss after kiss against her soft inner thighs, moving closer and closer to her softness. When he kissed the thick curls shielding her sex, she gasped. His caressing fingers soothed her before he gently smoothed over her feminine folds then he parted her to expose her dewy softness to his lips and gradually to the hot wash of his tongue.

Taylor moaned his name as wave upon wave of pleasure rushed over her. It was like nothing she had ever experienced yet offered the most exquisite pleasure. Her climax was quick and powerful. She recovered her breath in his arms as he soothed her, comforted her.

When she was quiet, he kissed her tenderly. "Are you all right?"

"Mmm . . ." she murmured tenderly, caressing the lines of his dark face.

She felt the urgency of his own passion. She automatically offered herself to him, closing her arms and legs around him as he sank deep inside of her. Neither one of them got much sleep that night as they loved each other through the night.

Taylor woke to Donald's warm kiss. "You're dressed," she said, her arms going around his neck. She rubbed her cheek against his hair-roughened chin. He felt so delightfully male.

"Come on, get up. Run with me." As usual he had a piece of fruit in his hand. Taylor was amazed at the amount of fresh fruits and vegetables the man consumed on a daily basis.

"Run?" she said in disbelief, taking a small bite of the apple he offered her.

"As in along the jogging path in the park," he teased, kissing her soft lips.

"Are you serious?"

"Yeah. Come on. We'll start out slow."

"How far?"

"Couple of miles," he hedged with a grin.

"I'll never make it."

"Sure you will. We'll start out really slow. Coming?" he asked with a playful glint in his eyes.

"Yeah," she said, pushing out her chin. "Give me five minutes to put some water on myself."

"You don't shower before you sweat. You shower after." He laughed at the look of disbelief she sent him, while enjoying the view as she rose.

"Put the coffee on. I have a feeling I am going to need it."

She showered and dressed in jeans, a turtleneck and one of her brother's oversized sweatshirts. She was glad she had packed her athletic shoes.

"Where'd you get that?" he asked, eyeing the University of Detroit shirt, handing her a mug of steaming hot brew.

"It's Scott's," she said, taking a fortifying sip.

He didn't like the idea of her wearing any man's clothes other than his own. He walked over to the bureau and pulled out an equally thick sweatshirt with the Chicago Bull's logo on the front.

"Here."

"You want me to change?"

More concerned about her lack of make-up than what she wore, she shrugged. Other than the quick comb she'd run through her thick curls and the coated band she'd used to hold it out of her face and the trace of lipstick she'd used, she didn't feel attractive. No—that wasn't exactly true. She may not look beautiful, but she felt that way. She had never felt so well loved.

"Yeah," he said, giving her a hard, possessive kiss

Taylor wanted to laugh, but she threw her arms around his neck and gave as good as she got.

"Keep that up and we won't make it to the front door," he said, forcing his mouth away from hers.

"Doesn't sound so bad."

He shook his head, his hands going to the hem of her sweatshirt. "Let's get going, girl. The morning is passing." He normally was up and out at the crack of dawn. This morning he'd been sidetracked as he lay holding her, enjoying her softness, refusing to even consider leaving her.

Taylor was limping on the way back, wondering how he did this day after day. But then his body was finely toned. "I should have stayed in bed."

"Come on, sweet stuff. Let me carry you."

"No way. I plan to return as I left—under my own steam."

He wasn't even winded but Taylor knew his workouts were much more strenuous than the miles he'd shared with her. She comforted herself with the realization that he had asked for her company. Perhaps he enjoyed her companionship as much as she enjoyed his. As long as they avoided certain topics, they got along fine.

"You didn't hurt yourself, did you?" He placed his arm around her waist. They had stopped on the way back to have breakfast and for Taylor to catch her breath.

"No, just wore myself out."

They walked back, holding hands, laughing and teasing each other. Donald left for practice while Taylor relaxed with a book while soaking her feet in hot sudsy water.

* * *

Taylor dressed carefully for their night on the town. He was taking her to a play, then a late night supper. She had selected the short, red strapless dress that clung in all the right places. A long-sleeved, high-neck, red lace jacket was buttoned to her throat and worn over the dress. The outfit drew the eyes to the graceful lines of her body. She was able to wear a high heel without a single concern about her height. Pearl drop earrings and a gold ankle bracelet were her only jewelry. Her hair was off her neck in a French roll and soft curls framed her face.

Donald was dressed in a black, three-piece suit, teamed with pale gray shirt and gray and black striped tie. He looked as if he'd just stepped out of the pages of G.Q.

She felt his lips on the side of her neck. "You look good, girl. Let's stay home."

She laughed, shaking her head. "Not a chance." She turned in his arms, her arms going around his waist. "Thank you. You look good yourself, handsome." She brushed her lips with his, careful not to leave red lipstick traces. "Would you really rather stay in tonight, rest? You really don't have to entertain me."

Donald could think of nothing he wanted more than to spend the evening alone with this lovely woman. Their time together was going much too quickly.

No, he wouldn't spoil the evening by thinking about her leaving.

He said, "Hey, I'm not so old, I can't show my lady my city." He placed a warm velvet cape around her shoulders, savoring their closeness for a few moments. "Ready?"

"Yes," she nodded, allowing herself to rest against him. He was so wonderfully big but more important, she truly enjoyed his company. If only their time wasn't always so limited. After this weekend how long would it be before they saw each other again? Two weeks? Three? More?

His voice was rough with emotion when he said, "Let's go."

He took her to the Briar Street Theater to see the play *Having Our Say.*

"I can't remember when I enjoyed anything more. Those Delany sisters were a marvel. Imagine living a hundred years!"

"Have you read their story?" Donald asked as he helped her into the car. He was glad he had only been recognized and not stopped for his autograph. He didn't want anything to take away from this special night with Taylor.

"No. Have you?"

"Yes, it was a good read. I'll lend you my copy; you'll enjoy it."

She smiled at him. "Thanks. Did you hear that one of the sisters passed?"

"Yes, Bessie in '96 at the age of 104. I understand her sister still lives in New York."

That was one of the things she enjoyed most about him: that he was well-read despite his busy schedule. He often relaxed with a book.

Dinner was supposed to be romantic, in a candlelit restaurant overlooking the city's bright lights far below. A flashbulb going off in their faces as they quietly talked, holding hands, was only the first in a series of intrusions. The annoying photographer was quickly ushered out by the management. By the time their meal had arrived, they had been interrupted a minimum of seven to eight times either for Donald's autograph or for his comment on the team's chance of winning another championship. The photographer had evidently let the entire restaurant know he was present.

"I'm sorry," he said, tightly.

"It's not your doing," she shrugged. Taylor only picked at the lobster and pasta in cream sauce on her plate, wondering how he could stand it. His privacy was constantly being invaded. They had said less than half-a-dozen words to each other since they arrived at the restaurant.

He did not try to hide his frustration with the way their evening had turned out. There wasn't a thing that the restaurant had to offer that could compare to being alone with Taylor. She made him smile. She brought a special kind of joy into his world and eased the emptiness.

He could be ruthless, a natural competitor. He had accomplished all the career goals he had set for himself. What he hadn't done was even come close to completing his personal goals. He wanted the same kind of closeness and love his parents had shared over the years. He wanted what his sister and Jess had, as well as Carl and Margie. He wanted that for himself. What did Taylor want? A lifelong commitment? Or a few weeks of being highly entertained by traveling the country at his side?

"You're not eating," she whispered.

"I have other things on my mind. This evening has not turned out the way I'd planned. We haven't been able to say more than three words to each other without being interrupted. How disappointed would you be if we left now?" He lifted an inquiring brow. He was more than ready to put an end to their so called night on the town. He wanted nothing more than to spend what was left of the evening alone with Taylor.

She didn't hesitate to nod her agreement. Donald had had the bill taken care of and had had the car brought around before she could collect her things.

"How can you put up with it?" she asked, once they were under way.

"You get used to it. Most of the time it really doesn't

bother me." He sighed, glancing at her momentarily before returning his attention to the road. "Tonight was different. This was supposed to be a special night for you."

"I think it would drive me crazy. People can be so rude."

"Yeah. Most of the time it's not a intrusion."

"Then you have no regrets?"

He shrugged. "I didn't say that. I hate the demands success places on my time. But I have plenty of perks. I've been able to live well and I've been able to help my family and others."

They had barely closed the front door when Donald cupped her shoulder, then said, "I'm sorry our evening was spoiled."

Taylor looked up into his dark eyes. "This is so silly. I know who you are, I've seen you play. All I have to do is look around in order to see the proof of your success. Tonight kinda of shoved the truth in my face. I suppose, I just don't think of you as famous, not since we . . ." her voice trailed away.

"Taylor, I don't know what you want me to say. It was bound to happen sooner or later. This is my town. I am well-known here."

"You're well-known across the entire country. No, the world," she paused before going on to say, "Your life is not your own."

He shook his head before saying; "You're wrong. It just takes some getting used to." He couldn't help wondering if she had found another reason to push him away. "Come here." When she didn't hesitate to take a step into his arms, he was able to let out a breath he wasn't even aware of holding. "Finally . . ." he sighed wearily.

Taylor relaxed against him, slowly accepting that this

was what she had wanted all evening, to be alone with him. "Hold me. Make love to me, please."

Donald trembled, his entire body suddenly taut with sexual excitement. As Donald's lips covered hers, he wondered if he would ever get his fill of this lovely woman. In just a few short weeks she had turned his life upside down. He remember how empty his world had been without her. He didn't want to go back to that.

Their kisses were slow and intense. Donald was the first to pull away. His heart pounding with excitement. The prospect of ending the evening with her within the shared intimacy of his home thrilled him to the core. Yet, there was so much left unsaid between them. Besides, he had only so much control.

When it came to Taylor, he could forget everything, even his resolve not to jeopardize his ability to play well and hard the next afternoon. It meant that he had to postpone his release until after the game.

He caressed her cheek. "Would you like something to drink? Wine? Coffee?"

"What is it? Don't you want to . . . make love?" Her body stiffen with tension.

Donald sighed. "I really don't want to go into the bedroom right now." He had loosened his tie and tossed his jacket and it over a chair. He sank down on the leather sofa kicking off his shoes. He dropped his head back against the cushions and propped his feet up on the coffee table. "Join me."

Taylor shivered, confused and hurt by his standoffishness. Something was wrong. What was it? What happened to cause such a drastic change in him? Suddenly, she was feeling decidedly unsure of herself and his behavior didn't ease her worry.

If she was a bold woman she would have demanded an explanation. That was not her style. It hurt to think he had tired of her. She told herself she was overreacting . . . making much to do about nothing. She'd taken a sizable risk when she decided to come to him. There was no way for her not to be vulnerable to him. Right now, the decision to come to him didn't seem like a wise one.

Instead of moving toward him, she firmly shook her head "I don't think so. Excuse me."

# Seventeen

Donald swore, realizing that he had hurt her feelings which was the last thing he had intended. "Sweetheart, wait."

She'd hurried toward the bedroom they'd shared the night before. He caught her before she could reach it.

"Taylor . . ."

Slowly, she turned to face him, angry with herself for wearing her feelings on her sleeve for him to knock loose. Although her instincts told her to pack her things and go home, get as far away from this situation and this man as she possibly could, she stood her ground, trying to ignore the tears burning the back of her lids.

"Yes?"

"You don't understand."

"And you are not interested in explaining," she surmised.

"Hell! I'm doing this badly. This has nothing to do with not wanting you. Girl, you had me so hot that all I could think about was having you nude beneath me as soon as possible."

"I don't remember offering an objection," she said, unaware of the way she twisted her hands nervously.

Why was she putting herself through this? She'd known from the first that his attention span when it came to women was, no doubt, limited. She certainly hadn't gone into this with hopes of a rose colored future. She hadn't expected it to last longer than their first weekend. Now here she was, a few weeks later, still involved with him and caring more for him than she had ever believed possible. She had no one to blame but herself because she had gone into it with her eyes wide open. Her only saving grace was that she had not done the unpardonable. She had not fallen in love with the man.

By remaining involved with him, she had set herself up for a hurtful mistake. She had begun to expect too much from him. If he was tired of her, he was doing a lousy job of telling her. Although she could not help wondering what could have made him change his mind so unexpectedly. Just last night, he had welcomed her with open, hungry arms.

"I lost my head, sweetness," he said, gently stroking the curve of her cheek.

"Like I said, I don't re . . ." she stopped abruptly, forcing herself to meet his eyes. She had made a painful error in asking for his lovemaking.

"You're not the problem. I am." He cupped her shoulders, ignoring her attempts to move away. "Don't. Let me hold you."

To her horror, she realized she did not have the will to protest. She wanted to be in his arms as much as he suddenly seemed to want her. She had no choice but to accept the truth. She had no pride as far as he was concerned. As angry and upset as she was with him she found her cheek against his chest, her face buried in his throat. When it came right down to it, where he was concerned, she was downright pitiful.

"Donald, just tell me what's happening here."

"Okay, but let's sit down so we can talk more comfortably." Once they were seated side by side on the sofa, his arm around her shoulders, he said, "My game was really off at practice today. Lately, I can't seem to concentrate on anything but you. I won't go out on that court tomorrow afternoon and make a fool of myself."

"What does that have to do with us? I asked you to make love to me and you pushed it aside as if it didn't matter."

"There's nothing I want more than to make love to you, sweetness." He placed a warm kiss on her soft lips, but he made no effort to deepen the exchange. "I want to take you again and again as I did last night," his voice huskier than normal. "Sweetheart, my control around you is just plain lousy. I have to work tomorrow. I can't be up all night making love to you. I can't do that if I come inside of your sweet heat."

Taylor blinked in shock. "Really?

"Really. I have to be at my best on the court, so . . ."

"So we don't make love." She looked up into the darkness of his eyes. "Why didn't you tell me? I thought that you didn't want to be with me."

"How could you possibly believe that after what we shared last night?"

"I don't know. I'm sorry. I suppose I overreacted." She pressed her lips tenderly against his. "Rejection hurts."

"I never rejected you. How could I?" He kissed her throat, lingered at the sensitive base. "You know how to press all my buttons," he whispered throatily.

She trembled in his arms, unable to sort out her jumbled emotions. All she knew was that she cared about him and didn't want to lose him. She would no doubt live to regret it, but she didn't even want to think of a time when he was not a part of her world.

"You are staying until Monday, aren't you, baby?"

A few minutes ago Taylor didn't think she would ever feel like smiling again. Now her laughter flowed freely.

"Well?" he persisted.

"Yes."

His mouth was red-hot with need as he ravished her mouth. "Thank you. We wouldn't have this problem if you lived here in Chicago."

"We wouldn't have this problem if you lived in Detroit."

They both laughed holding each other close. For now they were together. For now it had to be enough.

"Let's make popcorn and curl up and watch videos," he suggested, knowing full well that that was the very last thing he wanted to do. But he was badly in need of a diversion.


"Denzel was the best choice." They shared a double lounger in the recreational room in front of a wide screen television.

"Yeah, sure. You just can't see past the man's good looks like all the other sisters in America."

"The man is fine!" she said with emphasis, determined to ignore the way her body automatically responded to his closeness. Her head had been on his shoulder as she leaned back against him.

"If you say so." His gaze lingered on her pretty mouth. She was dressed in his blue silk pajama top which stopped at her knees leaving a good portion of her long shapely legs bare while he wore the pajama bottoms. "More apple juice?" The huge bowl of buttered popcorn was almost gone and only a quarter of the pitcher of juice remained.

"Not for me. I don't want to be up all night," she said, covering a yawn. "Ready to turn in?"

"Go on. I won't be long."

She touched her mouth against his before she left.

He sat staring out at the lake, marveling at the complexity of his emotions. He had forgotten everything, even what was best for him under the strain of wanting her so badly. He had come close to hurting her because of his embarrassing lack of control. He had been functioning on hormones instead of brain power. For the first time, she had shown initiative in their lovemaking; as a result, he had completely lost his head for a while there. He had been concentrating on nothing more than that overwhelming hunger.

He'd been lucky. She had accepted his explanation. For a few minutes there he had been afraid that he had lost her, something that had nearly sent him into a panic. They had just really found each other, just become lovers. He was not about to do anything to jeopardize what they had. It was too special, too rare. He worked hard to get past her resentment and he was not fooling himself into thinking it was in the past. Even though they were lovers, she was devoted and loyal to her family. Both qualities, he adored in her. He wanted those feelings directed his way. He told himself he needed to be patient. It would come in time. She was more than worth the wait.

She was asleep when he quietly entered the bedroom. His disappointment was all over his face as he stood studying her beauty. He enjoyed looking at her, especially enjoyed seeing her in his bed.

The bed was certainly large enough for them to sleep independent of each other. He did not even entertain the thought. No way was he going to deprive himself of the pleasure of holding her all night long. When he slid in beside her, she didn't wake but curved her body to fit against his. Her breath was warm against his throat. He sighed heavily. Eventually, he slept, a smile on his lips.

Taylor woke to Donald's sweet kiss on her throat. "Mmm, I could get used to this," she whispered. "No running, please."

He chuckled. "Did you sleep well?"

"Wonderful," she stretched.

"So that was you snoring," he teased. Her outraged expression had him roaring with laughter. "Come on. I'm hungry. Let's make breakfast together."

"One of us can't cook," she reminded him with a grin.

"Then one of us should get moving. You want to shower first?"

Taylor and Donald enjoyed a leisurely meal of pancakes, eggs and slices of turkey bacon; they shared the Sunday editions of the papers. Donald was scowling so at one section that she asked, "What is it?" She had been reading the book section of the New York *Times*.

He handed over the society section of the Chicago *Sun Times*. Taylor was shocked to find a photo of the two of them seated at dinner last night. Her head was thrown back as she laughed at something he said. His hand covering hers where it rested on the table. They clearly had eyes only for each other. The caption beneath the piece said, 'Williams evidently has a new lady love. Who is she?"

When her eyes met his, he said, "Sorry, sweetheart. I know you're not used to being exposed to the media. Unfortunately when you're with me it's unavoidable."

"There is no need for you to apologize. You didn't take the picture. How have you managed to take it in stride? I was ready to scream at those people last night who kept interrupting us."

"Believe me, so was I. But, seriously, it takes years of practice. Gradually, I've actually gotten used to it. I've gotten to the point where I'm grateful when they don't say anything too damning. It's part of the territory."

Taylor viewed it as a terrible invasion of privacy but decided to keep the thought to herself. Changing the topic, she asked, "How do you feel? Are you nervous about the game?"

He laughed. "I'm ready. Actually, I'm looking forward to coming up against Patrick Ewing. This is our last game of the season. We're going to kick some butt this afternoon. The Knicks are going home hurting." As a fierce competitor he was clearly in his element.

Taylor giggled, giving him a soft kiss. "I love to watch you play." She also hated it because she couldn't help worry about him on the court. They played to win, not concerned with their own physical well being.

When they left for the United Center, where the games were held, Taylor was extremely quiet, lost in thought. Donald appreciated the quiet, using it to mentally prep for the game, refusing to let unwelcome thoughts of their inevitable separation intrude.

They ran into several of his teammates and their wives and sweethearts. Donald made the introductions before he gave her a quick kiss and left her with Joy Ransom, wife of his long time friend and team forward Eddie Ransom.

The ladies had barely walked out of earshot when one of the security guards in front of the team's locker room called his name.

"One of your lady friends left this for you." He smirked as he handed over the pink, sealed envelope.

"Who?"

The other man shrugged. "I can't keep up with you guys."

"Thanks, John," Donald said absently.

"Keep your mind on the game, man. We need this win," the guard said, whistling as he walked away.

"Hey, I like your lady, man," Eddie said slapping him on the back. "She seems like good people." At six-eleven the light-brown-skinned man was one of the few who made Donald seem short. His ready smile and easy manner were only a few of the things Donald liked about him. His quiet strength and fierce determination was something they shared.

Donald kept his voice low when he said, "Yeah, she is. She's not only gorgeous but she's also down-to-earth."

"She the one from the big 'D'?" he asked quietly, so they wouldn't be overheard.

"Yeah. She seems to care about me, not the dollar signs."

"Your Mama didn't raise no fool. Hang on to that one, my man."

"I plan to."

"Hey, you serious?"

"It happened to you, didn't it?"

"Sure, but there is only one Joy."

"All I need is one. I been telling you that for some time.

"So you have. "What's it say?" Eddie asked curiously indicating the envelope.

His name was typed on the outside. Donald quickly broke the seal. Inside was a note asking if he was available tonight and a telephone number.

"Well?" Eddie asked.

Donald crumpled the note. "I have no idea who she is. I don't have time for this nonsense."

"Goes with the territory, my man."

"Yeah. Come on. Let's get a move on. We've got butt to kick."

Family and friends enjoyed the game from the owner's box. No expense had been spared. It was clearly a celebration of the end of a very successful season.

"I don't have to ask if you enjoyed yourself," Joy laughed, remembering how uneasy she felt the first time she watched her man play with the other wives. It was unnerving, not knowing anyone. Joy hadn't even known the rules of the game.

"I don't think I've screamed so loudly in my entire life. It was a great game," Taylor said with a smile. Everyone had been very friendly. She was Donald's friend and that was all that seemed to matter.

Watching him here on his home court was so exciting. She found herself reacting emotionally when he scored or when he was bumped or fell. She was only able to relax when he rested on the bench or during time-outs and half-time. The Bulls beat the Knicks and Donald had a sensational game.

"The guys will be along in a while. I remember how excited I was at my first game. Eddie and I were newlyweds."

"You two are still newlyweds," one of the other wives teased, joining them.

Joy blushed. "It will be a year next month."

"When it's seven years, then we can talk," another wife laughed, joining them.

An elaborate buffet was being set up while uniformed waiters were circulating drinks and refreshments among the growing crowd. It wasn't long before the men joined them.

"Miss me?" Donald said from behind her, close to her ear.

Taylor had no idea that her face lit up at the sight of him. He was sporting a bandage over his right eye. "Yes. You were wonderful on the court. Are you all right?" Her hand automatically going up to his temple.

"I'm fine. It's just a cut. Having fun?"

She nodded. "Are you sure you're okay? You came down really hard a few times."

"His head is too hard to break," one of his teammates added, joining them. "I want an introduction."

Donald laughed heartily before making the introductions. He, like everyone else, was holding a glass of champagne. Taylor couldn't take her eyes off him. It was like she finally realized the scope of his world was phenomenal.

"Come on, I want you to meet all the guys."

When he said all he meant all including the players, the coaches and the owner, everyone connected with the team. It was not long before Taylor lost track of all the names. Donald made sure her plate was full and that she was enjoying herself. Nevertheless, she was not disappointed when he asked if she were ready to go.

She looked up at him, her eyes lingering on his generous mouth. "Yes."

He forgot what he had been about to say. "Don't look at me like that, sweetness. I'm liable to embarrass us both." All he could think about was how badly he wanted to be alone with her. He wanted to celebrate the game with her in a very private way.

She blushed, then whispered, "Should I apologize for wanting to be alone with you?"

"Never," he said taking her hand and starting to weave their way to the door. He didn't talk until he had her in the car and on their way to his place. "Did you have a good time?"

"Wonderful. You have some great friends."

"Yeah," he brooded, as he thought of the envelope in his pocket. What if the witch who had stalked him a few years back was at it again. He would have to contact his lawyer. He was not about to put up with it again.

She called his name, but he seemed miles away. When she placed her hand on his thigh, his eyes met hers. "Is something wrong? You're not hurt, are you?"

He blinked in surprise. "I am fine. I didn't take on any more than a few new bruises. Why are you worrying?"

"You were frowning."

"Sorry," he smiled at her, momentarily stroking his hand over hers. He was not about to let anyone spoil the short time he had with Taylor. When she began to move her hand away from his leg, he held it in place.

Taylor didn't object. She was counting the hours before she would board the plane for home. Her eyes went wide when, while they were paused at a traffic light Donald moved her hand until she was stroking the length of his thickening shaft. Her eyes immediately went to his. She felt the heat of his gaze as she caressed him.

"Don't stop," he whispered throatily, his voice husky with desire. "I've been wanting to feel your hands on me since I joined you in the box. I need you, sweetness."

When the light changed and a horn blasted from behind them, he had no choice but to remove her hand. He was not reckless enough to chance losing control behind the wheel. In fact, he didn't so much as kiss her until they were inside the condo with the door locked. He wanted her too badly. He was shaking from the wanting and could not stop himself from holding her close against his long frame. His mouth moved hungrily over hers.

"Please . . ." she moaned, pressing herself even closer to him. Her soft full breasts provided a provocative caress against his chest, her hard little nipples enflaming his senses to the point of near madness.

"Now . . . I need you now." It wasn't a question, it was a statement of fact. He was functioning on pure male hunger.

They had only made it as far as the wide leather sofa in the living room. Taylor was left panting with desire as he paused only long enough to strip away his own clothes. Her hands went to the hem of her top but she was trembling so badly she could barely coordinate her efforts. She was only down to panties and bra when he said her name.

His hands replaced hers as he helped her undress. "Tell me you're mine," he whispered, kissing her.

"Yes . . . oh yes." Taylor offered no resistance because she had none.

When it came to Donald she had lost the ability to offer even a token protest. She wanted him too much . . . needed to be one with him.

There was no hesitation in their lovemaking. They came together, neither held anything back from the other. Taylor willingly accepted his weight, her softness open to only Donald's brand of lovemaking. He paused long enough to assure himself that she was ready for him. Her welcoming moist heat was answer enough. He stroked her intimately and deeply before his last tiny thread of control snapped. He nearly tore the condom in his haste to have her. His groan of pleasure was unmistakable as he slowly gave her what they both craved. She cried out causing him to stop.

Gritting his teeth, he practically growled, "Did I hurt you, baby?"

"No . . . Please, honey, don't stop. I need you so badly."

As her sweet heat welcomed him, he plunged to his full length. Only then did he hesitate, allowing her body time to adjust to his, while giving himself time to catch his breath. He held her close to his heart. This was what he had been hungering for. This was where he needed to be. No other woman even came close to giving him such sheer pleasure. Taylor . . . only she could make him feel so deeply, so strongly. She cradled him deep inside, her body perfectly suited to his.

Taylor could not tolerate the delay. She wanted him and she wanted him now. She rotated her hips, tightening her softness thus giving him a deeply erotic caress along his entire hard length. He shuddered in response, then gave her the unrelenting strokes they both longed for. The loving went on and on until they shared an exhilarating, mindless climax as one.

They collapsed in each other's arms. It was some time before either one of them recovered their breathing. Neither was interested in moving a single muscle. But Donald was forced to move first because he was afraid of crushing her. When he rose to his feet, she protested.

"Where are you going?"

"You're cold. I'll be right back." He returned in no time with a comforter and pillows.

She smiled as they cuddled together, her head on his shoulder. One sweet kiss led to another and another.

His stroking hand caressed her down her soft frame, whispering how much pleasure she had given him. He lingered over the soft outline of her mouth.

He said gruffly, "Talk to me. Tell me what's wrong?" He had heard her heavy sigh, felt her tremor.

Her full dark lashes fluttered up, then she looked away. "How could anything be wrong?" she hedged. She couldn't take her eyes away from the clock on the mantel.

"Tell me," he insisted.

"I'm going to miss you," was all she was willing to admit.

She was feeling so vulnerable when it came to what they shared. How could she put her faith in what they had? How could she believe it was enough when he faced temptation day after day as a matter of course?

Women made an art form of throwing themselves at professional black men, especially highly paid athletes. They were willing to do almost anything to gain their attention. There were no limits. None of the men were immune because they were all human.

Donald was a man, not a demigod. He had weaknesses. He spent so much time on the road. He was not only physically attractive, but he was extremely successful. On top of all that, they didn't even live in the same city. How long would it be before some tempting beauty turned his head? Was it realistically only a matter of time?

Taylor had touched on the very last thing Donald wanted to think about . . . their being apart yet again. And she was telling him only part of what he needed to hear. He longed to hear her say she cared about him. He wanted more from her than what they had. He wanted a commitment, but he knew the time was not right.

She had not totally moved past her resentment of him. Not once during the entire weekend had she mentioned her brother or his future now that his name had been entered in the draft. Unfortunately, it was still there between them. He cautioned himself not to push her, not to pressure her. What he wanted could so easily turn into an ultimatum. Something he didn't believe ever worked. She had to want him as much as he wanted her in order for them to make a go of their relationship.

"We still have several hours before I have to put you on that plane. Kiss me, Taylor. Give me your sweet mouth, girl."

She lifted her face to his, pleased to be able to satisfy him, while wishing for what could never be. Even though she knew that, in all likelihood, she was wrong for him, that she did not fit into his life anymore than he fit into hers, she opened her mouth for his forging tongue. She relished in the feel of him along the entire length of her body. The hard lines and angles of his masculine strength were more potent than any aphrodisiac . . . utterly irresistible.

His long fingered caresses were her undoing, she moaned his name, opening herself to him. Donald hesitated only long enough to protect her from unwanted pregnancy before he came inside of her. She was his woman, his heart. There could be no others. He would do whatever it took to hold her.

Taylor's breathing was quick and uneven when he rolled to the back of the sofa and eased her on top of him. "What?"

"Relax." His voice was as uneven as hers. He cupped her hips, guiding her movements. "That's it . . ." he crooned as she took more and more of him. He gasped her name when she accepted all of him. He fought his need in his effort to satisfy her first, thankful that he did not have long to wait for her release brought on his. His hoarse shout came as he tightened his muscular arms around her. She could barely breathe but she didn't complain as he convulsed in her arms. His hold on her did not ease until he collapsed, exhausted.

"You're wonderful," he murmured groggily, his caressing hand moving absently over her back.

She smiled, her face buried between his shoulder and neck, her lids too heavy to lift. In spite of their best efforts to stay awake, they both slept.

The telephone woke them near dawn. It was his pilot; the plane was ready. They were quiet on the drive to the airport. Taylor brooded over having to say good-bye yet again, while Donald worried that they were parting with no firm commitment between them. It seemed they had done little else than say good-bye during the few short weeks they'd known each other.

Even at this early hour the expressway was busy. When they reached the private hangar where his plane was waiting, Donald stopped her before she could take a single step away from the car or him. He had handed over her luggage to his pilot.

He said close to her ear, "I'm going to miss you, sweetness. When are you coming back?"

She blinked in surprise. "When are you coming to Detroit?"

"It depends on how the play-offs go. If we go all the way, I won't have any free time. And we are going all the way," he said confidently before burying his face against her neck. He whispered throatily, "Will you come to me, if I can't get away?"

"Yes," she pressed her lips against his cheek and then the fullness of his lips. They kissed each other thoroughly, oblivious to the waiting pilot.

"Take care," he said gruffly, shoving his hands into his pockets.

"You too. And good luck," she called, forcing herself to smile when she really wanted to cry. She hurried inside the plane before he could see her tears.

# Eighteen

"Mama, please don't cry," Taylor encouraged, feeling as if her own heart was breaking. "Yes, I promise. I'll talk to him again but I don't see what good it will do." She switched the telephone receiver from one ear to the other, nodding silently as she listened to her mother's pleas. "Yes . . . yes. I know, but you have to stop or you're going to make yourself sick. Okay. Kiss Daddy for me," she said slowly hanging up then.

Nothing was going smoothly. The entire week had been tough. Not one single night had she gotten a full night's sleep. She had gotten into an argument with a co-worker over nothing. Donald had not called even once. Oh, she knew he was involved in the play-offs. But the last time she looked, Chicago was still part of the Union and still had telephone access.

And to top it off, her brother had been going around acting like he did not have a concern in the world. Their parents were growing more upset by the minute as the NBA drafts approached. Scott wasn't listening to reason. Added to her troubling heap, she felt guilty because she was involved with Donald.

Why hadn't she told her parents about her relationship with him? She could continue telling herself that she did not really care what they might think. She knew it wasn't true. She cared, too much. She especially cared what her mother thought. They had always been so close, despite the distance separating them.

Unable to tolerate her own unhappy thoughts, Taylor grabbed a jacket, her purse and her car keys before hurrying out of the house. Traffic was not bad for early evening, but then again it was Sunday.

She pulled up to the two-story house where her brother seemed to spend more time than he did at home. Jenna was the attraction. Normally, Taylor didn't ever come by unless she was invited or called first. But tonight, she was too upset to worry about her brother's precious privacy. He had messed up her life, it was time to shake his up.

Scott answered the door before she could ring the bell more than twice. "Hey, Sis. Come on up. You okay?" he asked in concern.

"No. Give me a hug."

The two shared a warm hug, something they had not done of late.

"I missed you today," she said referring to his absence from Sunday dinner. Taylor had shared the meal with her elderly neighbor, having prepared more than she could possibly eat.

"Yeah. Me too. I was tired of arguing over this."

"It can't be helped and you know it," she flung over her shoulder before she stamped up the flight of stairs that led to the upper flat. "Hi, Jenna. I hope I am not intruding."

Jenna smiled, getting up from the small desk in the corner of the combined living and dining area where she had been working at the computer. She gave Taylor a quick hug. "No problem. You know you're always welcome. Can I get you something to eat? Drink?"

Taylor shook her head, shrugging out of her coat and tossing it to her brother. He'd apparently been camped out in front of the television, his chemistry text book face down on one of the sofa cushions.

"I just got off the telephone with your mother. I couldn't get her to stop crying." She glared up at him.

"Aw, Sis. Don't start with me."

"Mama isn't here to knock some sense in your head, so I've been elected." Her small chin lifted as she faced him toe to toe. "You're making a mistake."

"Oh, really? 'What a surprise." His voice was dripping with sarcasm.

"I love you. Mama and Daddy also happen to love you. So sue us for being concerned, you big knucklehead!"

He looked as if he were grinding his teeth when he said, "I'm a grown man. I can't let the three of you run my life. Face it, kiddo. Your baby brother is not a baby anymore."

"I understand that, but you're making a huge mistake."

"Okay, we disagree."

"Absolutely."

"Will you please stay out of my business?"

"The day you stay out of mine."

Scott knew Taylor didn't want to discuss her relationship with Donald Williams any more than he wanted to discuss his decision to enter the draft. Besides, in a few more weeks the draft would all be over. As far as he was concerned it was no longer an issue. Her involvement, on the other hand, was still an open subject. He didn't want to see her hurt. Guys like her pro-jock had women all over the country. As far as Scott was concerned, Donald was not to be trusted with his sister's tender feelings.

"I don't want to see you hurt by this guy."

"Really? Do you think I would like to see you penniless and uneducated?"

\* \* \*

Donald was furious when his knocks on Taylor's door went unanswered. It seemed as if this trip was fruitless effort. Damn! It was obvious that she wasn't home. Where the hell was she? Who was he kidding? He knew he should have called first. He had wanted to surprise her. Unfortunately, he was the one with an unpleasant surprise. What now?

A sound from the house next to Taylor's caused him to turn. Although it was after dark, Taylor's porch light had been left on.

"Get away from there, young man. Can't you see she ain't home," said the elderly woman peering out her side window.

"I didn't mean to disturb you. I'm Donald Williams, a friend of Taylor's." He was glad she had left the porch light burning and for once he hoped his face was recognizable.

"Oh, yes. Her young man. I'm Mrs. Burns. Taylor sure will be sorry she missed you," Mrs. Burns said. Taylor had mentioned his name several times. "She probably won't be long."

"Do you have any idea where she's gone?"

She shrugged. "Probably went to see her brother. They usually share a Sunday dinner, but not today. He didn't come by. She invited me over. That girl has a heart of gold."

Donald couldn't help grinning. "Thanks. I'll try there."

"But what if she isn't there?"

"Then I'll be back. Thanks, Mrs. Burns. It was a pleasure meeting you."

"Hope you find her."

"Me, too." He called, heading for his rental car. He was grateful that at first Scott had been quite open with him and they had exchanged addresses and phone numbers. It didn't worry him that Taylor wasn't expecting him. Spending time with her was his number one priority.

"Enough. Both of you sit down and stop yelling at each other." Jenna had had it with their silliness. When they were both seated at opposite ends of the sofa she insisted. "For the first time in my memory, you two didn't share Sunday dinner. How can you let anything come between family? You both are being mule-headed."

"I just want what is best for him," Taylor defended herself.

"And I want what is best for you," he added as the doorbell sounded. He and Jenna shared a look before she shook her head. He said, "Be right back."

"Expecting company?" Taylor asked.

"Not that I know of."

Taylor's heart accelerated at the sound of Donald's voice from below. Her hand automatically went to her hair which was pushed up in a braided ponytail. She didn't have a drop of make up on her face and she was wearing her oldest pair of pink sweats and her feet were in heavy pink cotton socks and sneakers. She didn't need to glance in the hall mirror to know she looked like a fright.

"Taylor?"

"I had no idea he was going to be in town. I certainly wouldn't have showed up here looking this bad if I expected him. How did he find me? Maybe I should go down before they come to blows?"

Jenna shook her head. "Give them a few minutes to talk. Come on in the kitchen with me. You can help me put on some coffee and get plates for the pie."

Taylor reluctantly followed, not wanting to know what they were saying . . . wanting not to care that he had finally found some time for her. He hadn't bothered to call in a week and it had been weeks since they'd last seen each other. She felt like yesterday's news.

Had she made a fool of herself over him? Had she made too much of his tenderness? It was possible that she had read all his signals wrong. He might be the kind of man who cared for a woman as long as she was readily available to him. The instant she was out of his sight, she was also out of his mind. She trembled at the possibility. What other explanation could there be for his gross neglect? The trouble was it did not change how she felt about him! She could not stop caring about him.

"We weren't expecting you," Scott said, at the door, his arms crossed over his chest.

The two men were at eye level, neither was forced to look up at the other. Donald did not flinch from Scott's unwelcoming stance.

"Taylor is here. That's reason enough for me. I suggest you get used to the idea because I'm not going anywhere until I've seen her."

Scott read the possessive gleam in the other man's eyes. He understood it well. He felt that same way about Jenna. He would not step aside and let any man take his place in Jenna's life, not brother or uncle or father or even ex-lover could get rid of him. Donald Williams was not Scott and he wasn't certain he could trust the other man with his beloved sister's love. He didn't have to be told that she was in love with the other man. He had seen it in her eyes, although she probably didn't realize it herself.

Scott said tightly, "I don't want to see her used or hurt."

They both knew what it was like to be a successful athlete. They both had been on the receiving end of numerous unwelcome advances from women. It was part of the territory. The problem was: did Scott believe that Donald could keep his head in spite of the temptations.

"Neither do I, Scott."

"You're serious about her?"

"Yeah. I'm in love with her. I plan on being around for quite some time. I suggest you get used to me." Donald surprised them both with his frankness. For the first time, he was able to put a name to his feelings for Taylor. It had taken weeks of isolation for him to sort out his emotions.

For three of the loneliest weeks, he hadn't come near her. In the last week he hadn't permitted himself even to so much as speak to her. It had been a true struggle to comprehend what had happened to him. It had been the most painful time of his life. He knew that Taylor was his and that was all there was to it. He didn't plan on giving her much choice.

"You better treat her well." Despite the fact that he was grateful for Donald's solid advice concerning the game, he was not about to back down. This was about family.

"You have my word." Donald offered his hand. It took a few moments but Scott clasped it.

Even after she told herself he should be the last person she wanted to see especially after weeks of being ignored, her breath quickened and her heart fluttered in anticipation.

"You okay?" Jenna asked as Taylor nearly dropped yet another of her limited supply of cups.

"No. I'm a nervous wreck. Why is it taking so long

for those two well-toned hunks to climb a single flight of stairs?"

"Scott isn't what's upsetting you. This is getting complicated. Did you and Donald have a fight?"

Taylor shook her head. "That's the trouble. He was so tender, so loving when we were together. Then I come home and I don't hear from him for weeks at a time. I don't know what to think," she ended in a bitter whisper, forcing back tears.

"I'm sorry," Jenna said, coming over to give Taylor's hand a squeeze. "You're in love with him, aren't you?"

"No! Oh, Jenna. I can't be that stupid. Why am I feeling like this? Oh, hell." Taylor practically hissed. She did not want to love him. How could it be love when she trusted him about as far as she could throw him. The jerk! It was all such a mess.

"Did you try calling him, Taylor?"

She shook her head. "I'm not about to chase him down like one of those sports groupies."

"I don't think he will see it that way."

"Who cares what he thinks!"

"You do, girlfriend."

"Hey, where is everyone?" Scott boomed.

"In here," Jenna called, rolling her eyes. In the tiny flat, there weren't a lot of choices to pick from: the kitchen or the bedroom or the hall closet since they were clearly not in the front room.

Taylor might have giggled if she were not so upset. She had no idea what she was even going to say to the man. Her breath stopped altogether when he entered the kitchen, filling it with his huge proportions.

"Good evening," he said, walking over to Taylor. He leaned down and pressed his mouth to hers in a brief caress before he straightened and nodded to Jenna.

"How did you find me?" Taylor asked when she had regained the use of her vocal cords. It was all so confusing. She had no choice but to accept how deeply she cared for him. She had responded to his kiss when she really wanted to throw something at him. It didn't make a whole lot of sense.

A brow quirked, but he answered easily, "Mrs. Burns. How you doing?"

"Fine. I wasn't expecting you."

She acted as if it were not a pleasant surprise. Donald stiffened, but he did not move away.

Scott interrupted, "You fellows goin' all the way?"

"Absolutely," Donald boasted. "The Celtics are tough but we're not about to let them stop us, especially with the championship on the line."

The conversation switched to basketball and Taylor was almost relieved. She was not sure how she felt about him being here. She certainly had not gotten over the shock of him following her, yet she couldn't keep her eyes off of him.

It had been so long since they'd seen each other . . . long empty weeks without him. Her hungry gaze returned time and time again to collide with his as she studied his strong, African features, while his lingered on her soft features and pretty mouth. They didn't stay long.

When Taylor said her good nights, she whispered in her brother's ear. "Call the folks. They need to talk this over with you." At his frown, she said, "I don't care if you don't want to hear it. They deserve better than you've been giving, kid."

Taylor didn't say a word to Donald until they were alone on the front walkway. "Why are you here?" she asked as he walked her to her car.

"You're here," he frowned. It had certainly not been the reception he had hoped for. He suppressed the flare of temper fueled by hurt at her lack of warmth. Instead he caught her arm before she could open her car door. "What's wrong, sweetness?"

"What makes you think something is wrong?" she hedged, dropping her eyes while holding her arms protectively beneath her full breasts. There was nothing she could do about the way her body was stiff with tension, yet pulsed with awareness.

"For one thing, you have barely looked me in the eye since I arrived. What's going on?" When she didn't answer, he sighed heavily then said, "Let's talk about this at your place." He locked and closed her door before jogging to his rental.

Donald was beat. He'd had a tough game that day and an especially rotten couple of weeks of doing without even seeing her. His temper was simmering. The team was doing well, but he wasn't. His day to day life was empty of the one person he cherished.

They had to do something about their situation. They just had to. He didn't know how much longer he could put up with not even seeing her. Yes, he had prolonged his agony by giving himself time to understand what was going on inside of him. He had hoped she might call, for once. Lately, he'd been feeling as if he was doing all the caring. The only time he felt confident about her having tender feelings for him was when she was in his arms.

Damn, she was driving him nuts with longing and emotional frustration. If she expected him to beg for her attention, then she had another thing coming. He was not about to let her pull him around by his heart strings.

He waited until they were inside her house. He followed her into the living room and watched as she busied herself switching on lights. Impatient with the delay, he said, "Well?" A muscle jumped in his cheek.

"Well, what?" she said, "I thought you would be on

your way to Boston?" She made a point of sitting in one of the armchairs and not the sofa.

He didn't mention the fact that he had been there long enough for her to have been in his arms where she belonged. He was literally shaking with need for her. Why couldn't she see that? But then this wasn't about him. This was about her.

Taylor could have easily told him that he was the problem. It would probably cause an argument, something she could not handle right now. What she longed for was to be pressed against his chest, with her arms around his waist. She longed to be doing nothing more complicated than absorbing his warmth and strength. Unfortunately, her hunger for him was not the issue.

"You watched the game?"

"Yes. Your timing was off. What was wrong?"

"I have no idea. Evidently I wasn't entirely focused on what I was trying to do." His voice was tinged with impatience. He couldn't afford to mess up professionally. There was absolutely no margin for error in pro ball.

Donald's frustration was directed inward. She had never been far from his thoughts. In fact, she was all he could think about. Did she have any idea what she did to him? She turned his emotions inside out. He'd been fighting his feelings; as a result, he was thoroughly exhausted from the wasted effort.

He had to be with her. He could not have survived another day without seeing her. He felt as if he were dying for the taste of her. He was dizzy with longing to be inside of her. She, on the other hand, was as cold as ice!

"Oh," she said, trying to look everywhere but at him.

"Taylor, I'd like to know what in the hell is wrong. Are you ticked at me? If it's because I didn't call, I'm sorry. It's complicated. I needed time to sort myself out." His black leather jacket landed on the back of an armchair. He stood over her in black jeans and black cashmere turtleneck sweater. He had too much pride to remind her that she could have called him.

"What makes you think I'm upset with you?" she said in a huff, still not looking at him. It was taking all her energy not to cry all over the man. How had she gotten so caught up in him emotionally? If she weren't careful she would end up hopelessly in love with him. Jenna was wrong. She was not in love with him, yet. She assured herself that she didn't have that to worry about. She cared for him, but she was not hopeless, yet.

"You haven't been near me since we've been alone. I did shower after the game," he retorted sarcastically. "Or have you got another man in here, hiding somewhere?"

Taylor looked at him then, her lovely eyes wide with disbelief. "You're welcome to look."

He swore heatedly. "Talk to me!"

"I have nothing to say."

"You're angry."

"Why should I even care whether you call?" she asked hotly.

"We both needed time. Everything was happening too fast."

"You are the one who needs space, not me."

"Oh, really? Does that explain why you barely spoke to me when I arrived? You've been nursing your resentment, letting it build. Or wasn't I supposed to notice?"

For the first time, Taylor looked into his dark eyes. She couldn't help herself. She read his confusion, but she also saw much more. His unmistakable concern for her softened her heart thus weakening her defenses. Motivated by feminine instinct as old as time itself, she rose and went to him. Sliding her arms beneath his arms, she encircled his trim waist. Resting her cheek against his chest, she inhaled his fresh male scent.

"Taylor . . ." he whispered.

She didn't have the words to explain herself, but then again she didn't need words to express her need of him. He was solid and strong. She leaned against him, letting him support her. She craved the assurance of his long, hard male body. Did he still want her? Had he missed her? Had he even thought of her?

Donald sighed heavily, cradling her before he dropped his head as he sought her mouth. Although he ached to deepen the kiss, he did not. He longed for her sweet offering, but it was not forthcoming.

"Sweetness . . ." he whispered, craving her heat as urgently as a plant seeking the life-giving force of the sun. His mouth was hot and loving on her skin as he laved the sensitive place behind her ear, thrilled by the sexy sound she made deep in her throat. No matter how angry she was with him, she still wanted him . . . needed him. She rubbed her breasts against his chest, letting him know where she wanted his attention. It had been so long . . . too long.

"Kiss me," he commanded in no uncertain terms. Her mouth was incredibly soft against his but not open. "Do I have to beg for your sweetness? Kiss me back, damn it." He stubbornly refused to deepen the exchange.

Powerless to resist, Taylor opened to bathe his wide, generous mouth with her tongue before she slipped inside to stroke his tongue with hers. Donald moaned his enjoyment as tremors shook his hard frame. A simple kiss from her could drive him wild with desire.

One by one her clothes fell to the carpet as he removed piece after piece, until he could pull her close, cup her sexy round bottom. He focused on nothing but her sweetly scented flesh. Goodness, she felt so good, so right in his arms. He squeezed her tight little nipples, leaving a hot trail of desire deep inside her feminine core. Hungry for the taste of her, he lifted her until his circling tongue could savor her highly sensitive brown nipple before taking it into his mouth to thoroughly enjoy. Her urgent pleas that he take her caused him to burn from the fiery heat of his own passion.

"No," he groaned aloud before continuing to lick and pull at her nipple, his large hand massaging her incredibly soft bottom. Her whimpers of delight fueled his own pleasure.

Taylor was beyond coherent thought, she was quaking with desire for his arousal. Her hands were not still as she touched him, stroking his chest, worrying his tight little nipples with her fingertips. She moved a leg between his in order to rub her aching mound against his hard, muscled thigh.

He lifted her until she was where they both wanted her most with her sweetness moving along his steel hard length. The erotic caress was too much. It pushed him over the edge. It would have been different if he hadn't known what it felt like to be inside of her, surrounded by her unbelievably tight sheath. He was shaking so badly that he took care to place her back on her feet. He was in so much need that he didn't trust himself to bear his own weight, let alone hers as well.

# Nineteen

Taylor's hands were not very steady as she pulled the sweater over his head. She said, "I want to touch you, honey," her voice husky with feminine yearning. Caressing down the thick pads of his muscular arms and chest, she clung to him. His lips were hot, needy before she pulled away to kiss his bare chest. She moved over his skin, her lips and tongue generating a wondrous heat as she tongued him.

The velvety softness of her open mouth aroused him to the point where he didn't even consider resisting. Suddenly her mouth warmed his nipple, then kissed it before she slowly licked the entire flat surface from the dark circle of flesh to the puckered tip. Donald groaned heavily, his shaft jerked so insistently that she felt the movement.

"You are driving me out of my mind," he grated roughly. His hands were at his waistband to ease the discomfort from his burgeoning sex.

"Let me," she said breathlessly, brushing his hand away. Her nimble fingers worked the buttonhole, then carefully eased the zipper down. She was as eager to fully caress him as he was for her touch. She could not help feeling flattered that his male hunger was directed her way. He was here with her. She told herself that this moment was all that mattered.

When her small soft hand eased inside his silk briefs

moving the material away, her fingers giving him the softest caress, he moaned thickly. She pushed his clothing down his long legs until he could kick free and was as bare and ready for her as she was for him. Although impatient for her hands on him, he swallowed the demand. He cautioned himself to accept all that she was willing to give. Her intimate caress was a rare and priceless gift and he would treasure it.

Taylor stroked him, her soft brown hands caused him to clench his teeth. Her movement along his length was painfully slow and caused his pulse to race with excitement. He had no idea that she was closely watching his face, trying to gauge his reaction. When she quickened her strokes, his breath hissed from between his lips and he growled his enjoyment.

"Like this?" she asked, as she lovingly pleasured him.

"Y-Y-e-s," he barely managed to get out, as she palmed, then squeezed his fullness below.

Taylor smiled, thrilled by his obvious enjoyment.

"Stop!" he breathed thickly. "I'm too close to coming."

She stopped immediately but she was far from finished with him. She longed to please him as unselfishly as he had pleasured her. She dropped her head and replaced her soft hands with the wet heat of her mouth. She caressed him with the damp, soft wash of her velvet tongue until he could not bear any more.

Donald clasped her upper arms and forced her up and against his chest. One hot kiss led to another and another, each hotter than the last. They sank down to the carpet holding on to each other.

She was on fire for him, so when he asked if she could take him now, she whimpered in response, offering herself to him. His hand was boldly caressing her sex before worrying her fleshy folds. She would have told him she was ready for him, but at that moment speech was beyond her. Her eyes were tightly closed as she moaned her consent as he slid his finger in and out of her tight heat mimicking the eventual thrust of his body.

Suddenly, he replaced his hand with the unyielding pressure of his penis moving against her vulva. He did not penetrate. "Taylor . . ." he crushed her mouth beneath his. "Answer me." Beyond words, she lifted herself against his sex until he was only part of the way inside of her. His harsh groan came from deep in his chest. "You want more?" he moved against her, teasing her, but all too soon his control eroded. Her wet heat eliminated his control and he guided her hips until he was sheathed within her. He held himself perfectly still, giving her time to adjust to him and giving himself time to harness the force of his desire. "Don't move."

Taylor could not tolerate any delays. She placed a series of damp kisses on his throat. "Donald . . ." she whispered, "please . . . love me." When her body instinctively tightened around him, offering him the sweetness of an inner caress, he growled his enjoyment. He began hard, insistent thrusts, stroking her from deep inside. There was no way either one of them could hold back any part of themselves. They were finally one, in perfect accord. The thunderous approach of his release triggered hers. His hoarse shout mirrored her own cry as they held on tight shuddering in the sweet aftermath of release. They rested, their bodies still intertwined, too tired to move even a single muscle . . . too fulfilled. The only movement between them was his hand along the rich smoothness of her back.

"I missed you. I had to see you," he said, his cheek against her hair.

Her face was buried between his neck and his shoulder. She was too choked up between warring emotions to verbalize her thoughts. She told herself that for now all she wanted to concentrate on was him and their brief time together. There would be time later to make some sense of it. Soon he would be gone. She would be alone yet again.

"Baby, talk to me. Was I too rough? Did I hurt you?"

"I'm fine." She kissed the base of his throat. They were still intimately joined. She savored the feel of him.

Donald shuddered at the erotic caress. "Take care," he warned huskily. "Or you will get more."

"More?" She pressed her lips behind his ear, tonguing his strong neck before taking his lobe into her mouth and sucking, while rubbing her breasts into his chest.

Donald shifted his weight as his shaft thickened and surged heavily, surrounded by her heat. His mouth was rough with desire as he thrust his tongue against hers. He lifted her thighs high around his waist, pushing his manhood even deeper.

Taylor nearly screamed from the exquisite friction he created so effortlessly. She was so close to climaxing, but she wanted to wait, wanted to wait for him. She laced her hands with his, holding nothing back.

He groaned thickly as he worked to keep their loving slow and thorough. He had waited weeks to have her, weeks to share the ultimate pleasure that only she could give him. They had been lovers for such a short time, each time was more exhilarating than the last, more fulfilling. She filled his heart and left him craving more. The brilliance of his climax was coming much too quickly. It took all of his concentration to be able to hold back the raging force of his desires. Taylor's tight heat lured him beyond the restriction he had placed on himself.

"Donald . . ." she crooned, "oh, baby," into his ear as she tightened around him.

It was too much. There was no turning back for either of them. They rushed ahead with blind trust in each other, they felt as if they were being hurled through space with such incredible force as they reached completion as one. They clung to each other, their hands still laced.

Their hurried breathing was the only sound in the room. He was the first to recover. "I'm crushing you." Yet, he couldn't bear to move. He didn't want to leave her. When they were like this it all made perfect sense.

"Mmm," she murmured, willing to bear his weight.

He sighed, collapsing on his back. When he spoke his voice was gruff with emotions. "I'm sorry it has taken me so long to get here. I have missed you."

"I've missed you, too."

He said, holding her against his side. "We spend too much time apart."

"It can't be helped."

"I don't agree."

Shaking her head, her hair soft against his throat, she said, "There is no easy solution. We both live very separate lives."

Donald did not agree, but decided not to push or rush her into a quick decision. Unfortunately, it wouldn't solve their current problem. He cupped her chin, lifting until he could study her eyes. "We need to talk, Taylor. We've put it off long enough. We have to talk about your brother. How long can we pretend it is not an issue between us?"

"That's hardly my fault."

"I'm not blaming you. Our living apart sure makes it difficult for us to talk. Even for us to believe in each other, trust each other."

"Yes," she agreed.

"What was wrong when I arrived? You seemed upset."

"I was. My parents are crushed because of Scott's decision to quit college." She sighed. "My mother was crying on the phone. I happen to love my folks. I went over there mainly to yell at him for dropping the bad news and leaving it to me to clean up the mess."

"I'm sorry."

"No, you're not," she said, moving away from him.

He caught her and held her at his side. "Yes, I am. Why must you always think the worst of me just because I disagree with you? Scott's a grown man. He's old enough to decide what he wants to do with his life."

"Does he have the right to destroy our parents' hopes and dreams for him? I can't forget you've taken his side in this over mine," she glared at him. "I've felt guilty about being involved with you when I know you've influenced him. I haven't even told my parents that I'm seeing you."

"Are you telling me you're ashamed of what happened between us?"

"I didn't say that."

"But it's what you mean, isn't it?" he demanded.

"Scott is going against everything our family believes in. By being with you, I am doing the same," she said in a tight whisper.

"You can't believe that."

"But I do." She managed to pull away from him. She grabbed her clothes, and rather than try to fumble into them, she went into her bedroom for a robe. He was right behind her.

"What about what we feel for each other? What about what we just shared? Are you saying that doesn't count?"

Instead of answering him, she concentrated on shrugging into a rose floor-length terry robe.

"Damn it! Answer me!" he roared his frustration. She was tearing him apart emotionally.

She was not sure what she heard in his voice other than anger. Compelled to look into his eyes, she searched for an answer. "I . . ."

"You what?"

"I care for you. I could not make love with you if I didn't."

He told himself it was enough for now. It had to be, but it felt painfully inadequate. He needed so much more.

"Perhaps it would be better if you left," she said, fighting back tears. Too much seemed to be happening at once. She was not sure how she felt about any of it. His showing up without warning. Her inability to resist him despite her hurt. She had no defenses against him. She couldn't help how she felt. She knew her parents would never understand her disloyalty. She didn't understand it herself.

He swore, his hands balled into fists at his side oblivious to his nudity. "What is this? Are you punishing me for not agreeing with you? For upsetting your parents?" This whole conversation was going nowhere fast. He knew he was exhausted because he was letting his temper get the best of him.

"No!"

"That is exactly what you're doing. You're letting something that we have no control over come between us. This should be about you and me. Not about Scott or your parents!"

"Please, just go. I can't talk about this anymore. I need time to sort it all out." Taylor turned her back on him, her heart weighed down with grief. She heard him leave the bedroom. It was all she could do not to break down. She yearned to run after him, tell him all that mattered was what they felt for each other. . . . but it wasn't true.

They didn't exist in a bubble. She was only a tiny part of his life while he was shaping her life for years to come. Someday, she would be nothing more than a faint memory for him while her world would be crushed. Caring about someone else wasn't supposed to hurt, but it was tearing her apart.

She was curled on the armchair and ottoman in the corner of her bedroom near the window. She glanced up when he returned. Donald was fully dressed. He walked with such grace for such a big man.

Squatting beside her until they were eye level, his voice raspy with emotion, he said, "I don't want to leave with things so strained between us."

"You shouldn't have come," she said unhappily.

"Do you mean that?" He recognized the anger in his voice, but he knew he was more hurt than angry.

Tears rolled down her soft brown face as she realized that she had the power to hurt him just as he had that same power over her. She shook her head, biting her lip. "Too much has happened in such a short time. First meeting you, then the difficulties with Scott and finally the two of us becoming lovers. Donald, it has all happened too fast. I don't know what I feel . . . what I want. I don't know what's best anymore."

She wasn't sure about anything anymore. It was all so confusing. She didn't want to care about him, didn't want to need his tender lovemaking. He was a celebrity for heaven's sake. He was amusing himself with her. How long could it last? He wanted her now, but how long would it be before some beautiful model or movie star turned his head?

Donald sighed wearily, but all he said was, "Walk me to the door?"

She nodded, following him. "How long will you be in Boston?"

"Depends on how we do. A week if we're lucky and take a sweep."

"Good luck," she said unhappily. He wasn't even out the door and already she was hurting.

"Thanks." His gaze was on her mouth. He needed her so badly that he couldn't stop himself from opening his arms to her.

She surprised them both by moving into them. She pressed her face into the warmth at the base of his throat.

"Take care of yourself," she whispered.

He nodded. "Take the time you need. Think about what we have. The next move is yours, Taylor. If you want to try and make it work, then you are going to have to come to me." His lips ever-so-briefly brushed against hers before he pulled away. "I won't accept third place in your life, behind your parents and your brother." He closed the door quietly behind him.

As he walked to his car, he felt as if his heart had been ripped from his chest. There were no guarantees, but he had done all that he could. It was up to her.

Taylor leaned against the door. Was that what she was doing? Was she wrong to let the situation with Scott come between the two of them? Scott had been between them from the first. Even when they hadn't discussed the situation with Scott, it was still there. What was she going to do? It felt as if she had been caught up in a whirlwind.

Tears filled her eyes and spilled down her cheeks. She had fallen for the wrong man, yet again. Only this time it was much, much worse. She had fallen for a man who lived in a fantasy world. They didn't share the same value system. She didn't spend her days flying from one part of the globe to the other or spend her weekends on luxurious private sea islands. She came from working folks. That was all she knew. That was all she wanted to know.

Her feelings were such a jumbled mess that she didn't know what was truly in her heart anymore. All she knew was it felt as if her heart was breaking. In spite of everything, she couldn't stop caring so deeply for him. Was this mistake enough to cause her a lifetime of pain?

He was gone. She had pushed him out of her life,

certain their differences went too deep. She should have never become involved with him. They should not have become lovers. It had only made an impossible situation more painful.

What if he were right? What if she had put her family ahead of him? What then? Donald made himself clear. If she wanted him, she would have to go to him. He had done all he was willing to do. The choice rested with her.

Taylor could not afford to question her actions too closely. She had managed to avoid examining her own feelings until she was on a plane headed for Atlanta. She had gone for over three weeks without seeing or speaking to Donald. The loneliness was unbearable. Being without him had caused her to take this last desperate measure.

If not for the sports channel or television interviews, she would not have seen him at all. She knew he was terribly busy and was traveling in and out of Chicago. The pressure was on because the Bulls were on a winning streak. They were close to reclaiming the championship.

She suspected that she had hurt him. He had made his point. If she wanted to see him, talk to him, be with him then she would be the one making the moves . . . every last one of them. She hated ultimatums. The first thing she would do when she saw him was tell him so. Taylor covered her face with her hands. The first thing she should do was tell him how sorry she was for the way things had turned out between them. She had been the one to push him out of her life. She was the one who hadn't valued what they had.

Taylor had no idea how many times she had reached for the telephone, yet never made the call. What could she say? That she was sorry she had judged him so harshly. That she had been wrong for only wanting the best for her brother? Not likely.

She had done what she felt she had to do. Even more, she would do it again. She had to stand up for what she believed was right. Yet that did not change her feelings for him or that she missed him desperately.

She not only craved his warm and witty conversation, longed to see his sharply handsome African good looks, but hungered for his especially tender and wildly sensual lovemaking. Perhaps, he wasn't the best man for her. But he was the one she adored. The man she loved? Had she truly fallen in love with him without even realizing it? Why couldn't she find the answer within herself?

She had worried about going to him until she could think of little else. She just wasn't sure she was going until the very last minute. Even though she had dressed and packed with care, she had been shaky until she actually walked on the plane.

She justified her behavior by telling herself that she needed to see him, needed to settle things between them. She couldn't go on wondering and worrying that he might not want to see her. She forced herself to see the total picture. It was possible that he was seeing someone else by now. Donald was special. His choices were not limited. She had to know if his feelings for her had changed.

She had been so upset by her brother's decision to quit college that she had put the blame on Donald's wide shoulders alone. She had also been angry with him for not calling after the romantic weekend they shared in South Carolina. And she realized after weeks of nothing to do but to think that she had been trying to punish him for neglecting her.

The worst of it was that she had let her own fears

overshadow what they had shared. By choosing to protect herself from the kind of hurt and callousness that Alex Adams had inflicted on her, she had in essence given up on living. If she didn't see Donald, didn't let him get too close then he in turn couldn't hurt her, couldn't break her heart.

She knew that being in the play-offs and the conference Eastern finals put incredible pressure on him and his time. She also knew that if it were not for their disagreement, he would have made arrangements for her to come to him wherever he was. If nothing else they would at least have been able to see each other.

She had been so embarrassed when she had to call Joy Ransom in order to find out where the team was staying in Atlanta. But Joy had been so cordial and pleasant, instantly putting Taylor at ease.

She had made Joy promise not to tell that she was planning on joining Donald in Atlanta. Joy was enthused, claiming the idea was wildly romantic and encouraged her to go after her man. The two found they had a lot in common besides being crazy for two popular basketball players.

In spite of her fears, Taylor's heart raced with excitement at the prospect of seeing him again. What was she going to say to him? How could she make him understand?

They had never gotten around to defining their relationship. Nothing was mentioned about a commitment or the future. For all she knew, they could want two very different kinds of relationships. She had no idea what he ultimately wanted. It was time she found out. She longed to be number one in his life and she was ready to give him that same honor.

For so long she had had no one, no one of her very own. All of that had changed when he had come into her world. Donald had brought with him so many wonderful possibilities. If only she hadn't been so fearful of the unknown.

It was late afternoon when the plane touched down. She was trembling with nerves. She was breathless when she told the taxi driver to take her to the Twin Towers in downtown Atlanta, her stomach tight with tension. She was in Atlanta and there was no turning back.

Taylor was not certain her legs would hold her when she approached the registration desk in the bustling lobby. "Mr. William's room number, please. Donald Williams," she quickly clarified.

"I am sorry, Miss but I can't give out that information."

"He is registered here, isn't he?"

"I am sorry, but I can't give out that information."

"I don't believe this," she muttered wearily.

"If Mr. Williams were staying here, it would be necessary to maintain privacy and security," he offered as explanation.

Taylor understood the necessity to protect and secure the hotel's guests. But she needed to see Donald. The idea of parking herself in the very public lobby in the hope that he would chance to pass through was not the least bit appealing. She felt like some kind of groupie, as if she were chasing him down. Perhaps she wouldn't be so upset if she were sure of her welcome? She fretted that she had waited too long to decide to come.

After spotting a bank of telephones near the elevators, she asked, "Can you at least connect me to his room?"

"It is against hotel policy to . . ."

"I know," she interrupted, not wanting to hear his whole litany of reasons why she was not allowed to contact Donald. What was she supposed to do now? She had come too far to just turn around and go back home without even talking to him. She had to see him. That was all she was willing to entertain at the moment.

Straightening her spine, she said, "I'd like a room, please." She reached into her handbag to locate her credit card, telling herself she would worry about the expense later. She was not about to give up now. After filling out the registration form, she wordlessly accepted the room key. Before she could ask for a bellman, she saw Eddie Ransom crossing the lobby. She called to him, waving.

He glanced over his shoulder, then grinned. "Hey Darlin," he said, reversing his steps and coming over to her. "Hi, beautiful," he said, kissing her cheek. "You just get in?"

"Yes. How have you been?"

"Great. Man, am I glad to see you." He lowered his voice, moving her aside. "Your man has been hell to be around. Like a bull with a sore . . ." he caught himself in time, then laughed uproariously. "You know what I mean. He didn't mention that you were coming at practice today."

Taylor took a deep breath before she shrugged, saying, "He doesn't know. I wanted to surprise him."

Eddie howled with laughter, waving away the bellman. "This your gear?" At her nod, he collected the garment bag and makeup case himself. He escorted her toward the elevators. "He needs to see you. If you can't sweeten him up then nothin' going to help. The guys are ready to throw his ornery butt off the team and he's our best scorer right now. This is not the time to lose the man. We want him sweet and happy. We got a damn championship to win day after tomorrow."

Eddie kept up a steady stream of chatter while they waited. His brows shot up when she punched the button for the fifth floor. "Where you goin', girl?"

Flushed with embarrassment, she admitted, "They

wouldn't give me his room number. Wouldn't even connect me to his room. Hotel security."

"What the hell is a phone call going to hurt? But that's the usual procedure with the team. If you don't know, they ain't tellin' you nothin'."

"I don't know how I was going to contact him if I hadn't run into you in the lobby. In fact, I considered hanging out in the lobby."

"He's in nine-twenty-three. Darlin', you're wastin' your money reserving a room. He ain't about to let you out of his sight." Eddie found the concept hilarious and roared with amusement. "He might be mule-headed, but he sure ain't stupid." He pushed the button to close the doors on the elevator panel when it opened on five, then pushed nine.

"Thanks, Eddie," she sighed, grateful for his reassurance.

"Joy will be here in the mornin'. Maybe we can all get together? Celebrate the win Sunday night?"

"Sounds wonderful." Her mind was not on entertainment as they got out on Donald's floor. Her nerves were back with a vengeance.

"Joy mentioned you called. We're pulling for you two," he said earnestly.

They stood in front of Donald's door. "Thanks, Eddie." She smiled, reaching up to give him a kiss on the cheek.

When he raised his hand to knock, she stopped him. "You've done enough. I have to do the rest on my own."

He nodded. "Good luck. Not that you're going to need it. The man is crazy about you, girl." He walked on down the hallway, whistling cheerily.

# Twenty

Taylor took a big, fortifying breath before she lifted her hand to knock. When there was no response, she tried again. Frustrated that he might not be inside, she had raised her hand to try one more time when she heard movement from behind the door before it opened.

It wasn't Donald's large frame that filled the doorway, but a petite light-brown-skinned woman wearing nothing more than a bathtowel. "Yes?"

Taylor blinked in total dismay. It took her a second to catch her breath and say, "I'm sorry. I must have the wrong room."

The woman smirked. "If you are looking for Donald Williams, he's in the shower. May I tell him your name?"

Taylor gasped aloud. She could hear the shower going from the next room. Only her reserve of common sense and her belief in herself kept her from grabbing the other woman by the hair and shaking her bald.

She said, lifted her chin regally, "I must have the wrong room."

This just could not be happening to her. Something was terribly wrong. Why would he invite her to come, then have another woman in his room? He was not a cruel man. Then the realization that she had waited too long nearly caused her eyes to fill. Evidently, this was his new playmate.

"I assure you this is Donald's room," she grinned, opening the door enough for Taylor to see Donald's handcrafted leather cases beside the dresser with his initials monogrammed on the handles. His brown leather jacket hung over the back of a chair. His sweatshirt with his team number and logo was carelessly tossed on the bed. There was no mistake. This could be no one else's room.

Taylor had no memory of grabbing her bags or running down the hall toward the elevators. All she recalled was the sound of the shower in the background as she raced to get away. She was trembling so badly by the time she reached the lobby that she barely managed to leave her room key on the registration desk.

She didn't care if they charged her for the unused room. All she cared about was getting out of there as fast as she could. She was so close to breaking down that tears burned her eyes. This was what she got for believing in fairy tales.

She stood on the front walk, quaking with emotion. She looked up when she was asked, "Do you need a taxi, miss?"

"Yes." She was numb with shock. She did not glance around and was relieved to be able to sink into the backseat of the taxi before it sped away toward the airport. Scalding hot tears came, ran down her face. She couldn't see the taxi that pulled up to the hotel as hers eased out into the busy downtown traffic.

A tall muscular man got out. His long ground-eating strides took him through the glass double doors and the hotel's lobby. As he passed the registration desk, a clerk called, "Mr. Williams!"

"Yeah," he paused, trying not to show his frustration. Three damn weeks and she still had not even picked up the telephone to call. He had no choice but to accept the obvious. She had no faith in what they had. She didn't feel what he felt for her. This thing with her brother had been between them from the first. There was not one damn thing he could do but continue to wait and hope she reconsidered. He had probably put his big feet in his mouth with that ultimatum. It was stupid.

"Sir, your fiancée is here. I know she wanted to surprise you, but it's highly unusual to allow anyone into . . ."

His heart skipped a beat. Taylor? "What are you talking about?"

"I let her into your room," he whispered. "It's not our policy, but considering your status we made this exception."

It had to be Taylor. It just had to be. He had the good sense to ask, "Does my fiancée have a name?"

"Yes, a Ms. Jones."

"Describe her."

"Ah . . . Mr. Williams . . ."

"Did you see her? Well then describe her. How tall was she? What was her figure like?"

"She's about five feet tall. Very slim black woman with a light complex . . ."

Donald barked. "Get hotel security up to my room. Now! Then call the police! I want that woman out of my room." He swore heatedly.

That was all he needed. Didn't he have enough on his mind? He was not about to get into a sticky mess because of some love-sick groupie.

He got to the room before the security guards but he didn't enter. He paced the hall while he waited. There was no way in hell he was going inside. She could end up accusing him of anything including rape. It would be her word against his. Damn!

The woman he wanted more than anything else in the world would not give him the time of day. The ones he didn't want were always throwing themselves at him, their boldness never ceased to amaze him. Damn! He felt like ramming his fist through the closest wall. Why couldn't it have been Taylor?

They had made love not once but twice before she had tossed him out of her house. Didn't their closeness mean anything to her? It had to have meant something. How could she have responded to him with such warmth and depth and not care about him? It made no sense. She wasn't a cold or callous woman. He had gone over and over it and always came up blank.

"Taylor, why?" he whispered aloud. He needed so much more from her than sex. He needed her in his life on a permanent basis. His feelings for her were deeper than even he had imagined when he issued that ultimatum. He wanted her to have his name. He wanted there to be no doubt in either of their minds concerning who came first in their lives. He was crushed that it had not been Taylor masquerading as his fiancée.

What was taking so long? Deciding he did not even want to see the woman being dragged from his room, he continued down the hall and around the corner. He knocked at nine-thirty-four.

"Who is it?"

"It's me, man. Let me in." He was impatient with himself. His cellular was in his room. He should have been on the telephone with his lawyer instantly, straightening this mess out. He didn't want the media to get a hold of it. He didn't want it to get back to Taylor.

Eddie's tall frame filled the door. "What are you doing here when you have a beautiful woman in your room? Have you lost your mind?"

"Have you lost yours? What do I want with some groupie? Hell! Let me use the phone. I've got to call my lawyer. I need him here before the mess hits the fan—or rather the tabloids," he ended, reaching for the telephone on the desk.

"What in the hell are you talkin' about?"

"There is a woman in my room. Probably butt naked stretched out on the bed."

"Hold it, man. You don't know the woman in your room?"

"No! How could I?" His lawyer came on the line. "Larry, look. I need you here, man. Some groupie told the hotel staff that she was my fiancée. They let her into my room."

"Did she take anything?" his lawyer asked.

"I'm not worried about her stealing. She can have anything she wants but me. If this crap is leaked to the press, it will be all over the place," he said into the telephone.

"Donald, think, man. Could she have access to credit cards or receipts while she was in the room?"

"I have no idea. I'll have my secretary call and cancel everything immediately. But that is not my problem. I need you here, handling this mess. Hotel security should be on the way up to the room. I didn't go in."

"Have the police been notified?" his lawyer asked.

"Yeah. I insisted."

"Good. I'll be on the next flight out."

"Call my secretary and have her arrange for the jet to be at your disposal. I need you here as soon as possible."

"Okay. I'm on my way."

Eddie was swearing as he paced, waiting for Donald to hang up the telephone. "Donald, how do you know it's not Taylor?"

"What?"

"Taylor is here. I left her at your door, man." He glanced at his watch. "Not half an hour ago."

"What!" Donald roared.

"Yes! Man, you better find out and quick."

"I don't believe this! It's not her. The manager described the woman to me. Five foot, light skinned. Oh hell!" He was stunned with disbelief. This could not be happening to him. "Taylor's in Atlanta?"

"Listen, she is here. She has been to your room. The registration clerk would not give her your room number. So she checked into the hotel. In fact, she was on the way to her room when I ran into her in the lobby and brought her to your door."

"And!" he prompted, certain he didn't want to know the rest. If Taylor saw . . . "Did that witch answer my door?"

"I have no idea. She wanted to surprise you, so I left her in front of your door."

"This is not funny, Eddie!"

"Man, I am not jokin'."

Donald was shocked at how unsteady his hands were when he picked up the telephone. "Yeah, front desk. Would you connect me to Taylor Hendricks's room?" He was pacing as far as the phone cord would allow while he waited. "What! She checked out? That's impossible. She just arrived not half an hour ago. Let me speak to the manager." He waited impatiently. "This is Donald Williams. Look, there must have been some mistake. I'm inquiring about Taylor Hendricks. Yes. I see." He carefully hung up the telephone instead of ripping it out of the wall like he wanted to do. Damn!

"Well?"

"Taylor turned in her keys and left, not twenty minutes ago." His voice reflected his fury. "I don't believe this!" He looked haggard, as if he were in shock.

"You think she knows about . . ." He found he could not voice the thought, especially considering the devastation he saw on his friend's face.

"She has to. Why else would she leave like she did?" Donald asked as he headed for the door.

"I'm sorry, buddy." Suddenly, there was no doubt of how deeply Donald cared for Taylor. It was all over his face.

"I've got to try to see if I can catch her at the airport. If I don't, I don't stand a chance in hell of getting her back."

"What about this mess? How can you leave with everything so up in the air?"

"I don't have a choice. Taylor is more important to me than even clearing my name. If this makes the tabloids or the eleven o'clock news, I'll deal with it. I have to go after her. I won't willingly let her walk away from me. I love her too damn much. Bloody hell!"

"You can make her understand."

"That's easier said than done. Will you deal with the hotel security and the police until Larry gets here? I'll be back as soon as I can."

"Sure. You'd better hurry."

"Here's hoping that there won't be any flights to Detroit until late tonight. Better yet until tomorrow morning." Donald wondered, as he bounded down the stairs, if it wasn't already too late. There was no telling what that woman had said to Taylor.

The only thing that gave him hope, helped him keep his head, was the realization that Taylor had come to him. That had to mean something.

Taylor's eyes burned from unshed tears. Her throat was clogged with them as she settled down to wait for her flight. She'd been lucky, in that respect. She'd gotten a seat on a plane leaving within the hour. She had been willing to wait all night if necessary, to leave Atlanta. She wasn't prepared to remain a second longer than she had to considering the painful situation she had found herself in.

She felt as if her heart had broken into a million tiny pieces. It was only as she left the hotel that she was able to put a name to her feelings. It hurt so badly because she had done the unpardonable. She had fallen in love for the first time in her life. Once again, she had walked in on her man with another woman. Only this time it was much much worse, because her feelings for Donald went far deeper than anything she had ever felt for Alex Adams.

From the very first she had turned away from his good looks and easy charm. Her actions had captured his attention, provided nothing more than a challenge to his enormous male ego.

If she had encouraged him, maybe thrown herself at him, he probably never would have paid her the least bit of attention. It was all a game to him. A wicked hurtful game, she decided as she whisked away a stray tear. She had to stop. Hadn't she shed enough tears in the cab on the way? Must she make a fool of herself in the middle of a crowded airport?

She had foolishly let flowers, telephone calls and romantic weekend trips weaken her defenses. Once she had capitulated and agreed to date him it was only a matter of time until they became lovers. It hadn't taken him long to lose interest in her. Becoming involved with him had proven to be a terrible mistake on her part. She should have known that she was way out of his league. She felt as if she'd been slapped in the face with the realization.

Thank goodness, she had not left her name. He had no way of knowing she'd even been in the hotel. That she had chased him down like an eager puppy, desperate for his attention. Eddie! He was bound to tell Donald that she had been looking for him! Taylor moaned in misery. Well, what difference did it make now? It was all over between them. Nothing mattered now but putting hundreds of miles between them.

It certainly hadn't taken him long to replace her in his bed. No time at all! He had his pick of lovely women from all across the country, willing to do his bidding. She had been such a blind fool ever to trust him with her heart. Her own brother had warned her against him, but she had been too much in love to listen.

Yes, she now realized that she had been in love with him for some time. She never would have made love with him in the first place if her emotions had not been involved. She just had not realized until now. What a mess.

She had spent the last few weeks chasing after a man who had no idea what the word commitment meant. He had overwhelmed her with his charm and masculine appeal and had effectively erased her common sense. She had been functioning on pure emotions for weeks now and hadn't even realized it.

Why had he used her this way? Why had he given her an open invitation, if he was not sincere? Nothing could ease the stark hurt inside of her. Presently, she didn't even have the luxury of tears. She had mopped her face dry when she had arrived at the airport. There wasn't much she could do about her swollen eyes. An application of lipstick and powder would not repair the damage. Frankly, she didn't care what she looked like, certain that her heart was broken beyond repair.

Apparently, all he had been interested in was the sex. That had been what this whole thing was about. She was offering and he was taking. The thought of him as her lover made her tremble in misery. They had made love often and she had enjoyed every second of being in his bed. He had been considerate of her needs. He had made sure that she reached completion each and every

time they made love. He often held back in his determination to satisfy her. Despite this horrible heartache,
she would be less than truthful if she labeled him a selfish man.

The problem was he was just too damn generous with
his body. When it came down to loyalty, he clearly had
none. He valued his own needs above all others. He was
a man who couldn't resist the tempting allure of a
woman's body . . . any woman's body. Three weeks!
They'd been apart for only three short weeks. And he
hadn't given her time to recover her hurt feelings before
he replaced her in his life.

She sighed wearily, telling herself that it had been
bound to happen sooner or later. It was better that it
happened now before she became any more emotionally involved with him. Long ago, Alex had taught her
that when it came to sex, men were not to be trusted.
Donald had just confirmed that, damn him.

With his keen sexual appetite it wasn't any wonder
that his new woman had answered the door nearly nude.
Taylor blinked away tears, her hands balled into fists of
outrage. Their entire relationship had been a waste. Her
outrage couldn't change what had happened this day.
Nor could it soothe the pain deep inside. Nothing could
make it go away.

She told herself that she had survived the loss of her
Alex and she could survive the loss of Donald. What she
had had with Donald was obviously not meant to be.
She was better off without him. If only she could make
herself believe it.

The traffic was a monster this late in the day. Donald
could barely sit still by the time he reached the airport.
It was all he could do not to vent his boiling rage at the

taxi driver. He was like a powder keg ready to blow at the least sign of trouble.

He couldn't believe that his entire world had been turned upside down because of one desperate woman. He had suffered the unpleasantness and inconvenience of over ambitious fans before, but he had not been personally threatened by their antics until now.

If Taylor would not or could not believe him . . . then—No! He couldn't make himself finish the thought. It was much too painful to even consider being without Taylor in his life. It had taken him so many years, long empty years looking for that one special woman. There was no doubt in his mind that Taylor was that woman.

There were so many things he loved about her. Her main focus in life was not motivated by financial gain or selfishness. She possessed a warm and loving heart and cared for others deeply. She had a strong sense of self and family. She deserved nothing less than complete love and devotion. He intended to give them to her, if she would just let him.

There was no way on earth he could stand back and let her walk away from him. She was worth fighting for. If it came down to it, he would follow her back to Detroit. He was willing to put his career—everything—on the line to get her back. None of that mattered without her to share it with.

As his long, muscular legs moved purposefully through the airport, he was grateful that he had remembered the name of the airline she had flown on on her trip to Chicago. Hopefully, that detail would give him a fighting chance to catch her. The Atlanta airport was one of the largest in the country. When he checked the monitor, he nearly stopped breathing when he saw that a plane was leaving for Detroit shortly. He had less than thirty-five minutes to reach her before her plane started loading. That is, if she was taking that flight. He wouldn't allow himself to entertain the thought that she might have taken an earlier flight.

As he quickly moved through the terminal, he nearly stepped on a toddler left unattended for a moment. His quick reflexes saved the situation as he scooped the baby up and then handed him over to his frantic mother. Donald let out a breath he didn't even know he was holding when he spotted Taylor near the Northwest departure gate. She sat alone with her head down and her shoulders hunched. His heart skipped a beat as he approached. He paid no attention to the curious onlookers who had obviously recognized him. He had eyes only for her.

She either sensed his scrutiny or heard his approach. She lifted lovely dark eyes filled with sadness, which instantly changed into sparks of indignation. "Go away. I have nothing to say to you."

"Taylor, please. Let me explain."

"Leave me alone," she hissed.

When he went to sit beside her she jumped to her feet. "Can't you hear? I said leave me alone."

"I can't. There is an explanation. Please, just give me a chance to clear this up."

Taylor couldn't believe they were standing in the midst of a crowded airport arguing. Nor could she believe that, in spite of everything that he had done to hurt her, she was even speaking to the man. He had used her!

She grabbed her bags and rushed toward the ladies' restroom. Donald was right behind her. He had no trouble keeping pace with her.

He was not even winded when he said, "I know what you must be thinking. You're wrong. I can prove you're wrong, if you'll just give me the chance."

Taylor yanked the ladies' room door open, thankful

that he could not follow her inside while trying to manage her luggage and not burst into tears all at the same time. Why was he here? Hadn't he hurt her enough? Must he also embarrass her in public?

Taylor was wrong. Donald caught her arm before she could get inside. He firmly blocked her entrance with his large solid frame.

"Don't you dare touch me! Haven't you hurt me enough already?" Tears were trickling down her cheeks and she dropped her luggage in order to cover her face with small trembling hands. "I hate you for this," she said in a bitter, furious whisper.

He ached to hold her, take her into his empty arms. Instead, he held his arms stiffly at his sides. "Please, baby, don't cry. I am so sorry. I never meant for you to be hurt like this."

"Why can't you understand English! It's over. I don't want anything else to do with you!" She yelled at him, furious by the way he was blocking her with his body. She sniffed, trying desperately to control her tears. This could not be happening to her. It had to be a nightmare.

"I know you're upset, sweetness, by what you think happened. If you ever cared anything at all for me and what we shared, you will allow me to explain. I don't know what she said to you, but you can believe it was a lie."

"I'm not interested in your explanations. I saw with my own eyes that you're nothing but a liar and cheat. Now let me go past!"

"Gladly, once you have listened to me."

"No! Leave me alone before I call security."

"Go ahead. I'm staying right here until we've talked this out." His hands were balled at his sides as he fought the urge to touch her. He hated the fact that his touch would not be welcome.

Taylor knew better than to try and push past him. He

was solid muscle. His body was in peak condition. She would need a crane to move him.

"What did she tell you?" he asked softly, ignoring the curious glances they received from onlookers.

"There was no need for her to say anything. I've got eyes in my head. I heard you in the shower! Look, I saw enough to convince me I was a fool to believe in you."

He sighed heavily. "It's quite simple, Taylor. It all boils down to trust. You can let this destroy what we have. It's up to you. Do you honestly have so little faith in us? In what we've shared?"

Taylor wanted to scream that she was not the one at fault here! He was the one who'd cheated, not her. He was the one who had encouraged her to come here.

"How can you dare to ask me to trust you? I came here by your invitation. And what did I find? A half-naked woman in your room covered only by a towel. Damn you! The point was—you have been sleeping with that woman! Which means that whatever happened with us was a serious mistake! It's over, Donald. Now move. I don't want to miss my plane."

"Taylor, I was not in that hotel room. I didn't invite that woman into my room," he was amazed at his ability to hold on to his temper. His voice was tight with emotion as he tried to use his head, not his heart.

"In a minute you are going to tell me, it wasn't even your room."

"I have no reason to lie. If I wanted her, I would be with her." His voice dropped huskily. "Sweetheart, all I want is you. You are my world. Please don't let this come between us. I love you." He was past caring that they now had an audience. There was only one thing he cared about and that was Taylor. He was putting it all on the line in order to keep her.

A fresh wave of tears filled her gaze. If he wanted to hurt her, he could not have found a better way. She felt as if he'd thrust a knife through her heart as she accepted that that was all she ever wanted . . . his love. But nothing was the way it should be. Nothing!

"No . . ." she whispered as tears flowed down her cheeks. "Please, don't say that. It should not matter anymore. Nothing matters . . ."

"It's true," he said, taking her into his arms, carefully he cradled her against his body as he whispered into her ear, "I do love you. Baby, I need you so much. I need you in my life . . . only you, my heart."

"But . . ."

"No buts. Stay with me. Let's work this out together. We can get past this, sweetheart. I know we can. The question is, do you care enough about me to try?"

"No!" She hit at his chest, her face buried against his shoulder. "It's not about me."

"Do you love me, Taylor?" he whispered, his voice brimming with emotion.

Taylor was unsteady on her feet, she could hardly remain standing. His strong arms kept her from falling flat on her face. "Do you have any idea how I felt when that woman . . ."

He pressed a finger against her lips, his heart pounding with dread. "Do you love me?"

"Yes . . ." she whispered, unable to hide the truth. "I can't help it."

"Then trust me, sweetness."

"Excuse me," someone said from behind him. He nodded, moving them over.

Taylor was not sure she was strong enough to do that. She felt as if history was playing a horrible trick on her by repeating itself. She had also found Alex with another woman. Suddenly, she remembered that Alex had never claimed to care for her. Donald was saying the things she yearned to hear. Was he telling the truth? Could she believe?

"Taylor?"

"You expect too much."

"I'm asking you to believe in our love." His gaze was locked with hers, both ignoring the curious glances sent their way.

It would be so easy to walk away, so easy to try and put this behind her. But the trust he demanded was the hardest thing she had ever done. He was asking her to risk her heart . . . her well being. Was she strong enough to even try? Just then her plane was announced and she had to decide that instant.

"From the very first, you've had doubts about me. All those doubts have come down to this moment. We can either try to work this out together or stand back and let this destroy what we have. I want a commitment with you, Taylor. No one else."

Up until a few moments ago she didn't think they even had a future. Had she been wrong? Had she been guilty of judging him too harshly? Was she letting her fear color what was right in front of her?

"Last call for Northwest flight 456 leaving for Detroit, Metropolitan Airport," came from over the loud speaker.

# Twenty-one

Donald dropped his hand as he waited for her to decide. He had purposely not told her that he didn't even know that woman. It really didn't matter. What mattered was if she truly believed in him and his love for her. For the first time he had let down his defenses with a woman. She had been allowed to see what was in his heart. She was the only woman who knew the real man. She had seen him up, she had seen him down. He wanted her to know all of him . . . his fears . . . his anxieties . . . his hopes and dreams.

Taylor was not infatuated with the image. She knew what he valued and what he treasured. He loved her too much to just walk away. He adored her down to earth approach to life, her clear view of the importance of money. If he lost it all tomorrow, she wouldn't care. She would be there for him. He was what mattered to her and she was what mattered to him.

If she truly could not put her trust in him, it was better if they discovered it now. Donald wanted her to be his wife, but that could not happen if she didn't have absolute faith in his integrity and believe in his unshakable love for her.

Overzealous women were a hazard in his profession, something she would have to accept. He could again be forced into a difficult situation by a reckless fan. That was a risk he faced every day. Yet, that didn't mean he didn't love Taylor or that he would dishonor their love. She was his heart. As badly as he wanted her, he knew it wouldn't work if she didn't believe in his commitment to her and their love.

Neither took notice of the people that streamed around them as they stared into each other's eyes. Donald waited, determined to hold on to his self-control. This was not the time to hold anything back. He could very well leave the airport with his heart shredded like confetti all over the place. It seemed to take an eternity before she reached down for her luggage and gave it to him.

"I'm ready."

Donald grinned. The cases stopped him from wrapping her in a fierce possessive hug. "Oh, baby. You won't be sorry. I promise you that," he said caressing her cheek. "Come on, let's go somewhere where we can have some privacy."

Taylor nodded. It wasn't until they were seated side by side in the back of a taxicab as it pulled away from the airport that she asked, "Why was she in your room?"

"I'm afraid I can't answer that. I suspect she was a misguided fan."

He was watching Taylor closely when he went on to say, "I evidently just missed you. When I returned to the hotel this evening, the registration clerk told me that my fiancée insisted that they let her into my room. I thought it was you, until I asked him to describe her, naturally then I knew it couldn't have been you. So I had them call hotel security and decided it was best not to even go inside the room—to let the authorities handle it. I was so ticked, I asked for a room change. Anyway, I went to Eddie's room to use the telephone. He told me about you baby, being here in Atlanta." He kissed her throat, whispering, "I nearly went out of my mind when I was told by the desk that you had checked out."

Her head was thrown back as she looked up at him. "She was acting as if I was the intruder and she had every right to be there with you."

Donald whispered close to her ear, "I was furious when I realized what happened. I will never deliberately hurt you. I love you."

"I love you, too," she said so softly that if he had not been listening closely he wouldn't have heard.

His eyes locked with hers. He whispered, "Are you sure?"

"Yes. That's why this hurt so much." She shuddered.

He lowered his head toward hers. "Forgive me?"

She lifted her chin in order to press her mouth to his. Their kiss was brimming with love and ripe with promise. Their lack of privacy caused them to end it much too quickly and didn't come close to easing the longing they shared.

"Yes, but it wasn't your fault."

"It can happen again."

"What?"

"It's part of the risk of being in the public eye."

"Does that kind of thing happen with everyone?"

"Just about. Pursuit is the normal method overzealous fans use to get close to you. Most of the guys have had some unpleasant incident they can recount." He would be glad to put the entire incident out of his mind.

He kissed her cheek, careful to resist the seductive allure of her beautiful mouth. Right now, he was too needy and they didn't have nearly the privacy that the kind of kiss he had in mind required.

"Thank you," he said, knowing she was to be treasured.

"You're welcome," she smiled, unable to take her eyes off of him. "Now what are we talking about?"

"Thank you for taking a chance on me."

Taylor's caressing hand traveled the length of his jaw.

"That was one experience I don't ever want repeated."
She could not control the distaste in her voice.

With his arm around her, he smoothed down her arm.
He sadly said, "I wish you hadn't had to go through it,
my love."

"I know." She wanted nothing more than to be alone
with him, to show him what was in her heart. The sheer
relief that came from releasing her emotions was overwhelming.

When they pulled up to the hotel, Donald was the one
to help her out. He groaned when he spotted the police,
television cameras, reporters and players through the plate
glass window in the front of the hotel's wall. The lobby
was like a zoo even before they walked inside. He held on
to her with one hand and balanced her luggage with the
other, determined not to allow them to be separated.

He was spotted instantly. A camera was shoved in his
face. "Don, what do you have to say about all this. Is it
true that . . ."

"Just a moment. I'll answer all your questions in a
moment."

"Mr. Williams, sir," the hotel manager had to push
his way through the crowd. He said, "I'm sorry about
this inconvenience." He give him the new room key.
"You have every reason to be upset due to our mistake."

Before he could respond, a half dozen microphones
were shoved into his face. "Mr. Williams, this is WZ . . ."
Donald ignored them. He saw Eddie talking to a group
of players. Motioning to him, he whispered into Taylor's
ear. "Don't worry baby. This shouldn't take long." To
Eddie he said, "Here, take these and Taylor up to the
new room."

"Sure thing," Eddie cupped her elbow and steered
her away before the reporters realized her involvement
in all of this, while Donald prepared to face the media
alone.

"Are you okay?" Eddie asked once they were safely in the elevator and out of earshot.

Her smile was a bit weary. It had been an emotionally exhausting day. "Better than I was when I left here. I can't believe the press. They're everywhere."

"Donald is news. Don't worry about it. He's a pro. He knows how to handle them. I'm glad you came back. Donald went charging out of here. He didn't care about any of this, nothing but getting to you. Taylor, I'm sorry you were hurt. Unfortunately, these things happen. He was not responsible for this. He doesn't know that woman."

Taylor smiled, patting his hand. "I know now. He explained everything." She was touched by Eddie's concern.

The elevator stopped on seventeen. She was grateful when they reached the room. She was exhausted. "Thanks, Eddie." She stood inside the doorway of what appeared to be a beautiful suite and watched as he carried her luggage into the bedroom. "I appreciate your help. You're a good friend."

"No problem," he said with a smile. "Just remember, Donald is wild about you."

She gave him a bright smile and a hug. "You're a very special man. Give Joy my love. Good night," she said, letting him out.

Kicking off her shoes, she padded on bare feet into the bedroom and collapsed in the closest armchair barely able to keep her eyes open. She felt as if she had been on an emotional roller coaster. Her emotions had been twisted first one way then another.

From the instant his door had been opened by that woman, she had felt as if her heart had been crushed. The taxi ride from the hotel, her wait in the airport were a blur of anger, jealousy and grief. She had mourned his loss. When she'd left Detroit, she most certainly had not expected to find herself in such a horrible situation. Nothing had gone as planned. Yet, suddenly her life had changed drastically yet again due to Donald's declaration of love. He gave her hope for the future. He loved her as much as she loved him.

It was too much. Heartbroken, she had not been prepared to see him ever again. She had no reason to expect him to follow her. She sighed dreamily, thrilled that she had been so wrong in her estimation of his emotions. He had been unrelenting in his determination to win her back.

He had ignored the cost to him personally. He had not hesitated to fight for her even in the midst of one of the largest airports in the country. There was no way she could not know how deeply his feelings ran. He had risked public humiliation in order to change her mind. Their argument—and their reconciliation for that matter—had not been private. He had taken considerable personal risk in going after her. There wasn't a doubt in her mind that he would have followed her back to Detroit if necessary.

Knowing her love was returned was worth every unpleasant emotion they had both suffered this day. "Whatever the future held for them, together they would work out all the kinks.

It was later than he expected when he'd finished with the reporters, then given his statement to the police, and finally met with his lawyer and the hotel management. The woman had been retained in the security office until the police had taken her to the station.

Donald was glad for the quiet as he let himself into the suite. Although the suite was an upgrade in hopes of pacifying him after that mix-up, he still was not appeased. All the unpleasantness could have been avoided if they had just followed hotel policy and not let anyone inside his room.

. He was disappointed when he found the sitting room and bedroom empty.

"Taylor?" He knocked at the bathroom door but doubted she could hear him over the sound of the shower. He walked over to the separate stall and opened the door. "Hi."

"Oh!" She jumped. "You scared me," she scolded.

"Sorry, sweetness." He couldn't wait a second longer to see her. His dark eyes glinted with an unmistakable hunger that only she could eliminate. She was so beautiful, so perfectly lush and he had come dangerously close to losing her.

"You look tired," she said, her eyes stroking his face.

When he didn't speak, but shrugged, she asked around a sweet smile. "All finished?"

"Yeah. You?" His voice was husky with unmistakable need.

"Almost . . ." She blushed as he leaned back against the sink content just to watch her.

He ignored the way his body prepared itself to make love to her. Even that did not interrupt his absorption. He longed to hold her . ... keep her safe out of harm's way. His emotions were running high, but he didn't want to alarm her. Dear God, he needed her so desperately.

Taylor turned on the spray, rinsing her soap-covered frame. He held a warmed bathsheet out for her and quickly wrapped her inside. Encircling her in his arms from behind, he placed a gentle kiss against her nape. He lingered, pressing his face between her damp shoulder and neck while his arms tightened even more around her.

Tossing her showercap into the sink, she asked, "Honey, are you okay?" Puzzled when he did not allow her to turn nor did he respond but held her firmly against him, she questioned, "Donald?" With her back to his front she couldn't fail to feel the hard evidence of his arousal against her back.

"No," he whispered heavily.

"Honey," she persisted until he permitted her to turn so that she could see his face, his eyes. She could not read anything in his face, yet his self-absorption worried her. He had faced the press alone. Maybe she should have stayed.

"Was it so terrible?" she asked caressing his beard-roughened cheek. He needed a shave but that didn't matter, nothing mattered but his well being.

The look he gave her was filled with anguish.

"Tell me," she whispered, pressing soft butterfly kisses on his wide generous mouth.

Donald groaned thickly, capturing her mouth, to hold her still as he deepened the kiss. His hot foraging tongue sought the sweet warmth within, needing the reassurance of her softness. He had thought he had lost her. He had been desperate for a while there, certain he had lost everything, if he had lost her.

"It was a terrible ride to the airport. I'm not sure what I would have done if I'd lost you, baby. I love you. I need you in my life. I have no life without you."

She held him tight feeling him tremble with emotion, knowing she was a fool to have ever doubted his love. He was a strong man, but his emotions made him vulnerable to her, just as hers did the same.

"I'm here. I am not going anywhere, my love." She kissed him over and over again as if she could kiss the hurt away. "I'm so sorry I scared you. But you have to know I would never have left if I had known you loved me. I had hoped you cared for me, but love—it was too much to hope for."

"Believe it. Taylor . . ." he paused. "Promise," he

mumbled insistently against her sweet scented throat. "Promise you'll never leave like that again."

"I promise. I will always give you a chance to explain."

"Thank you." He sighed heavily.

"But if I ever find you in a hotel room with a half-naked woman, I will break both your arms."

His laugh was deep, soothing to her ears. "You have nothing to worry about. Remember, I was never with her."

"Yes, I know."

"I only want you. Make love to me, sweetness." He wasn't certain he could ever let her go. She owned his heart.

"Yes . . ."

They interlaced their fingers and walked hand in hand into the bedroom. When they reached the bed Donald began undressing. Taylor pulled back the sheet, wanting to be in his arms as much as he seemed to want her there. She let her towel drop to the carpet then slid beneath the comforter. He sighed heavily when he settled beside her and pulled her close.

"Comfortable?" He closed his eyes, enjoying their closeness.

"What will happen to that young woman? Will they charge her?"

"I don't know. To tell you the truth I don't care." He said angrily.

She was so used to him taking things in stride that she was disturbed by his intensity. "It's over. She didn't come between us. We didn't let her." Taylor's caressing hand smoothed up and down his arm.

"Only by the grace of God. She came a hair's breath away from destroying our relationship."

"No one can do that. We won't let it happen."

"No . . ." he echoed.

She soothed him with the soft brush of her lips along his collarbone. "It's over."

"I can't tell you how important you are to me. I never felt this way about anyone else," his dark eyes caressing her small African features.

"Oh . . . Donald," she whispered, cuddling even closer. "I hadn't planned to fall in love with you."

He chuckled a deep throaty sound that caused her to giggle. "Unexpected, huh?"

"Something like that."

He rolled over until she was flat on her back while he looked down at her. His sex nestled between her softly parted thighs. He moaned, "Sweetheart . . ." moving in order to relish the softness of her mound against his pulsating shaft. He needed the reassurance of her welcoming heat . . . assertion of her love.

"Aw . . . Donald . . . my love," she said breathlessly. "I want you so badly . . . please."

He easily lifted her until he could nestle her breasts, pull the sweet, berry hard nipple into his mouth. He laved the entire peak, circling over and over again only when he was thoroughly satisfied with the way it stood out like ripe fruit did he apply suction. The powerful sensation sent desire spiraling throughout her entire system and pooling in her moist womanly center. The dazzling pleasure went on and on as he concentrated on enjoying her.

Taylor sobbed out her enjoyment, not able to breathe until he paused only long enough to move to the other breast and resumed driving her out of her mind with pleasure. She was so very close to climaxing when he allowed her to catch her breath.

Intent on drowning his senses in the same kind of hot pleasure, her soft hand moved over his body, stroking his flat nipples until they stood out like tiny pebbles on the beach. She surprised him when she laved him, slowly . . . sweetly.

She adored his sharp, pleasurable gasp. His breath stopped as she continued down his muscular torso. When her soft fingers played in the thick nest of curls surrounding his sex he nearly came off the bed, his pulsating need was so great. Finally, she caressed him where he wanted her soft hands the most, she moved over his shaft from the ultra-sensitive peak to the broad base. She used both hands to encompass him; long, purposeful strokes soon had him close to peaking. Unable to bear more, he caught her hands, kissing the center of each soft palm.

"No more," he cautioned hoarsely, positioning her in order to ravish the sweetness of her mouth. The kiss was so wonderfully wet that he didn't want it to stop, but he needed more . . . much more.

He rolled until they lay on their sides, facing each other. He draped her thigh provocatively across his waist, leaving her open to his caress, his keen male hunger.

"Sweet . . . so sweet," he said as he lovingly parted her damp soft feminine folds with the firm peak of his sex. He teased her, using his manhood to arouse her. He didn't rush, even when she whimpered her excitement.

"Donald . . ." She trembled from the firm caress, purposefully moving her hips determined to force him where she ached to have him. "Honey . . ." she craved his strength, ached to have his full hard length deep inside. "Hurry . . ."

Donald whispered a rough throaty moan unable to bear the feel of her wet heat on the crown of his sex without giving in to that natural urge to be deep inside. Carefully he penetrated her tight sheath, determined not to hurt her in his eagerness to be buried to the hilt inside of her.

Taylor sobbed out her relief, calling his name. At long last . . . She trembled in his arms. They were intertwined, each breathing deeply, reluctant to move relishing their joining, their intimacy. Their bodies were not only joined, but also their hearts. Their loving generated from deep inside, a result of what they felt for each other.

She unwittingly tightened around him, giving him a rhythmic massage that caused him to let out a throaty groan. Unable to remain still a second longer, he began giving her the deep, hard thrusts they both adored. Her name was a rough caress on his lips as he gave her the full force of the urgency of his need. As her soft arms and legs clung to him, she quivered as each stroke was more forceful, more compelling than the last. They fit so perfectly together. With her eyes tightly closed, she was not prepared when he slid a hand between them and began stroking the tiny heart of her femininity.

She screamed his name as she shuddered, climaxing ahead of him. The sweet inner caressing strokes of her body caused him to lose control, his hoarse shout of triumph signaling his rush of release. He convulsed heavily in her arms. They clung to each other savoring the sweetness of the moment. He placed a lingering, loving kiss on her soft, kiss-swollen lips.

"Taylor . . ." he said close to her ear, "You feel so good . . . so good." His breath was warm on her throat. "You are one of a kind. Girl, you sure know how to keep me coming back for more."

She returned his kiss, whispering, "I love you."

"Does that mean you're finally going to stop blaming me because Scott decided to enter the draft?"

"Donald!" she exclaimed, trying to put some space between them. "I don't believe you asked me that now!"

Donald cupped her lush hips not allowing her to separate her body from his. "Well, you do. Be still." He was in heaven, and he was not interested in changing positions any time soon.

She sighed deeply, not wanting anything to spoil their lovemaking. She pressed her lips against his throat.

"Well?" he prompted.

"Not any more. Scott made his choice. I don't like it, but it's his choice," Taylor said playfully, "I still love him." Then she said, more seriously, "I'm sorry, honey. I was wrong to let it come between us. Can you forgive me?"

"If you marry me."

"What?" she said, her heart skipping a beat, doubting she heard correctly.

"You heard me. I need you with me. I want to build a life with you. I want you to carry and raise our babies."

She just looked at him, too overwhelmed to speak. She had not expected this. She wasn't even sure that she'd secretly hoped for it. She had been fighting her feelings for him for so long that she didn't even know when she'd lost the battle. She loved him so much that she knew her heart belonged to him. There was nothing she could do or for that matter even wanted to do about it.

"Say something."

She stroked the generous curve of his bottom lip. "How can it work? Honey, our lifestyles are so vastly different. You are constantly traveling. We don't even live in the same city. I want to finish school and someday teach on the college level." Yet, even as she offered the explanation she knew she could not live without him. She needed him so badly.

"There is no reason why we can't eventually live anywhere you choose. Sweetness, I only have two more years in my contract with the Bulls. Then I'm retiring from pro ball. The business goes where I go. If you want to stay in Detroit, I have no objections. I was born and raised in that city. My family is there. It doesn't matter where, as long as we're together. I love you, Taylor. Never doubt it. I need you."

Her large pretty eyes filled with tears.

"Don't, baby," he cradled her against his chest, stroking her back . . . soothing her. He had known how he felt about her much longer than she had. Time he hoped would ease her fears and uncertainty. He could not let her go. They belonged together.

She smiled through her tears, surprising him when she whispered, "You're going to make such a wonderful father." She felt him flex inside of her.

His chest swelled with pride. "Shall we work on it," he whispered huskily. He automatically surged forward his body thickening and lengthening at the thought of making love to her. Suddenly he was once more crazy with need for her. She pleased him each and every time they made love. Her body felt as if it had been made for his . . . her sweet womanly sheath tightly caressed him from aching crown to pulsating base.

Taylor gasped, loving every minute of the hot, wildly erotic loving he gave her. She hung on to him as he took them both to new dizzying heights. When their release came it was as one—they shared all the promise and pleasure of their loving. As their breathing slowed he stroked her.

"Marry me, Taylor," he persisted, his lips pressed to the base of her throat.

"Yes . . . yes. Oh, yes." She rained soft kisses over his hair-roughened cheeks and jaw. When she reached his lips, he opened for her, allowing her full access to him. "I love you so much. I promise I'll make you a good wife."

"Thank you." His voice was filled with emotion. "I promise to take good care of you."

"We'll take care of each other. I know you have to travel a lot, but I hope to go with you as much as I can."

He smiled thoroughly pleased. "I'd like that. I know you want to finish college. Honey, you will be able to go to college full time if you want. By the time we're ready to leave Chicago you may be ready to start teaching."

"You are so sweet."

He chuckled. "No, you're the sweet one. I have something for you."

She didn't want him to leave the bed. "I have all I need. I have you."

He couldn't help smiling. "I've had it for some time. I'll be right back."

Reluctantly, she released him.

True to his word, Donald returned with a square shaped jewelry box. He was right: it was familiar. He had hoped to give it to her on their first real date.

"Donald! You kept it!" she said in amazement.

"When I first saw it, I thought of you. I had to keep it, in hopes you would accept it someday."

"Oh, honey." She kissed his cheek. "You've been carrying it around in your pocket?"

"Yeah, I hoped you would change your mind. As I said, it reminds me of you, sparkling, pretty, lush." He didn't wait for her to open it, but flipped the lid himself. Inside was a square cut diamond and emerald tennis bracelet set in eighteen-karat gold.

"Well," he urged, when she simply stared at it.

"It's beautiful."

He didn't hesitate to place it where it belonged, on her pretty brown wrist.

She pressed her lips against his. "Thank you. I love it."

He leaned back against the pillows, content just to hold her close to his heart.

She remembered how intensely she feared the women who hunted him, seeing him as easy prey for a life of riches. She suddenly realized she was no longer afraid. It did not matter what someone else wanted. Other women were not a threat to her because of the way he felt about her. The reality of his love for her gave her the confidence to face each new day at his side. He was her partner in love and life. Her friend . . . her lover, soon to be her husband.

"You're going to spoil me," she teased, snuggling even closer.

"Why not? You could use a little spoiling. There is no such thing as too much love."

She agreed with him deciding to do a little spoiling of her own—only with sweet loving kisses.

"Mama, will you please stop fussing," Taylor said with a touch of impatience. "I'm sorry. I'm just a little jumpy." A nervous wreck would be more like it, she thought. She had been planning this special day for months and now that it was finally here she wasn't sure she could go through with it.

"With good reason. Bridal jitters," Virginia Hendricks said as she kissed her daughter's cheek before fluffing out her veil.

They were in the small room off the main corridor of the church that Taylor and Scott had both grown up in and where the wedding was to take place.

"It won't be long now." Jenna squeezed Taylor's hand. She looked lovely in her slim pale pink bridesmaid's dress.

Taylor hugged her, knowing how difficult it was for

Jenna to be her maid of honor considering the situation with Scott. "Thank you so much for doing this."

In the months since she and Donald decided to marry, Scott and Jenna had stopped seeing each other. It had been a painful separation for them both. Things hadn't gone as Scott expected when he was drafted by the Charlotte Hornets. He was making plans to move out of state and Jenna was not going with him. They had been both hurt by her refusal to follow him. He was starting a new life, but he was starting it on his own. Their parents, like Taylor, had no choice but to stand back and let Scott choose his own path.

Now today was Taylor's special day. She told herself it was only the beginning. But she was so scared, scared that she wouldn't be able to make Donald happy. His love had certainly made all her dreams come true.

A soft knock on the door made her jump.

"Ready?" Scott asked, peeking his head around the door. His hungry gaze lingering on Jenna.

"Yes." Their mother answered for all of them.

Jenna didn't look up, she busied herself with helping Taylor with her bouquet of pink and yellow roses.

"Where's Daddy?"

"Right here, baby girl." George Hendricks said, taking his daughter in his arms for a brief hug.

"What about me?" Her tall, handsome brother asked before he took her into his arms. He whispered close to her ear, "Be happy."

She nodded, unable to speak. Taylor felt as if her legs were going to give out; they were shaking so badly as she waited while Scott escorted their mother to her seat. Jenna was next. The wedding march was Taylor's cue but she was trembling like a leaf in a whirlwind. She wasn't sure she could do this, even as the double doors were opened. In fact, she was certain she could not until her eyes locked with Donald's. In that instant she knew everything was going to be just fine. The love in his eyes and smile on his dark handsome face had her quickening her step. There could be no doubt about the love they shared, a love everlasting.

## About the Author

Bette grew up in Saginaw, Michigan, and graduated from Saginaw High School. She obtained her bachelor's degree from Central State University in Wilberforce, Ohio. Bette began her teaching career in Detroit and completed her Master's degree from Wayne State University. She is currently teaching in the HeadStart program for the Detroit Public Schools. You may write her at P.O. Box 625, Warren, MI 48090-0625. If you wish a response please include a self-addressed stamped envelope.

Look for these upcoming Arabesque titles:

November 1997

ETERNALLY YOURS by Brenda Jackson
MOST OF ALL by Loure Bussey
DEFENSELESS by Adrienne Byrd
PLAYING WITH FIRE by Dianne Mayhew

December 1997

VOWS by Rochelle Alers
TENDER TOUCH by Lynn Emery
MIDNIGHT SKIES by Crystal Barouche
TEMPTATION by Donna Hill

January 1998

WITH THIS KISS by Candice Poarch
NIGHT SECRETS by Doris Johnson
SIMPLY IRRESISTIBLE by Geri Guillaume
A NIGHT TO REMEMBER by Niqui Stanhope

*The author acknowledges Vertamae Grosvenor for VER-TAMAE COOKS in American's Family Kitchen, for her tales and recipes from the low country.*